THE NEW BILLIONAIRE BOSS

TINA GABOR

Join the Sparks Fly Romance VIP list for free by visiting this link:

https://sparksflyromance.com/bronson1/

01-06-22

To Edie and Briana -
The book wouldn't be as good without you.

LAUREN

I'd woken up early this morning and jogged down a fricken mountain to get to this Starbucks in time for our call—the call that was supposed to tell me the deal had closed and everything was fine. The call that still hadn't come even though I'd texted Carolyn, my close friend and real estate agent, a half hour ago.

Why did the closing for this property have to fall during my day job's stupid corporate retreat?

What made it worse was the retreat center didn't have cell reception or internet access. I get that the place was built a million years ago by Franciscan friars, but they updated their Instagram with pictures of "Franky," the retreat dog. Someone there must have internet, but they didn't make it available to retreat visitors.

They say it's so we can disconnect, unwind, and relax. But watching old infomercials on YouTube is what I do to relax. Not having cellphone reception made me feel like someone trapped me on a desert island.

I gulped my skinny vanilla latte as my gut churned. Was it from stress or drinking coffee on an empty stomach?

Yes, I knew better. But when I'd gotten here, I couldn't help myself. The smell of espresso made me do it.

No wonder every cup has a siren on it. It bothered me I hadn't put that together sooner. There's nothing like dairy, espresso, and stress after a run down a mountain to make you question your ability to make prudent life choices.

I blamed my weakness toward caffeine on withdrawal. The Malibu Retreat Center, where I'd been staying for the last two days, seemed to specialize in tepid, light brown liquid that could not be confused with coffee.

This retreat had shot my daily routine to hell, and my internal stress levels threatened to show. I'd been working on being "less rigid" as my ex used to say, but I'd never be a "go with the flow" type. Changes in plans, or frankly, any major changes, tended to freak me out. Being on this "retreat" had been torture.

I checked the time on my phone. The first meeting of the morning retreat started in forty-five minutes.

I debated calling Carolyn. But if there was a wrinkle in the deal she was ironing out, I didn't want to get in the way. She'd call me as soon as she could. I trusted her.

Don't think I'm a huge real estate mogul. This is only my third house. I like to buy in the cheap area where I went to get my undergrad degree. I rent out the rooms to college students. Ultimately, I'd like to have enough money to quit my job and build more revenue streams.

Real estate rental is something that doesn't take as much time as some of my other ideas. The deal on this house in South Florida had been too good to pass up, even though it was a tad out of my price range. I'd already paid for the inspection and appraisal. That money would be down the drain if this deal didn't close.

I'd broken one of my cardinal rules for this house, which was I'd dipped into my emergency fund. Well, more than dipped. Instead of nine months' worth of expenses in savings, I now had just under two.

I vowed to build it back up again soon. That's if this deal didn't go south.

My phone rang. I snatched it up. "Please, just tell me the deal went through," I said to Carolyn.

"We've hit a snag," she said.

My entire body tensed. Snags and I do not get along. I like a plan and things going by that plan. I exhaled and willed my voice to remain calm. "What's the bad news?"

"The seller doesn't want to sell."

"That's more than a snag." I took another deep breath and steered my thoughts away from dwelling on why this snag shouldn't be happening. Denying reality is a trap that would no longer ensnare me. I reminded myself to deal with what is not what I thought it should be.

"Yeah, I'm standing alone on the lawn right now, trying to calm down," Carolyn replied.

"Did Tess give a reason?" I asked. Tess was the seller. If there was some type of family emergency or something where she needed us to wait, I could compromise.

Carolyn exhaled. "Tess said that she didn't feel good about the deal."

"I bet she thinks she can get out of our purchase agreement because she got a better offer."

"That's what I'm thinking." Carolyn's voice was tight and higher than usual.

"Did you do some fishing to make sure we're right on that? Did you ask her if she needed more time?" I asked.

"You know I did," Carolyn answered.

"Did you tell her—"

Carolyn interrupted me. "That we have a contract? Yes, of course I did."

It made my insides shake when I had to be the bad guy, but I played the part well.

"Put her on the phone," I said to Carolyn.

I heard Carolyn walking as she spoke. "I'll go back inside, get her, and call you back."

We hung up, and I glanced at my watch to check the time. I needed to call an Uber and have it waiting to drive me back to the retreat. Mr. Damien—that's what everyone called my boss, Damien Bronson—hated anyone for being late, and so did I.

We called all the sons "Mr." plus their first name, because there were too many Bronsons working at Bronson, Inc. The only one we called Mr. Bronson was William Bronson, their father, who founded the company after buying a small chain of convenience stores.

Mr. Bronson himself was supposed to be at this retreat. Being a stickler for punctuality myself, being tardy to an event with the boss of all the bosses would be something I could never live down.

I admired Mr. Bronson. He grew the company into one of the largest grocery companies in the country, and now the company even had its own product and development division.

A part of me wished I worked in that part of the company, but I'd rather focus my efforts on building wealth for myself. I learned from my parents that you never got rich working for someone else. No matter how nice the people you worked for seem to be, when it came to choosing between you and their own profit, your employer will choose profit.

A man talking loudly on his cell phone entered the Starbucks. He sported that cliche, Malibu rich guy look— tousled black hair, shades indoors this early in the morning, expensive suit tailored exactly the right way to show off his broad shoulders and tight ass.

Mr. Malibu looked like he'd been out all night. Probably banging some chick or dude ten years younger than him.

He looked familiar. Was he somebody famous? Celebrities infested Los Angeles and the surrounding areas—especially here in Malibu. The glitterati ceased to be interesting to me years ago. All they did was drive up real estate prices so people like me couldn't afford to buy anything here.

It bugged me I couldn't figure out where I knew him from. I have an excellent memory.

"I'll be there. I just stopped for a coffee!" he growled into his phone and then hung up.

He took off his sunglasses and looked around the shop as if to see if anyone had caught him getting pissed on the phone.

Yup. I caught you being a douchebag, Mr. Malibu.

He turned in my direction. Our eyes met. He looked me up and down and then smiled.

Ugh. He must have thought I was into him. He probably thought everyone was into him with the way he looked, but I had a deal to close.

I swallowed the last of my latte, got up, and headed for the door. There was no way I was going to concentrate on setting my seller straight with him distracting me, and I wouldn't be a loud jerk arguing on my cell phone in the coffee shop like some people.

I exited Starbucks, dropping my cup in the trash on my way out.

My legs were killing me from running down that damn hill to get cell reception. My quads and calves were so tight they teetered on the edge of cramping.

There was no place to sit outside, but I didn't care. I squatted down in the parking lot and inelegantly sat on the cement parking bumper.

Yes, I did that in my cheap clothes, wearing zero makeup in the middle of Malibu. At this moment in my life, I gave zero fucks.

Time was running out. The morning meeting would start soon.

I opened my ride-hailing app and hit the button. If the car got here early, I'd just have him run the meter until I finished my call. It would've been easier if I could close this deal on the drive back, but I couldn't risk losing reception in the middle of my call.

My cell rang just after I saw a driver was on the way via the app. Time to get my game face on.

"Hey!" I answered.

"Here she is," Carolyn said, and then I heard her handing her phone over to the seller. Carolyn knew I was in a hurry. I could always count on her.

"Hello," Tess grunted.

"Tess, what seems to be the problem?" I asked, forcing my voice to be calm.

"Listen, there's no way I'm selling to you and that's that."

"And why is that exactly?" I emphasized the word exactly.

"I don't need to tell you. It's none of your business."

I tried to calm myself, but Polite Lauren was about to leave this chat.

"If you need to stay longer, or you're having financial problems, I'm willing to work with you, but I'm not walking away from this house. We have an agreement," I said, my voice firm but not raised to the point of yelling.

"My business is my business," Tess barked.

That was it. I didn't have time for this shit.

"Your business is going to take a big hit, Tess. We have a purchase agreement. You can try to sell it to another buyer. But whatever extra you think you're going to make, you're gonna pay more in court costs, when I sue you and win. So just sign that damn document, and let's get this over with."

"I don't think we have a fair price, and I can get better," Tess confessed.

"I'd recommend you call your lawyer, but I bet you don't have one. Find out how much it's going to cost you to hire one. And then from there, have your new lawyer figure out what it's going to cost you when you lose.

"Because you're going to lose, Tess. You signed a contract. I will enforce that contract. It won't even cost me a dime to do it, because you'll be paying damages and court costs, and we both know only one of us can afford to go to court. And it's not you."

"You're bluffing," she said.

I was pseudo-bluffing. I couldn't afford a lawyer, and I doubted a deal this small would be worth a lawyer taking this on contingency.

"Tell me what it's going to be. Are you honoring your contractual obligation and signing now, or do you want to see me in court?" I asked, my voice stern and serious. Then I stopped talking.

The weakest point in a negotiation is to talk after you've made your ask. It's the one thing that I'd learned from my ex-boyfriend, Ivan. Well, that and never to trust a man again.

But I learn my lessons even when it hurts. Like Dad used to say, the more painful it is to learn the lesson, the more thoroughly you can learn it. And boy, did I learn from that relationship.

Tess waffled and complained without answering my question. Then she paused, as if she was waiting for me to respond.

I remained silent.

She babbled for god knows how long, and I didn't speak. Not. One. Word.

Some people have a hard time with remaining silent. I used to be that person, but I vowed not to be like that anymore. It's hard, though.

People will call you names. They'll swear at you. They'll cry and yell. But you've got to hold the line no matter how much it makes you uncomfortable.

I'd never back down and sell myself short again—especially if someone was trying to manipulate me over their own wrongdoing. To paraphrase a Taylor Swift song, the old Lauren can't come to the phone right now... 'cuz she's dead.

My car arrived. I got up from the parking bumper and hit the mute button on my phone as Tess continued to chew me out.

"Start the ride," I said to the driver. "I need to finish my call, but I can't risk losing reception. I'm going up the hill."

The driver nodded and started the ride as I waited to see if my bluff paid off. Tess had stopped talking. I even had to check to see if the call had dropped or she'd hung up on me. But she was still there.

She was thinking.

"You know, if you were nicer, you could've gotten a better price," Tess said, breaking the excruciating silence.

I fought the urge to tell her if she was smarter, she would've gotten me to pay more, but I remained quiet. I heard the phone rustle.

"Hey," Carolyn said. Had Tess walked away?

"Is she signing?" I asked.

Carolyn didn't answer right away, so I stayed quiet.

"Just signed," Carolyn said.

Thank god! I checked my watch. Twenty minutes until nine.

"All right, I'm going back to the retreat, so you won't be able to reach me. But I'll check in with you tomorrow," I said.

"Don't worry about this deal, it's done," she said.

I hung up my phone and exhaled. That was close. Then I heard a car door shut right next to me. I turned to see that Mr. Malibu was trying to jack my Uber.

"Hey!" I yelled at him, "that's mine."

"I'm going to have to take this. I'm running late," he said, reaching for his wallet.

"Apologize to whomever you're going to be late to meet, because this is for me. The meter is already running," I answered.

That was when I got the notification on my phone. The driver had canceled my ride. What the?!

2

AIDEN

I stared at the woman standing outside of the Uber. She looked pissed. But I needed to get to our West Coast corporate retreat.

She opened my door, which took me by surprise. Did she have some type of mental imbalance, or was she on drugs?

She opened her mouth to speak, but her phone beeped. She looked down at her phone and then turned to the driver. "You canceled my ride!"

The driver shrugged. "He offered me $100."

She stomped her foot on the ground and threw up her hands. "You'd already started the meter!"

Damn. I thought she was just keeping the man waiting. I didn't know she was paying him to wait. That meant I was the asshole here.

I sighed. Time to turn on the charm.

I stared directly into her green eyes. "Please forgive me." I saw her lips part just a little. Yup, she wanted me.

I shot her a flirty smile, reached into my wallet, and

pulled out a $100 bill. "Take this, for what was already on the meter, and get yourself breakfast on me."

She didn't reach for the money. "I don't need your money. I need this car. So get the hell out."

Seriously? Judging from her big box store athletic wear, which I had to admit hugged her figure well, I couldn't believe she didn't need, or at least want, the money.

"Listen, lady, I'll come back for you," the Uber driver said.

Her head snapped to face the driver. "I'll deal with you in a minute."

I wanted to be contrite, even though I really didn't have the patience for this. "Get in the car, and I'll pay him to take you wherever you want to go after I'm done."

She folded her arms across her chest. "How about you go wherever you're going after I'm done?"

"I don't have time for this." Yes, I was in the wrong, but the driver wanted my business more than hers. Just as I was about to lean forward to tell the driver to leave, she swung the door open wide.

I stared at her. "What do you think you're doing?"

She tried to push her way into the backseat. "I don't have time for this either!"

I refused to budge.

She attempted to push me across the seat with her little body, and when she didn't succeed, she opted to climb over me.

Her butt grazed my lap as she took the place next to me in the backseat.

The move was insane, but it turned me on. I am a dude, after all.

Her long, light brown ponytail swayed back and forth as she panted from the effort of forcing her way into the backseat with me. If I wasn't in such a hurry, I'd think she was kind of cute. Not my regular type and possibly insane, but definitely cute.

"Take me to the Malibu Retreat Center," she instructed the driver.

"The one just up the hill?" the driver asked her.

She refused to even look in my direction. "Yes, it'll only take five minutes. Then you can take him to his Assholes Anonymous meeting or wherever he's going."

I couldn't help but smile. She worked for my father's company. Wouldn't little Miss Angry Pants be so surprised!

"All right, then that's what we'll do," I said.

She glared at me.

"You won," I said to her. "Can't we be friends now?"

"I have a higher standard for my friends," she said.

I couldn't believe she was talking to me this way. People never spoke to me this way. I'd give her one more opportunity to play nicely. "Truce?"

"Listen," she said to me, turning to face me. Those green eyes and her button nose made her angry face look so cute. "I know you're so sure you're important or some-thing, but there are a lot of us little people who are just trying to get to our shitty jobs. So why don't you sit there and wait for your turn for once instead of jumping to the front of the line. It's what the rest of us have to do."

I wondered what job she had at my father's company that she considered shitty. But I couldn't help but smile. "Nice speech, but for the record, I don't like my job either."

She turned back to me and gave me the once over. "Maybe if you stopped throwing around your money, you wouldn't have to work at all." Then she turned away from me and put in her earbuds.

I was only trying to be nice. Who the hell did she think she was!

I would've argued with her, but she'd regret talking to me this way soon enough.

It surprised me how hard I had to work to look unfazed by her words.

But they stung. Big time.

I'd tried to do something with my life instead of working for my father, but it all went to shit. We sat in silence as the Uber driver took us up the hill.

I didn't even hear any music or noise coming from her earbuds. She probably had them in just for show.

She stared out her window without even looking in my direction. I knew because I watched her the whole time.

The car pulled into the retreat center parking lot. She jumped out without even saying a word or even turning to look back at me or the driver.

"Do you know her name?" I asked the driver.

"If I remember right, sir, it was Laura or Laurel," he said. "Something with an 'L.'"

Hmm. We had thousands of employees throughout the world, and over four hundred working at our headquarters here in LA.

Of course, none of us were the type of men who forgot a pretty face. Not that any of us would date someone who worked for us. Dad had a strict rule against it, and I'd been the only one of us who'd broken it.

Huge mistake. It was why I'd been brought back home.

I tipped the driver an extra twenty and stepped out of the car. Now, where on Earth was I supposed to go in this place?

"There you are!" Damien said, approaching me on the walk.

"Yes, here I am," I said. For reasons I never understood, Damien seemed to think that he was the boss of me. I was the oldest, and I'd always wanted to strike out on my own. But Damien, he loved Bronson, Inc.

"I have a team t-shirt for you to wear," he said to me, attempting to hand me some ridiculous rag.

"No," I said, refusing to take it. There was no way I was going to dress like someone getting ready to play beach volleyball.

Damien gave up. He knew better than to push me on something so small. He was lucky that I'd even showed up.

"I'll introduce you to the team at the morning kickoff, and then you can shower and change during the mini team building sessions. But I expect you to lunch with us."

I looked at my watch. Twenty minutes until nine. "What time is lunch?"

"Half past noon," he said.

"And how long is this kickoff thing?"

"Ninety minutes."

"How about I skip it and nap? I've been on a plane all night."

"No. This schmoozing is the stuff you're actually good at," Damien insisted. "I took a red eye from Florida to get here in time for the start of all this, and I stayed all day.

And that was business. You've had the whole week off. You could've taken an earlier flight."

I glared at my brother.

"I'll tell you what. I'll introduce you, you'll say a few words about being happy to be back, stay for fifteen minutes, and then leave for your nap. But don't you dare oversleep. Dad might be here for lunch."

I couldn't help but smile. Damien was threatening to tattle on me to Dad like when we were kids.

"Okay, Damien. I'll play along."

"Seriously, Aiden. We need things to go more smoothly over here than they did in New York."

I stared hard at him. "You know what she was threatening to say about me and what really happened are two totally different things."

"More prudence would've kept those threats from affecting the company."

"I could just leave the company," I said. "Then there'd be no risk at all."

"That's something you have to take up with Dad. But while you're here, you're on my watch."

Without waiting for me to respond, Damien started up the path. I followed him, even though I didn't want to.

As the youngest, Damien had a chip on his shoulder about being taken seriously. But he was right, so I let it go.

Then I remembered the girl.

"So tell me," I said, hastening my pace to catch up with him, "do you know a woman named Laurel or Laura?"

Damien stopped and stared at me. "Do you mean Lauren McCall?"

"I don't know her last name, but she's an intense, possibly insane person. Long, light brown hair, green eyes, button nose. She looks like she's not wearing makeup, not just that thing where women put on makeup to look like they're not wearing makeup."

"Yep," Damien said, shaking his head, "that's definitely my Lauren."

I did not know why, but hearing him refer to her as "my Lauren" bugged me. "What do you mean 'my Lauren'?"

"She's my assistant. How do you know her?"

"She was at the Starbucks down the street earlier this morning," I said, leaving out our Uber altercation.

"Really?" Damien asked. "That girl is a mystery. I've never seen her outside of work. She never goes to any of the company social events."

"That doesn't seem like the type of employee you'd have as your assistant," I said. That his assistant wasn't all in on Team Bronson made me like her more.

"True," he agreed, "but she's an excellent worker. Always on time, dots all her I's, crosses every T."

"Well, she showed up at this retreat," I said.

"I made it mandatory," Damien confessed.

"Wait! You made it mandatory that employees come in for a 5-day retreat that includes the weekend?"

"We gave them two floating holidays to make up for it."

I shook my head no. "I can't believe you, bro. Just because you want to work weekends doesn't mean the employees do."

"They seemed excited about it," he said.

"Like they would tell you what they really think."

Damien didn't respond and continued monkeying with his Powerpoint display and shuffling papers to get ready for the stupid, daily kick-off thing.

My brain flashed back to her, calling this a shitty job. Maybe this mandatory weekend function was part of the reason she'd said that. I couldn't help but smile. Did my brother know that was what she thought of working for him?

"Well, you'll definitely have time to see her. She's helping me run this morning's kickoff meeting," Damien said. "But don't get any ideas about Lauren."

"For crying out loud, of course I won't," I said. "She's not my type."

"Brother," Damien said, opening up the door, "it doesn't matter if she were your type. Lauren will not give you the time of day."

"Is she a lesbian?" I asked.

"Are you that conceited?" Damien laughed. "Not every woman is dying for a chance to be with you."

"I just meant why wouldn't I have a chance?" I said, following him inside.

"Because Lauren is a serious person who has her shit together, and you're you," Damien said.

"Translation, she has a stick up her ass, and I'm fun," I said.

"Whatever you need to tell yourself."

Now I know why he liked her as his assistant. With the chip on his shoulder about being young and the stick up his butt, I wondered how my brother walked upright.

Once we were inside, Damien started shuffling papers and doing whatever it was he was doing at the lectern to get ready for this meeting.

"I'm gonna step outside for a minute," I said.

Damien looked up from his paper, shuffling. "I thought you quit smoking."

I headed for the door and yelled back to him. "I did, but I haven't quit fresh air."

The truth was all this nature really made me want a cigarette. I knew Malibu was beautiful, but I missed the energy of New York.

Just as I was stepping outside, my brother yelled to me, "be back in five minutes. We start on time here."

I rolled my eyes and stepped into the "fresh air" of the retreat to calm down by staring at the dirt and mountains or whatever.

The view was pleasant, though. I could see all the way to the Pacific Ocean. It definitely could relax some people.

It was interesting to think of how serene it was up here, just a mile and a half up the mountain from the Pacific Coast Highway. Or the PCH, as we all called it around here.

I grew up here in Malibu, but ditched it for the East Coast. I wanted to get away from my family and all their expectations.

Last week, I turned 34. Dad told me it was time for me to grow up and get serious, which I thought I'd be doing by getting married and having children.

Dad was very much against any of his sons falling in love because he thought it would just lead to heartache.

But as the oldest, I remembered Mom the most. Dad and Mom had been very much in love, and I'd wanted that for myself.

Except now I understood Dad. Genuine love was rare, and its imposters masqueraded so convincingly—especially if you were rich.

Nope. Never again.

I don't want to sound like a ridiculous rich guy, but

sometimes having a lot of money made it hard to figure out who really loves you for you and not for the stuff that your dad is leaving you.

I sighed as I looked out at the ocean in the distance. What had happened to me? I wanted to be my own man, but here I was.

I turned from the ocean and looked up at the mountain. Even though I resented being forced to come here, I appreciated the silence. It was as if the quietness forced you to think about yourself. Although, in doing so, I realized how much of me I didn't like.

The sound of someone running across the gravel path behind me interrupted my pity party. I turned. It was that Lauren woman.

"Hey!" I called out to her.

She turned and looked right at me.

"Fancy seeing you here, Lauren!" I said, letting her know I knew her name.

Her jaw dropped, and then she let out a startled yelp as she tripped.

Shit!

I sprinted over to her. A few drops of blood speckled the walk.

"Are you okay?" I asked.

"Tell me I didn't lose or chip any teeth," she said, looking up at me.

Fuck! I'd been with the West Coast office for all of five minutes, and I'd already broken my brother's assistant.

3

LAUREN

*S*o far, I'd dealt with two assholes in one morning —Tess and Mr. Malibu. I hadn't handled either of them perfectly, but I'd won both battles. My nerves were shot. I needed to get to the meeting on time and get my head together.

Being at this retreat had really thrown me off balance. I missed my morning routine. By this time, I would have made my latte and watched an old Ron Popeil infomercial while I sketched out ideas for my own inventions. As dorky or weird as that sounds, it made me happy to start my day doing something just for me.

I left my hair in a ponytail and jumped into the shower, careful to not get my hair wet. I barely had time for the shower. There'd be no way I'd have time to wash and dry my hair. It took me only a few quick seconds to change into fresh clothes.

I glanced at my watch: 8:54. If I ran, I could get to the main building in three minutes, giving me three minutes to catch my breath and get organized.

Perfect.

I grabbed my clipboard, my room key, and my phone. Then I dashed out of my room, down the trail toward the main meeting hall.

From the looks of it, people had stayed up pretty late last night after the "Margarita Mingle."

I thought a margarita machine was a strange choice, considering a group of friars ran this retreat center, but everyone seemed to like it. I'd opted not to drink despite all the peer pressure to "loosen up."

For once, I was glad that my slacker coworkers would stagger in a bit late. The later they were, the earlier I looked.

I jogged further down the path. The building was even closer than I remembered. I smiled. Even if things didn't go according to plan, some quick thinking and hustle could get a girl back on track.

The key, for me, was to always have a plan.

"Lauren!" a man's voice called out to me.

I turned to see who it was. It was that guy that tried to steal my Uber. What was he doing here?

Then I realized why he looked so familiar. He was one of the Bronson sons—the one transferring here.

Fuck! Was I super bitchy or merely justifiably miffed about the ride-share? Was it his fault or mine? Was he the type of guy that would feel entitled to that car and get me fired?

My ankle rolled on a rock or something, and before I knew it, I was on the ground.

A gritty feeling in my back teeth, along with an iron taste, registered in my mind.

"Are you okay?" the asshole from Starbucks asked me.

"Tell me I didn't lose or chip any teeth," I said. I worried I'd knocked out a tooth when I fell to the ground. Dental implants were expensive and not covered by our company insurance. Would I have to get dentures?

"Smile, let me see," he said, squatting next to me on the ground.

What was with men telling women to smile? "I'm not in the mood to smile," I muttered and then bared my teeth so he could look.

"I didn't mean it like that," he said.

I wiped my mouth with my left hand, but it wasn't enough. I turned my head and spit on the ground. The spit was pure red.

He whipped out his cell phone. "I'll call an ambulance."

"Are they that bad?" I asked. I realized he hadn't told me about my teeth.

"Your teeth are okay, but we need to make sure the rest of you is, too."

I tried to get up, and the soreness in my wrist made me realize that something had gone wrong. "I landed on my wrist."

He stared at his phone. "There's no damn cell reception here!"

I was still laying on the ground. "Can you help me sit up?"

He turned to me and rushed to help. "Oh my God! Yes."

I sat up and stared down at the ground, seeing my clipboard snapped in half.

I'd fallen, still clutching the paperwork for this morning's meeting.

Mr. Malibu looked at my wrist. "That doesn't look good. We need to get you some ice."

My mind wandered for a moment, and then I remembered the meeting. "Shit! The meeting! I'll be late."

He shook his head. "We've got to get you to the doctor."

"I'll be fine," I said, even though I was anything but sure.

"Do you think you can stand if I help you up?"

I wanted to sound confident, even though I did not know. "Absolutely."

He put his arms around me. His aftershave smelled fantastic. He helped me up with ease. He looked down at me, his expression concerned. "Are you okay?"

I nodded yes. "Thanks."

I walked toward the main room for the meeting, but I took one step and wobbled big time.

The unknown Bronson brother steadied me against his side. I mumbled thanks again.

People headed into the kickoff meeting, and I saw Mr. Damien step out the front door and look around. Everything seemed like it was getting darker. I wondered if a cloud had just blocked the sun.

"Mr. Damien is looking for me," I said, worrying I'd be late. "We have to get over there."

"We have to get you to the hospital," Mr. Malibu said.

My mind immediately went to the cost of going to the hospital. I was at a work event, so was this covered by workmen's comp? There was no way I was going to a hospital. Hospitals were for last resorts only. Going there unnecessarily could break a person financially—a lesson I'd learned the hard way with my folks.

"No hospital," I insisted. "I'll just go home and take it from there."

"You're limping," Mr. Malibu said.

"I think I could still drive with it," I heard myself say. I wasn't thinking clearly.

"Damien!" Mr. Malibu yelled.

Damien spotted us and immediately ran over. "Lauren, are you okay? What happened?"

I opened my mouth, but I couldn't think straight. I could hear a sort of loud cricket noise. "Where are all those crickets?"

"She was running to the meeting when I called out to her. It distracted her, and she tripped," Mr. Malibu explained to his brother. I tried to remember Mr. Malibu's name from the memo, but my mind blanked.

"I don't have any cell reception, but I think I should take her to the hospital," he continued.

A co-worker came over, but my brain couldn't remember her name either. It unsettled me I was having a hard time focusing and remembering things. Deep down, I knew that my wrist and ankle probably would not heal on their own.

"Oh, my god!" I heard her say. "Your wrist looks terrible!"

I tried to look down at my wrist, but I lost my balance.

"Easy," Mr. Malibu said, holding me tighter. He turned to my co-worker. "Find some ice for us."

I wanted water to rinse my mouth so I could check on my teeth, but all I said was "and my teeth", which drew puzzled stares from everyone.

"Okay," she said, and I watched as she jogged toward the cafeteria. I bet no one would distract her and make her break her clipboard.

"My clipboard," I tried to say, but my words weren't coming out.

"I'll have someone take her to a doctor," Damien said.

"Listen, I haven't even been here, nobody knows I'm supposed to be here, it might as well be me," Mr. Malibu told Damien. "Plus, I feel like this is my fault. Give me your keys."

I heard them argue a little more about stuff I couldn't understand, and then I felt myself sort of sinking.

I heard them ask me stuff like "Are you okay?" but it seemed as if they were underwater.

"Yeah," I muttered, as everything got darker. How big was that cloud? How many crickets were around here? My field of vision narrowed until everything went black.

4

LAUREN

I woke up on a sofa of what I assumed was one of the friar's offices. How the heck had I gotten here?

"Don't worry, Angie is running to the front office to have them call an ambulance," someone said.

Angie! That was her name! And then my mind registered the word "ambulance."

My heart jumped in my throat. One hospital stay could ruin all my careful financial plans and attempts to get ahead in the world. "No ambulance!"

"It'll be fine," Mr. Malibu said.

Although I was a little woozy from passing out, I forced myself to sit up and made my voice clear. "It won't be fine, and there's no way you're getting me into an ambulance for what's probably a sprained wrist."

Angie entered the room holding a dishrag filled with ice. "One friar is already calling."

She must've heard me from the hall.

"Tell him to cancel it, and you can give me that," I said, motioning to the ice.

She handed me the dishrag filled with ice, and I placed it on my wrist. I forced myself not to wince too hard, even though the pain shot through my entire arm like a surge of electricity. "See, I'm fine."

Everyone looked at my wrist. It'd swollen to almost twice its size. It didn't look like they were buying my story.

"If there's some sort of ibuprofen or Tylenol or something like that, I'll take it. Then we'll go to the urgent care center covered in my medical plan." I turned to Mr. Malibu and stared hard at him, silently blaming him for my predicament. "I won't commit financial suicide because you all freaked out and called an ambulance."

He looked duly contrite, but too guilt-ridden to help me. So, I turned my attention to my boss, Mr. Damien.

"Mr. Damien," I said, forcing my voice to sound clear yet serious, even though I was on the verge of passing out again. "You know I know the right thing to do here."

He nodded and turned to Angie and gestured for her to take care of it.

"I'll tell them to cancel it," she said and dashed back out.

"Now that that's taken care of," I said. "I'll just need a ride to urgent care."

"I'll take you," Mr. Malibu said. "You guys should get back and get the retreat started."

The meeting! I looked down at my watch, and it was twenty minutes past 9 o'clock. My first instinct was to worry about being late, but then I realized as a person who wouldn't be attending the meeting, there would be no way for me to be late.

Angie returned. "Ambulance canceled."

"Perfect," I said, realizing I'd need my insurance cards. "I need to go to my room to get my purse."

"You didn't have it with you?" Angie asked.

I realized she'd been running around this entire time with her purse on her shoulder. What a hassle!

I looked down at the pocket of my yoga pants, relieved to see my phone hadn't fallen out. My phone had a wallet attachment on the back. "I didn't want to have to worry about carrying my purse around all day as we went from event to event." I'd slipped the keycard in it along with my driver's license.

"I'll go to your room and get your purse," Angie volunteered.

I reached for my cabin key with my right hand, but thought better of it. I dug my keys out of my pocket with my left hand, which was kinda difficult because they were in my right pocket.

After some wrangling, I got the key card out and handed it to her. "4C."

She nodded.

A friar entered with a glass of water and a bottle of ibuprofen.

I reached for the bottle of ibuprofen, but Mr. Malibu stopped me. I glared at him.

"How did you plan on opening it?" he asked as he popped open the child safety cap.

Crap! Having a broken wrist was totally going to suck. Please let it just be a sprain, I thought.

I looked down at it. My wrist throbbed. The swelling

and bruising made my stomach queasy. Mental note: Don't look at deformed wrist.

"How many?" Mr. Malibu asked, shaking the bottle gently to get my attention.

"Are they 200 mg capsules?"

He squinted at the bottle and nodded yes.

Damn. Even his squinting was sexy. I shook off that thought and focused on my basic math. "I'll take four."

"Isn't that a lot?" he asked.

"It's the maximum dose. Don't worry, I'll tell the doctor. He'll agree with me."

Mr. Malibu doled out four pills and handed them to me. When his hand brushed my palm, the warmth of it excited me.

I looked up at him, and he looked down at me with those intense, dark eyes.

I put one pill in my mouth, set the other three on the couch, and motioned for the water. My boss handed it to me. I took each pill separately and then picked up the glass with one hand.

"Why not just take them all at once?" Mr. Malibu asked.

"Because I don't want to choke to death after breaking my wrist," I said. I never understood people who could take several pills at once. It seemed like a one-way ticket to Chokesville. I took the other three, one at a time.

My coworker returned with my purse, and I tried to get up on my own. It was hard getting up from a low couch only using one hand. I really needed to work on strengthening my abs.

Mr. Damien and his brother helped me up. It relieved me to find that my ankle was already feeling better.

"Can you stand?" my boss asked.

"Yes, the ankle must've just been twisted funny. It feels better now," I said.

"Don't put too much weight on it anyway," Mr. Malibu said.

Sure, now he was Mr. Helpful.

I took a step for a second and wobbled a little.

"Aiden," Mr. Damien said.

"On it," he said, sweeping his arm under me and lifting me into his arms.

I gasped. My left arm shot around his neck to keep me from falling.

"Don't worry, I've got you," he said, his warm breath on my neck.

Holy fucking hell! Even annoyed and in pain, his hard chest, sexy voice, and hot breath made me breathe heavier. Thank god he was carrying me or I'd have gone weak in the knees.

I put my head down on his shoulder, hoping to hide any signs of me being turned on.

The group of us slowly walked toward the parking lot. As we passed the meeting room, my coworkers stared at me. So mortifying.

Finally, we made it to Mr. Damien's car. Someone opened the door, and Mr. Malibu placed me in the car. Damn, he was strong.

Angie popped in and handed me the ice-filled rag. The ice was melting everywhere, but I tried to keep it on my wrist to keep the swelling down.

After a few words, I watched Angie and my boss walk away, and then Mr. Malibu joined me in the car. "Where to?"

I tried to dig my phone out of my right pocket of my yoga pants so I could look up an urgent care center in my plan.

But between sitting down in the bucket seat of my boss's sports car and having my phone in the opposite pocket because I was usually a righty, it was nearly impossible.

"You have issues asking for help, don't you?" Mr. Malibu asked.

"Listen, Mr. Malibu, this is all your fault, and I don't need your criticism or your help," I snapped.

"Mr. Malibu?"

I realized I'd said the quiet part out loud.

5

AIDEN

"*A*iden," I corrected. "The name is Aiden Bronson."

She pretended to ignore me, but I caught a fleeting look of embarrassment when I corrected her.

I wanted to dig further into this Mr. Malibu thing, but the way she was twisting her wrist to get into that pocket made me nervous. I didn't want to have to deal with an employee with two broken wrists right off the bat.

"Would it be easier if you stood up?" I asked her.

"I've got it," she said, finally freeing her phone from her pocket. Then I heard the sound that every person knows so well. It was the sound of her phone hitting the side panel of the door and skating somewhere under the seat.

I got out of the driver's seat, walked over to the passenger side, and opened her door.

"Do you see it?" she asked.

It impressed me how well she was handling all this. That wrist looked terrible.

I was glad that my brother and the rest of the

employees had finally gone into whatever building that was over there to start their bullshit meeting.

"I see it," I said.

Luckily, it was just under the seat and I wouldn't have to reach over her to get it.

I forced myself to not let my eyes linger on her yoga pants. So they came with pockets now. Interesting. I hadn't appreciated just how hot she was when we were fighting over the Uber.

Her pride and self-sufficiency impressed me. I was used to women who depended on me for everything.

The helpless act had always made me feel important, more like a man. But looking back, that damsel in distress type felt burdensome, and at worst, manipulative.

"Did you find it?" she asked.

"Yeah, I see it. Just lift your right leg a little so I can reach it."

She lifted her leg, and I reached for the phone. The top of my hand grazed her calf, and it actually turned me on.

Damn. If that calf-graze did it for me, I'd taken too much of a break from having sex. My broken engagement and subsequent PR threat had demolished my interest in women. Maybe it was a good thing that I was getting excited. It could mean I was finally getting over Christine.

I handed Lauren her cell in her left hand and rushed to get back in the driver's seat. With every minute, it seemed like her wrist became more swollen. "I'm just gonna head down the hill since we're obviously going to go that way, while you look up where we're going," I said.

"Damn it! I forgot there's no cell service here!"

"This retreat is going to be a nightmare," I muttered to myself.

"My thoughts exactly."

I subverted my instinct to rev the engine and tear out of the parking lot. I wanted to make sure that I didn't have her sway too much and risk her hitting her wrist.

I took the corner easily and headed down the mountain.

"I appreciate that," she said.

"Appreciate what?"

"You're taking it easy on the speed, which I'm sure is not your nature."

I appreciated being appreciated, but I didn't like her tone regarding my nature. "What do you mean by that?" I turned out of the parking lot and down the private driveway, turning onto Cross Canyon Road.

"Men who drive sports cars like to drive fast."

"That may be true, but you forget, this is my brother's car." She thought she was so clever.

"And you don't have one just like it or similar?"

Okay, so she was right, but I'd get back at her.

"My name is Aiden, in case you didn't hear me earlier. You can call me that instead of Mr. Malibu."

Her face reddened. I enjoyed having one up on her, but a part of me worried she was only embarrassed about calling me Mr. Malibu because I was the boss.

"You've got to understand, Mr. Aiden, I'm not exactly in my right mind," she said, holding up her wrist. "The pain is a little much."

I smiled. "Understood, but you can call me Aiden."

"I prefer to keep things professional."

Damien was right about her, and that would make things easy for me. But I had to admit, it stung a bit. A change of subject was in order. "Which way should we go when we get to PCH?"

"Whichever way is easier for you. We can take Malibu Canyon and Las Virgenes over the hill, or we'll take PCH and then jump on the ten. But just to let you know we're probably going to end up in Van Nuys or some place in the Valley."

"Wait. How deep into the Valley? Why not some place here in Malibu?"

"Because that's where the urgent care center on my insurance plan is."

"There's probably an urgent care center right on PCH. I'll get directions as soon as we have cell reception again."

"There might be a place in Woodland Hills on my plan, but I'll look for it when we get down the hill," she countered.

I took a moment to think of a better solution than driving all over the Valley, and I remembered the urgent care center I'd gone to when I'd broken my collar bone mountain biking was just up the street. "Our family goes to an office close to here. You'll get your x-rays right away. At your Van Nuys place, you'll end up sitting there for ages."

"I will not go broke going to your fancy Malibu doctor. There's going to be worker's comp. forms to fill out and tons of paperwork. I'm not about to do this the wrong way and wind up paying through the nose by going to some doctor out of my plan."

"For crying out loud," I muttered under my breath. I was just trying to help her, and this was how she acted.

"I'm sorry my poverty is getting in the way of your

day," she said. "You know what. Just drop me off at the Starbucks at the bottom of the hill. I'll get an Uber to take me to the right place."

"Are you kidding me?"

"I won't be peer-pressured, or worse, boss-pressured into ruining my financial future just because you're an impatient asshole."

Did she just call me an asshole?

"I'm an asshole because I want you to get to a doctor sooner rather than later. And by the way, the longer you wait to get that checked out, the worse things could be for you."

"Well, that's just a risk I'll have to take. Just drop me off at the Starbucks at the bottom of the hill."

I wouldn't drop her off or be a chauffeur for the entire day because of a few thousand dollars. "I'm taking you to my doctor. You won't have to pay a dime."

"And how and why is that?"

"I guess I feel bad because I saw it all happen," I answered.

"We both know you caused it."

"I just called out your name. I didn't tell you to keep running without looking where you were going."

She glared at me. "You called out my name because you knew it would surprise me that you were here. Otherwise, you would've just waited until we got inside. You wanted me to realize that I was talking to my boss's brother, and then I'd have to feel bad for not letting you steal my Uber. This is totally your fault. You know what you were thinking when you did it. You didn't count on the fact that you were endangering me. Because you're a selfish prick who doesn't think about other people and only sees things from your own point of view, and the world lets it happen, because you're rich!"

I couldn't believe she'd dared talk to me that way. The phrase "Who do you think you are?" flew out of my mouth, which was completely not the right thing to say. It made me look exactly like the privileged asshole she accused me of being.

"I'm the person getting out of this damn car," she yelled. "Pull over."

I gritted my teeth. What the hell was happening? How had it come to this? Was I going to be written up to HR when I hadn't even officially started working yet?

"Listen, I'm sorry," I said to Lauren. "I didn't mean to be insensitive. I'm just concerned about your welfare. And if you'll allow me, I want to drive you to the nearest facility that will take care of you."

Tears rolled down her cheeks. "Listen, I don't mean to be rude. The pain is making me short-tempered."

"Please, forgive me," I said.

"Let's just pretend as if none of this happened," she said, her voice shaking.

This absolutely did not look good for me. This was my brother's personal assistant. She was obviously a straight shooter. And now, I'd completely fucked up my first day back on the West Coast. This couldn't go this way.

"I'll drive you wherever you want," I said. "If you want to go to Van Nuys, I'll drive you to Van Nuys. I don't know where that is exactly, but I will type whatever address you want into this navigation system. As soon as we get fucking reception. Please, please tell me what you need and what I can do."

She went quiet. I looked over at her and saw she was staring at her wrist. "This looks kind of bad."

That wrist looked like Frankenstein's wrist. My heart ached for her. "Lauren, can I take care of this for you?"

"I can't risk being stuck with some giant medical bill, which I know is not something that you're familiar with, but please stop making this harder for me. It really hurts and I'm scared, but I can't afford to make the wrong call here."

My heart dropped. I've always had money, and I never worried about how much it would cost to go to the doctor. It had to be a really hard way to live. And although I thought about it from time to time, watching this capable person moved to tears and in pain, trying to decide if she should hurt longer to make sure that she could afford care, broke my heart.

"Don't worry," I said. "I'll take care of it. I'll take care of everything. You're my brother's right-hand person," I said, using a gentle gender-neutral term.

"You don't understand," she said, her voice smaller than before.

A minor accident derailing someone's life was something I knew about only in theory, but to see someone wrestling with it right in front of me was gut-wrenching. "Let me take care of this."

The idea of her suffering a minute longer than she had to broke my heart. I told myself it was because I felt guilty for trying to steal her Uber and causing her to fall.

She wiped her tears from her face with her good hand. Nothing about her screamed drama queen. She didn't even make a sound when she cried, only one small sniffle.

There was no way any of my brothers or my dad

would think any altercation between us was her fault. I needed to fix this stat. I vowed that by the end of the day, Lauren would only have good things to say about me.

6

LAUREN

*T*he car went quiet as Aiden drove. I stared out the window and avoided eye contact. The part where I couldn't stop myself from crying didn't help.

I wiped away the tears. It was hard to wipe away my tears without my right hand, and my wrist hurt. Was I doing the right thing?

This day hadn't gone the way I planned. I wanted the deal to close and to get through the retreat with no drama. Why did I even have to go to this stupid retreat? Wasn't it enough to just want to do your job well and leave? Why did companies want to make you feel like "you're part of the family?"

I knew why. It was so they could lull you into false security and take advantage of you.

This company would not be "like family" no matter what the team building bullshit said.

I had a family. And I loved them. There would always be love in my heart from them, even though they were gone. There was no way I'd let some corporate bullshit try to replace them.

I had plans for myself and my future.

But had I put all of that in jeopardy? I didn't intend to be a bitch to Aiden. It was just the entitled way he stole my Uber and the fact that it didn't even occur to him that some of us, as in some families like mine, had genuine issues with medical bills.

My parents had worked their entire lives to save for retirement, and when Mom got sick, it was all gone. By the time Dad got sick, we had to rely on government aid. Even after they died, bill collectors tried to get me to cover the debt.

If it wasn't for Mackenzie and Carolyn, my two best friends who still lived in Florida, I'd be totally alone. But none of us were financially stable enough to provide much of a safety net for the other. But one day, I'd change that. I was going to make something of myself, build my fortune outside of my job.

It amazed me how many people tried to get ahead in the corporate world, thinking that being an exemplary employee would somehow pay off.

Businesses bankrupted all the time and left their employees in a lurch. Heck, when my mom got sick, her job wanted to cancel her health insurance because she wasn't eligible after so many days of not working because she was in the hospital. What good was paying for health insurance if they were just going to take it away when you finally needed it?

No. None of that would be my fate.

"We're here," he said.

I looked up and saw the valet. Damn. This was absolutely going to be expensive.

"I'm sorry. I made a mistake." I tried to stop him, but he was already out of the car.

A healthcare assistant in a pristine white jacket opened up my door. He held a wheelchair out for me. "Are you our patient?"

"I don't—"

Aiden interrupted me. "Yes, it's her wrist and ankle."

The assistant swept in and put his arm underneath my shoulder.

"I can walk," I said.

"This is just our procedure to make sure everything's okay. You just rest. We'll take care of you." He eased me out of the car and settled me into the wheelchair.

The kindness of the assistant put a lump in my throat. I wanted to relax, not think of the pain or the bills, and just get better.

He pushed me into the urgent care center, and instead of being pushed into a waiting area, he wheeled me directly into an actual examination room.

"The nurse will be with you in a moment, and then the doctor will see you."

"I'll be taking care of everything," Aiden said.

"Of course, sir," he said with a polite nod, and then left.

I looked around the immaculate office and took a deep breath. Please God, let him be true to his word. Don't let him go back to work, have his father yell at him, and then have me lose my job, or worse, be on the hook for these bills.

"Don't worry, Lauren."

I looked up at him.

"I'm a man of my word," he added, as if he could hear my thoughts.

I felt like it was the pain that was making me emotional, but his firm voice telling me he was a man of his word made me want to burst into tears and have him hold me. I'd been on my own for so long.

If it hadn't been because I'd gone to grad school out here, and then gotten this job at Bronson, Inc., I would've moved back to Florida to be closer to Carolyn and Mackenzie.

"Does it hurt a lot?" Aiden asked.

"No. Not much at all."

He nodded, but there was something in his expression that made me feel like he knew I was lying.

Somehow the room felt way too small with just the two of us in this doctor's office. Although, as far as examining rooms go, this was the nicest and biggest one that I'd ever been in. There was even a white lounge sofa.

"Do you need some water? They have a cappuccino machine in the lounge. I can make you a latte or whatever it is you like."

"No," I said. The latte I'd drank in lieu of water or breakfast was still disco dancing in my stomach. Almost on cue, my stomach let out a Chewbacca-like roar. Please God, don't let me pass gas right now, I prayed.

"We'll get you something to eat after this."

"They'll have lunch at the retreat," I said.

"Do you want to go back there with your Franken-wrist? I'm not in excruciating pain, and I don't want to be there."

I laughed. Neither of us wanted to go to that bullshit

retreat. "Do you think having this injury would be a good reason for me not to go back?"

Then, I regretted it. This was my boss's brother, after all. I couldn't be plotting get-out-of-work excuses with my boss's brother, who was also the owner's son.

"I'm sure the doctor will give you a note."

"No, I should go back."

"You'll do what the doctor says because you strike me as a person who always does the right thing."

I was a person who did the right thing, but the way he said it pissed me off. "Was that a dig?"

"For crying out loud! It's a compliment. Doing the right thing is what everyone is supposed to do. Or at least that's what everybody keeps telling me."

I wanted to cross my arms, but I couldn't without risking hurting my wrist, so I just looked away from him. "You sure as hell don't make it sound like it."

There was something about him thinking he knew me when he didn't that pissed me off. He knew nothing about me. And he never would.

The nurse entered the examining room and saved me from digging a deeper hole for myself. I needed to watch my temper. There was only so much shit I could blame on the pain before that got old.

"I understand you're having trouble with your wrist and ankle," she said, looking over some paperwork.

I held up my incredibly swollen wrist. "I think it's fine."

Aiden laughed.

"Sorry about that," she said with a smile. "I was buried in my clipboard."

"That's what I'm usually like, but my clipboard broke in half when I fell."

She made notes on her clipboard. "We're definitely going to need an x-ray for both the ankle and wrist."

The nurse took my vitals and then asked me some questions regarding my medical history. She was filling in the forms for me. In all my life, I'd never had those forms filled out for me by someone other than my folks. It was like rich people lived on another planet.

She looked up from her clipboard. "Do you have your insurance cards with you?"

"You won't need any of that," Aiden interrupted.

The nurse turned to Aiden.

"I'll be paying in full today," he said.

She smiled. "That cuts down on the rest of the paperwork, then."

It relieved me that Aiden was being aggressively certain that they wouldn't have any billing information on me. If doctors had billing information, they would definitely use it at some point. Well, not all doctors. Just the ones I was used to dealing with.

The assistant returned to take me to the x-ray room.

"The nurse said to x-ray her ankle, too," Aiden said.

"We will check her ankle and wrist, Mr. Bronson," the assistant said as he wheeled me away. Somewhere between the car and now, the assistant had learned Aiden's name. The Bronsons were that rich.

A half-hour later, the doctor had diagnosed me with a broken wrist and sprained ankle. Luckily, the fracture wasn't as serious as it could've been.

It looked like it would take about eight weeks for my wrist to heal.

"I was in the middle of a company retreat," I said to the doctor. "Can you write me a note for that?"

"You can pick it up from the nurse with your prescription. The nurse will outfit you with a splint now, and you'll come back for a cast in a week after the swelling goes down."

Cast! How the hell was I going to drive my car home? How the hell was I going to work?

"Will I be able to drive with the cast?" I asked.

"Driving is off-limits. Also, your right ankle is sprained, so you'll need crutches. Keep your weight off of it for now. You can use ice packs to bring down the swelling. Keep it elevated as much as possible."

The doctor turned to Aiden. "The nurse will schedule the follow-up visits. We'll see how the ankle and the wrist are doing then. Make sure she keeps the weight off that ankle and doesn't move that wrist around."

A cast! A sprained ankle! Follow-up visits. Shit.

7

AIDEN

*M*y gut sank, realizing that she not only broke her wrist but sprained her ankle. Why had I called out to her? I thought it would be a funny joke, but she was running so fast to get to the meeting on time. I should've known.

It was my fault that she was running late. If she hadn't been arguing with me over the Uber, she would've at least had a few extra minutes.

Maybe my ex was right. Maybe I was self-centered.

The orderly wheeled Lauren into another room with the nurse. I followed and watched while the nurse patched up Lauren's wrist and iced her ankle.

My telephone rang. It was Dad. The nurse and Lauren looked up at me.

"I'll take this outside," I said, scooting out of the room. I didn't want either of them to see me grovel.

"Hi Dad," I said, trying to sound casual as I strode through the lobby and headed outside.

"I take it by how long it took you to answer that things aren't going well," Dad said.

"As well as one could expect," I said, keeping my comments vague. What did he know? How much did I have to tell him?

"It's great you volunteered to take care of the situation. It'll show the employees that you care. We need you to make a good impression," Dad said.

I exhaled. As much as I wanted to be indignant with my recent romantic history, I'd given everyone cause to doubt me.

"I saw it happen and wanted to make sure she was okay," I said. I deliberately avoided mentioning the part where I'd distracted her and was partially responsible for her fall.

"Well, that Lauren is a good one—a straight shooter."

"She's very feisty," I said, and regretted it.

"Don't get any ideas about Lauren."

"Dad," I started, but he interrupted me.

"She won't have anything to do with you, anyway. But remember, Aiden, let's not have any of that nonsense that happened in New York here."

"You have my word."

Dad didn't respond to my assurance, which stung.

"So how is she?" he asked, breaking the silence.

"She has a sprained ankle and a broken wrist. She won't be back at the retreat, and I don't know how much she'll be able to do at the office."

"Well, she's never taken a vacation—always took the money—a girl after my own heart. But, as your mother used to say, nature doles out rest if you don't take the time."

It surprised me that Dad knew so much about Lauren.

"How long has she been working for us?" I couldn't help but ask.

I heard keys tapping. Dad must've been reading her employee file. "She did a paid internship here during her last year of getting her masters. Since then, she's been with us three years with four raises. It's strange. Most of the people who become assistants, especially the talented ones, keep moving up. But for reasons that I don't understand, Lauren has turned down her last two promotion offers."

"Maybe she enjoys working with Damien." I couldn't help but feel a little jealous.

"They're definitely a very efficient team. But there's no funny business with Damien and Lauren, that's for sure. Neither of them are the type."

My father's comment jabbed at my sore spot again. It implied that I was the type, and I had no defense. His disappointment with me permeated all of our conversations as of late.

"Make sure she gets home okay, and arrangements will have to be made for her car," Dad continued. "Double check her address. Make sure it doesn't go to the wrong place."

"Will do."

"Son," Dad said, his voice stern. "Get back to the retreat as soon as you're done. I'll be there tomorrow, and I expect you there, too."

I hung up the phone with Dad, went inside, and sat down in the waiting area. I figured Lauren could use her privacy, and I needed time to get all her paperwork settled.

If Dad wouldn't be there until tomorrow, then maybe I could spend the day "taking care" of Lauren. Plus, I'd turn on the charm and ease the tension between the two of us.

I wondered if Damien knew Dad wouldn't be there for lunch, or if he implied Dad "might" be at lunch to make sure I wouldn't sleep through it. My money was on the latter. Thinking about Damien made my resolve to smooth things over with Lauren more resolute.

It wouldn't do me any good if she complained about me to him. He'd go straight to Dad with it. Damien had always been a tattle tale.

Of all people to get into a fight with within seconds of moving to the West Coast, it had to be one of Dad's star employees and Damien's assistant.

An image of Lauren's adorable face popped into my mind. It would be fun to spend the day with her. But then Dad's warning not to get any ideas echoed in my thoughts.

He'd tried to warn me about my fiancée. But I hadn't listened.

This time I definitely would.

8

LAUREN

I slumped in my chair and exhaled when Aiden left. Not having to worry about what to say or do while he watched my wrist get bandaged up allowed me to relax. I wondered who called him.

It was all I could do not to stare at him and drool. I thought I was immune to good-looking men, having worked with three of the five Bronson sons. But the more time I spent with Aiden Bronson, the more my brain couldn't help wondering what his shoulders looked like under that expensive dress shirt and suit jacket.

"All right," the nurse said after outfitting my wrist with a splint. "That'll do it for now. I'll schedule your follow-up out front. Do not take this off until we give you the okay."

I nodded and admired her handiwork. The splint rendered my wrist immobile, and it felt more secure.

"The assistant will be here to wheel you out, and I'll have your prescriptions, paperwork, and crutches ready for you at the front," she said as she exited the room.

It was nice being in a fancy urgent care center.

Honestly, it felt like I was at a regular doctor's office, but bigger, brighter, and kinder.

Not that I thought doctors were mean, but it felt like they didn't have time to care. Too many patients. Too much paperwork.

When I made my millions, I'd only go to doctors like this.

Within minutes the assistant arrived, swept me back into the wheelchair, and wheeled me to the nurses' station. The nurse said she'd call my prescriptions into the pharmacy near my house and gave me some "samples" for now. Seriously?

I asked her what type of paperwork I'd have to fill out for work, thinking that I'd have a mountain of things to fill out, and she assured me she'd coordinate with HR.

She opened a drawer behind her, grabbed something, and handed it to me. "Here's an ice pack for later."

I was going to say I had one at home, but the one she gave me had a nifty strap on it—way nicer than any icepack I'd ever owned.

"Could I have another one?"

She reached back into her drawer and took out another one. "Of course."

The assistant wheeled me out to the lobby. "I'll be right back with your crutches."

Aiden stood up and greeted me. I couldn't help but admire his gorgeous body. Next to my wheelchair he seemed so tall.

"Don't worry, even when you return here for your cast, it's covered. They have my billing info."

"It'll be a little far for me to come out here next week—especially if I can't drive."

Aiden smiled. "I know you know how to call an Uber. Get one and submit your receipts to my office for reimbursement."

"If you say so."

He feigned a shocked expression. "Did you agree with me on something?"

The sooner I stopped acting like a total bitch to one of the owner's sons, the better off I'd be. "I can be a very agreeable person."

I looked at my doctor's note. It said I couldn't move my right hand for the next few weeks. "So how does this work come Monday? Do I come in?"

"When I return to the retreat, I will find out more details and have those relayed to you," he said.

"Because if there aren't modified duties arranged for me, there will be temporary disability paperwork for me to fill out."

"I assure you, HR will take care of it. In the meantime, let's get something to eat."

My stomach had been grumbling all morning, but I wasn't sure it was such a great idea to get lunch with him.

"We can go through a drive-through if you're hungry," I suggested.

He shot me a look like I was crazy.

"What? You don't like Taco Bell?" I teased.

He shrugged. "I've never had Taco Bell. I'm sure it's fine, but Geoffrey's is only three minutes from here."

Geoffrey's was expensive. I couldn't afford it, and I couldn't go in there dressed like this. "They'll be serving lunch at the retreat in about two hours."

"Listen, if you're in a hurry, I'll gladly take you home. But if you're worried about me buying us lunch, you'd be doing me a favor. My father has told me I have to get back to that retreat and take part in my brother's corporate festival of the ridiculous, but only after I'm done attending to you."

I exhaled and looked away. "I'm not dressed for it."

"Of course you are. This is Malibu. The less you dress up, the richer they think you are."

He had me there, and with all the embarrassing shit that had happened to me, why not get some free fancy food and an epic view out of it?

"I've never been to Geoffrey's," I admitted.

Aiden smiled. "You'll love it."

9

AIDEN

I pulled up to the restaurant's valet and jumped out of the car before Lauren tried to get out on her own.

I pointed to the valet opening Lauren's door. "Don't let her get up. Make her wait."

I rushed around the car, grabbed Lauren's crutches, and handed them to the valet. I reached into the car to help her up. "Okay, here we go."

Her arms wrapped around my neck as I lifted her. I hated to let her go, but I didn't dare linger a second longer than appropriate.

She stood on one foot and held onto the car for balance.

I reached for her from the valet.

"I don't need those," she said, waving off the crutches.

"Humor me."

She held up her splinted wrist. "I'll only take one because I have no actual way to grip the other just yet."

I handed one crutch back to the valet. "Put this in the back seat or the trunk."

I handed the singular crutch to Lauren.

She took it and slid it under her left arm. "Is it true that Marilyn Monroe used to eat here?"

"That's before my time, but I've heard stories to the effect."

She hobbled forward on one crutch. "You look old enough to know."

I looked down at her and saw her smiling. She was teasing me. Unbelievable. "I'm only five or six years older than you."

"Who says I don't look old?" she asked.

"I say," I answered, as I walked close enough to steady her if she lost her balance. If Dad hadn't told me she'd gone to grad school, I would've guessed she was twenty-two, and she looked even younger in the sunlight.

The hostess sat us on the patio where there was a gorgeous view of the Pacific Ocean. I'd been here hundreds of times growing up, but watching Lauren look out at the water made me enjoy the view all the more.

She wouldn't let me help her to the table or walk up the walk.

I admired her independence. Henry, the afternoon server, came to our table. "Aiden, you're back."

"Just got in this morning."

"We're glad you came to visit us so soon. What can I start you two off with today?"

Henry and I both looked to Lauren for her to order first. She looked so cute as she concentrated on the menu.

"This is my first time here," she said. "It all looks so good. What would you recommend?"

"Geoffrey's Benedict is always good. It's a toasted croissant with prosciutto, roasted potatoes, fresh fruit, and hollandaise sauce, or get it with lump crab cake," Henry suggested. "Also, if you're like Aiden here, you'll love the grilled filet mignon with your choice of scrambled eggs or fresh vegetables, roasted potatoes."

Lauren folded the menu. "I'll have the grilled filet mignon."

I couldn't help but smile. A woman after my own heart.

"I'll have the same, of course, and I'll take a Caesar salad," I said.

"Does the lady wish to have a salad as well?"

We both turned to Lauren.

She smiled. "I'll take a Caesar, too."

"And to drink?" Henry asked.

"A Diet Coke and some water," Lauren said.

I wanted to drag this out so I wouldn't have to go to the retreat until tomorrow and get on Lauren's good side. "Why don't we have a little fun? They have a great Malibu Mint Martini. If you like rum with mint and lime soda. They're perfect for a weekend afternoon."

Lauren looked at the clock on the wall. "It's only 11:25 in the morning."

"You've closed some kind of deal in the parking lot, gotten injured at work, had x-rays and a splint put on. Isn't the day long enough?"

"How did you know I closed the deal?"

Busted. "I couldn't help but overhear you barking at the seller of whatever it was. An impressive bit of work. Why not celebrate?"

"It was a bear to close that deal," Lauren said, half to herself and half to me.

That was my opening. I turned to Henry. "Two Malibu Mint Martinis and another water for me."

Lauren's eyes got wide, but she didn't stop me. Time to mount my charm offensive. She seemed proud of that deal. That seemed a good place to start. "Tell me about this deal you closed."

She looked out at the ocean. "I don't think it's as impressive as the deals you're used to."

"Nonsense. Dad always says, a deal's a deal. So what are we celebrating?"

"I bought a house."

"That's great. Los Angeles real estate is booming."

She shook her head no. "It's in Florida. I can't afford to buy here."

Was she leaving the company?

"I'm not moving," she said, deducing what I'd been thinking. "I'm going to rent it out."

I nodded my head. She was clever. No wonder Dad and Damien liked her so much.

"That's smart. Rental property can be tricky out here. I'm all for tenant's rights, but if you get the wrong tenant in California, it can really cost you if you don't have enough capital reserves."

She looked me straight in the eye. "Diplomatically stated as to avoid any pesky political or class issues over a friendly lunch."

Her directness and her lack of fear of me—I found it refreshing. "So where is this mystery deal?"

"In South Florida. Close to FAU," she explained. "Instead of renting out the entire house, I rent out each room separately to the kids at the college. That way I'm more flexible—"

"And it's easier to evict people who aren't paying. Plus, you spread out your risk," I said, finishing her sentence. I might not be as business savvy as my brother and Lauren, but I knew a few things.

She smiled and nodded. "But it's also a good value for the students who rent from me. I do excellent job vetting each of the applicants, and they don't have to pay for rent if they're only going to be there for the fall or spring semester. I sometimes do short-term vacation sublets in the summer."

"It sounds like you've done this before. How many houses do you own there?"

"This is my fourth."

Henry arrived with the martinis and set them on the table. I reached for mine and took a sip. "You're quite the tycoon."

"Hey," she said, her expression somewhere between crestfallen and offended. "It's a big deal for me."

"Wait! I didn't mean to imply it wasn't. I'm impressed."

She shot me a doubtful look.

"I tried to go out on my own, and I ended up just losing a fortune. You've probably invested a fraction of what I did, and it sounds like you're already turning a profit."

"I'm not sure," she started, and then paused.

"You've got to know your numbers. Otherwise, it's just gambling," I said.

She shook her head no. "Not that. I meant I'm not sure how much of what you're saying is real."

I reached for my martini and took a large sip. "I'm not sure I know what you mean.

Without hesitation, she said, "That's a lie."

Her comment stunned me. She was right. I'd known what she meant.

We drank in silence until the tension got to me.

"I don't know," I finally confessed. "Sometimes I don't know when I'm being genuine, or I'm just being what people expect me to be."

My confession surprised me.

"Now that I believe," she said.

"Can we drink to that?"

She held up her glass. "We can drink to that. And to my deal."

With that, we clinked glasses, took very large swigs of our martinis, and then finished them before the salads arrived.

I motioned to Henry for a second round. This was getting fun.

LAUREN

*H*is answer took me by surprise. It made me think there was more to him than being a spoiled rich kid.

I looked around the restaurant. Since the weather was SoCal perfection, 72 degrees, with a light breeze off the ocean, the place was packed. Despite that, we'd still gotten one of the best tables outside on the patio—right by the clear glass wall with the perfect view of the Pacific.

My martini tasted fantastic, and I decided I'd enjoy myself. I liked how Aiden was impressed by my deal. With an exception to Carolyn and Mackenzie, my two best friends, nobody knew about any of my deals.

It was nice to be recognized by someone, well, frankly, rich.

I would've thought I'd feel embarrassed being here with no makeup on and in my regular casual wear, but I felt perfectly at home here. Was it being with one of the Bronson sons that made me feel valid, or had I rid myself of my "poor kid" insecurities?

I looked out at the water, sipped my martini, and imagined what it would be like when I could afford to come to places like this as a casual lunch on my own.

The server brought our salads, and we dug into them. We ate in silence, both of us too hungry to talk. I never would've guessed that a salad could taste this good. Most of my Caesar salads were from fast-food restaurants and diners. I rarely ate out, and when I did, I kept it on a budget. This really was living.

"Oh," Aiden said, setting down his fork.

I stopped eating and looked up from my plate. "What?"

"I think I spotted you smiling. Are we actually having a good time?"

I stabbed the last bite of lettuce on my plate. "Don't get used to it."

He held up his hands in surrender. "I assure you, I'm just grateful for the reprieve. I've been a dick, and I'm sorry."

His frank apology surprised me. Then I spotted his empty martini glass and looked back at him. "Are you drunk?"

"I've been a flaky billionaire playboy all my life, it takes more than two Malibu Mint Martinis at noon for me to be drunk."

I laughed. "Weird flex."

"I suppose so," he laughed. "But you're falling behind."

He motioned to the server for a third round of martinis.

"I shouldn't," I said.

"You're the one that doesn't have to go back to that wretched retreat," he said, leaning back in his chair. "I'm the one trapped there for God knows how long."

"You're the one who's supposed to be driving us."

"It's not even my car," he answered.

"What? You have no problem crashing your brother's car? I'm so not riding with you."

"No, I mean I'll have my brother's assistant pick up his car, and we'll get my driver to come get us."

"Is that so?" I asked.

"It is," he said confidently.

Our server deposited two more Malibu Mint Martinis on the table.

"I think you've forgotten. I'm your brother's assistant," I said.

He burst out laughing. "I did forget."

Normally, I'd be offended, but the drinks, the view, and gorgeous man made the day too fun to be offended. I hadn't had fun like this in a while.

"You know, I haven't had this much fun in what feels like ages," Aiden said.

My eyes snapped to his. "I was just thinking the same thing."

"How weird is that? Because I thought we hate each other."

"We do," I agreed, smiling at him.

"We really do," he confirmed, his voice low and husky.

Mayday! Mayday! I was crushing on my boss's brother. Bad Lauren. Abort. Abort!

11

AIDEN

This was the most fun I'd had with a woman in ages. Lauren was smart, funny, and sexy. I was just thinking that I needed to hold off on the next round when I saw her signal to Henry for more.

"I've created a monster," I said.

"A Malibu mint monster."

"You are in pain from your injuries, after all."

"Oh, I'm not feeling any pain," she said with a smile.

I laughed. Sure, my plan was to make sure she would forgive me for being a jerk earlier, and I knew I had to be careful, but I couldn't help myself.

"It's like I can be myself with you," I mused out loud.

"Who are you when you're with other people?" she shot back.

"I have no idea," I laughed.

"Yes, you do. You're just too lazy, too proud, or too drunk to think about it."

I sipped my current martini and smiled. "There you go again."

"Again?"

"Calling me on my shit. You've been doing it all day. You're fantastic at it, you know."

"I'm just saying that maybe there is a part of you that feels like there's a person you have to be when everyone's watching."

I sat forward in my seat and locked eyes with her. "Is it because that's how you feel?" I asked.

"Now look who's calling who on their shit," she said.

Henry came and deposited two more drinks. I dusted my current drink and reached for the fresh one.

"Let's toast to that," she said.

"To our shit?"

"Yup. Let's drink to leaving behind all our shit," she said, laughing.

In my mind, all I could think was how much I really needed to do that. I desperately wanted to leave behind all that heartache, drama, and trouble in New York.

I took a deep breath. Maybe Dad and my brothers were right. This could be my fresh start.

We clinked glasses, drank our drinks, and shared dessert as we stared out at the water. I felt at peace for the first time in over a year, but I knew our lunch had dragged on long enough. My day with Lauren would be over soon, and I wished it weren't.

"The view here is beautiful," she said, "I hate to leave it."

"Who says you have to leave it?" I asked.

"We've been here way too long, and all good things end."

My heart skipped hearing her call our time together "good."

Maybe we could be friends. Maybe that's what I needed, a genuine friend.

"Then we'll go somewhere else," I said, deciding I needed to bond and explore this new friendship. I'd never been friends with a woman.

"But we won't have the view," she said. "Which is a shame because it's getting closer to sunset."

I looked down at my watch and it was 4:10. It was late winter, but a warm day in Southern California. The day could've passed as spring.

"I know exactly where we'll get the perfect view. I'll be right back."

I got up to make the arrangements.

Yes, I was going to bring Lauren back to my place, but I was going to keep it platonic.

Normally, I'd worry, but I had two reasons not to. One, I wasn't up for falling in love or even being with any women after the shit show of my last relationship. And two, Dad was right. Even if I was tempted, Lauren wouldn't give me an opening. It was freeing to be with the one of the few women I'd never have a chance with.

I'd make a new friend—a beautiful, smart, sexy, friend.

LAUREN

*A*iden got up from the table with his phone in hand. I couldn't help but stare at his butt as he walked away. Damn. Tall, broad shoulders, and a nice butt, too.

I giggled, thinking about it. Nope. No thinking about your boss's brother's butt. The phrase "boss's brother's butt" made me giggle again.

When I realized my behavior bordered on ridiculousness, I told myself to pull it together and turned my attention to the ocean. What a view!

My mind went back to my deal from this morning. I decided not to call Carolyn. No news was good news. And if there was bad news, I didn't want it to ruin my relaxed mood.

This was the best afternoon I'd had in years, and all I had to do was break my wrist to get it. Sheesh. I'd led a pitiful, dull life in the last few years.

I vowed to myself that I'd come back here when I

closed my tenth deal. Maybe what everyone said about me was true. I needed to lighten up.

But would it be as fun to come here without Aiden?

Nope. Not going there. What I needed to take from this is that I needed to make time to make friends. Of course, my mind went to making friends with Aiden, but he was a bigwig at the company. It would look like I was kissing up.

Did I care what people thought? It wasn't like he was my immediate boss, anyway. From what I could tell from the company memo, he'd be working on an entirely different floor.

I took another sip from my drink and put all these boring thoughts aside. I deserved fun, so no more over-thinking things.

And I really needed to pee.

I went to push myself up from the table and was reminded of my broken wrist and sprained ankle. With all the drinking, I'd forgotten my injuries.

How many had I had?

I swayed as I stood up and leaned over to pick up my crutch. Definitely too many. I needed to be careful.

Focus, Lauren, focus.

I carefully used my one crutch with my left hand and tried to advance a little with my left foot. Why couldn't I have twisted my left ankle instead of injuring both my right ankle and right wrist? It was almost impossible to use my crutch. Or maybe it seemed impossible because of way too many Malibu Mint Martinis.

Halfway to the restroom, I felt a warm hand on my shoulder.

"Are you trying to escape?" Aiden asked me, his hand remaining on my shoulder and his breath on my ear.

I turned to look up, and he was kneeling down to whisper in my ear. Damn. His dark eyes practically smoldered, and he smelled so good.

"Trying to come up with an alibi, I see," he said with a smile.

I realized that I'd been so dumbstruck by his good looks that I hadn't said a word. Did he know that what it was, or did he just assume I was drunk? It was a weird day when I was hoping to appear just drunk.

"I need to use the ladies' room," I said, hoping that I wasn't slurring my words.

"Likely story. Listen, I don't mean to be critical, but you stumbling around on this crutch is making me nervous."

He put his arm around me and grabbed my crutch.

Before I knew it, he'd swept me into his arms and was carrying me to the bathroom.

I stifled a giggle. "You can't go into the ladies room."

"I'll wait outside, but if I hear a thump, I'm coming in."

He took me to the door and gingerly set me down.

"I'll be waiting right here," he said.

"Take a few steps back. A woman needs privacy," I heard myself say. What was I doing? Who was this giggling person who didn't care about making bathroom demands to her billionaire boss? Not my direct boss, but one boss, for sure.

I decided it was easier not to care. Not to mention I was too drunk to keep my self-conscious thoughts straight.

I hopped to the toilet, did my business, washed my

hands, and dried them. It took some time to do this all one-handed.

A gentle knock on the door got my attention.

"I'll be right out," I said, not sure if it was someone waiting to use the restroom. Had I been in here long?

"Just making sure you're okay," Aiden said.

"I don't need any help in here," I said.

"As your new best friend, I promise you, I'll be helpful," he said.

"Thanks, new best friend," I called back, "but I've got this. I'm a very competent person."

My heart soared at the concept of him even jokingly calling me his new best friend. I hopped over to the door. He swept me back in his arms again, and we headed to the parking lot.

Normally, I'd worry about how heavy I was. But he was so strong, and I was feeling no pain, so I enjoyed the ride. "Where are we going?"

"It's a surprise," he said. "Quick question, is your home address the same as the address on file with HR?"

My heart sank at the idea of going home.

"Is next stop home?" I asked.

"No, I just needed to know where to have the company send your car," he said.

"Oh," I said, relieved. "Yes, all of my stuff is up to date with HR."

"Of course it is."

"I'm a very competent worker," I said.

"More than competent, from what I hear."

I nodded. "Damn straight."

He laughed. "Okay, competent worker, we're going to wait here for a ride, and then be ready for a surprise."

"If it is good as the Malibu Mint Martinis and lunch, I'll be amazed," I said.

"It'll be even better," he said.

I decided not to worry about anything. Today, Lauren McCall would be literally and figuratively along for the ride. See, I could go with the flow. Well, at least as long as the drinks were flowing.

AIDEN

*I*t felt good holding Lauren in my arms. Her head rested on my shoulder while we waited for Gerard, one of the family's drivers, to pick us up. He arrived driving the Mercedes-Maybach I requested. Typically, I preferred to drive myself or take a ride share, but I thought this car would be best so Lauren would have leg room for her bad ankle.

Gerard stepped out of the car and opened the back passenger door for me even though the door could've been opened electronically. I handed him the crutch. "Put this in the back. I'll get her settled."

"Nice ride," Lauren said, as I helped her into the car.

My chest swelled. Was I trying to impress her? Was it working?

I put her into her seat, and she slid her legs gingerly into the car, making sure not to hit her ankle.

"Thank you," she whispered.

I smiled as I knelt by the car and leaned over to help

her with her seatbelt. She probably didn't need it, but I enjoyed being close to her.

"Let's make sure you're safe and sound. We've already had one trip to urgent care, let's not become regulars."

She let me help her, which, for reasons I was afraid to think about, made me smile even wider.

My face was inches from hers. "All set."

"Safe and sound," she said, turning up to look at me with her green eyes.

Damn. If this were a date, I would have already kissed her.

I closed the small distance between us. I was about to kiss her, but the sound of another car pulling up behind us got my attention. With the spell broken, I pulled back. Better get moving.

"Make sure everything is clear from the door," I instructed.

I waited while she tucked her feet into the car, and once it was clear, I shut the door and jogged to the other side of the car. Gerard was ready and waiting. He opened my door electronically, and I hopped into the backseat.

I reminded myself that there would be zero funny business between me and Lauren. We were going to be friends, and friends looked out for each other's safety. That's what I told myself.

Gerard turned back onto PCH, and we were off. A giddiness came over me. I couldn't put my finger on why, but I suddenly felt hopeful that I could truly have a fresh start back here at home.

"How long till we get there?" Lauren asked.

"Patience, patience," I said. "Good things come to those who wait."

"But I want an Oompa Loompa, and I want it now!"

I burst out laughing. "That's that bratty girl from Willy Wonka, right?"

"When I grow up, I want to be Veruca Salt."

"You know they deemed her a bad egg," I reminded her.

"Maybe I want to be bad," Lauren answered in a caricature of a vampy voice. But damn, hearing that breathy voice made my cock stir in my pants.

Our eyes locked for a moment, and I thought I saw her take a little breath. Was Lauren attracted to me? I couldn't deny that my heart sped up at the idea. I never doubted if women were attracted to me before, but this definitely excited me. We hit a damn pothole, and it shook the car hard.

"Wait, does this seat recline?" Lauren asked, noticing the leg rest.

"I thought you might want room to stretch out," I replied.

Lauren quickly figured out how to extend the seat and leaned back. "Let's just drive to the beach and open the windows."

"We can do that, but I had something else in mind."

"I can't believe it's better than this seat," she said, luxuriating in the leather.

I smiled. It was nice to have the seats, but I never appreciated them as much until I saw Lauren enjoying the space.

"We'll be there in about fifteen minutes, but I could have Gerard take us to the beach if you prefer."

"Let's go wherever we're going and get there in time

for the sunset. Besides, it'll give me longer to enjoy lounging here."

"You haven't seen nothing yet," I said, leaning over and turning on the calf massage.

"Ooooh," she moaned.

"It's not harsh on your ankle, is it?"

"No, it's the opposite," she said with her eyes closed.

I enjoyed having time to look at her while her eyes were closed. I could take my time absorbing her adorable button nose, soft cheeks, and full lips.

Gerard continued up the hill and then stopped at the gate to our private street. She opened her eyes to see why we stopped.

He used the remote instead of the keypad.

"Wow," Lauren said, looking over the side of the cliff. "Are we going to throw a ring into the volcano when we get to the top?"

"Are you a movie fan? That's the second reference today."

"Only the stuff they stream online for free."

I smiled. There was something about Lauren's realness about money that I appreciated. People would be surprised to know that my father was actually a very frugal man. He said the reason he became a billionaire was because he knew the value of a dollar.

To be honest, I wasn't sure that I did, but I appreciated Lauren did.

We got to the private gate that led to my Malibu house, and the driver used another remote to open it.

"A second gate. Are we going to a prison?" she kidded.

Her joke was more accurate that she could've imagined, but I never wanted to be one of those oblivious rich people who complained about how hard it was to have money. "A very well decorated prison with a view," I replied. When we got to the house, I saw Lauren's jaw dropped ever so slightly before she closed it again.

"No funny quips?" I asked.

"No, I've been thinking about buying one of these, but I was looking for something bigger and closer to the water. You know, like in the ocean itself."

Gerard triggered the doors, and I turned to Lauren. "Stay right there."

"No problem. I'm thinking about using this as my winter home."

"Well, before you rearrange the furniture, let's see the sunset," I said, hopping out of the car.

I met Gerard outside the car. "Grab her crutch, and I'll lift her out."

Lauren had already unfastened her seatbelt and was now making her way out of the Mercedes.

"I thought I told you to stay," I chuckled, reaching into the car to lift her. Her arms slipped around my shoulders as if they belonged there. I picked her up. It was much easier to do with the SUV's height than my brother's low-riding sports car, not that she was hard to lift.

Gerard walked up the long pathway with us and opened the front door. The house staff wasn't expecting me home this weekend. I was supposed to be at the retreat.

"Carrying me over the threshold? How romantic!" Lauren joked.

I looked down at Lauren in my arms. A pang of sadness struck at my heart.

I'd bought this house in a rush when I realized I

wouldn't be moving into the Connecticut estate I'd bought for Christine and me last year. My ex had spent so much time and money decorating that damn house and planning the wedding. I thought it was because she was excited about building our life together, but it was more about impressing other people.

By now, I thought I'd be on the way to having a family.

Lauren rested her head on my chest, and I let the pain fade. No marriage for me, but friendship with what my father would call a "level-headed girl" could be my cure. Dad seemed to be in much better spirits now that he and Auntie Mary had become friends. It might work for me.

LAUREN

I rested my head on Aiden's chest and let out a long sigh. My body relaxed in his arms.

The feeling of the softest leather in the world under my behind brought my attention to the fact that I'd closed my eyes. Had I dozed off for a second there?

An amazing view of the Pacific Ocean greeted me when I opened my eyes. The entire back wall of Aiden's living room was glass from top to bottom.

"I think we are five miles out in the ocean," I said. All I could see was the Pacific.

"Not quite, there's a pool, a deck, a cliff, and a highway before you get to it," he said, walking behind me. I glanced over to where he was going and realized it was the bar. Another drink would be nice.

I sat forward on the couch and looked around at the rest of the living room. The sleek, modern furniture, the wood floor, the recessed lighting—I love it all. The place was bright, uncluttered, and spacious. It amazed me how large it all was. Waterfront property anywhere in Southern California didn't come cheap.

"So do you live here alone, or do you share the place with a modest-sized army?"

"I guess I live here alone," he said, stopping to think. "Actually, this is the first time I've been here. But the servants live here or rather, in the house next door."

"You bought a house for your servants to live next to. Interesting choice."

He laughed, but then he went quiet. I turned to look at him at the bar. He was looking off into the distance as if lost in thought. I worried I might have upset him. I turned back to the view of the ocean to give him some mental space.

He cleared his throat and broke the silence. "You might have read about my engagement?" he asked.

My heart dropped at the idea of Aiden being engaged, but I wouldn't let it show. "I remember seeing your name in some headlines in my newsfeed, but I didn't read the articles. Congratulations on your engagement."

"The engagement's off," he corrected.

I fought the urge to smile, even though I knew that was a shitty thing for me to be happy about.

"I moved back to the West Coast and bought the house that I liked that was closest to the family," he continued.

"It's good to be near family when things don't go as you hoped," I said, missing my folks. I stared out at the beginning of the sunset. It reminded me of Florida and vacations on the beach with them.

"I'm better off," he said.

"True," I agreed. "If things wouldn't work out, it's better

to know before you're married—especially in your financial position."

"I can't believe you said that."

"I didn't mean to be rude," I said, turning to see him again.

Honestly, I wasn't sure what part of what I just said had offended him. Maybe I shouldn't have another drink, I thought.

He waved off my apology. "Don't be sorry. Most women never acknowledge that it's a dangerous proposition for me to get married."

"Oh, that." I turned back to the view. "Never get married without a prenup. But I'm sure you knew that."

"Do you plan to have a prenup when you get married?"

"I don't know that I'll ever get married. But I sure as hell wouldn't do it without one."

The sound of a cocktail shaker made me wonder if he was making more Malibu Mint Martinis. Although I thought I might be in the mood for something less sweet.

Aiden brought two cocktail glasses over the couch. "I think I really dodged a bullet. Marriage isn't for me."

They were clear with olives. My guess was vodka martinis, which were perfect.

He sat down next to me. I could feel the heat between the two of us. I looked out at the amazing view. Touches of pink striped across the horizon.

"Looks like we made the sunset," I said.

"Another toast?" he asked.

I raise my glass. "To sunsets and never getting married."

Aiden smiled. "To sunsets and prenups," he corrected.

We clinked glasses. I looked out at the gorgeous view

and sipped my drink. Yup, martinis. Although maybe it wasn't great that I was in a strange man's house, letting him make a drink behind my back.

I looked for a place to set my drink down, but didn't see a coffee table.

Aiden took my drink out of my hand. "It's behind us." Then, he set the drink on the table just behind our heads.

I turned to look for it, but it was directly behind me.

"I'll put it over here so it's easy for you to reach," he said, scooting closer to me and allowing the drink to appear over my left shoulder so that I wouldn't have to use my bad wrist to lift it.

His body pressed against my shoulder, and I couldn't help but enjoy how close he was to me.

"Thanks," I said.

"My pleasure," he replied, his voice just a tad huskier and sexier than it had been a moment before.

Our thighs were touching, and his arm was behind my neck. I didn't know why, but I leaned my head in the crook of his shoulder. It seemed like a natural thing to do. After I'd done it, I thought I'd made a mistake, but Aiden's arm continued to rest on my shoulder.

I relaxed and told myself to enjoy the view. Nothing to worry about here.

15

AIDEN

*W*hen she put her head on my shoulder, I couldn't resist putting my arm around her. Friends did that, right?

Alright, I was kidding myself, but I couldn't resist. Holding Lauren stirred an odd combination of excitement, contentment, and joy inside me. I watched the sunset and didn't dare look in her direction. I didn't want to break the spell.

The sound of a slight snore told me she'd fallen asleep. I looked down at her long, light brown hair and kissed the top of her head.

The sunset faded to black. I told myself that when she woke up, I'd take her home, but she remained asleep. As much as I wanted to stay like this, I figured I ought to wake her up.

I shook her gently, but she didn't wake up immediately. Had she passed out?

Fuck. What medication had they given her? I thought

it was ibuprofen or some type of anti-inflammatory. If they gave her Vicodin, I could've damn well killed her.

No. Lauren would never drink after taking Vicodin. I shook her harder. "Lauren! Lauren!"

Her eyes fluttered awake. "Hi!" Her voice sounded groggy.

"What kind of medication did you get from the doctor?"

"Ibupro—" she started, but didn't finish.

I shook her. "Ibuprofen? Did you say ibuprofen?"

She nodded.

"Are you sleepy?" I asked. "Do you want me to take you home?"

She put her head on the side of the couch and looked up at me, smiling. She looked adorable. Like a tired kitten.

"So handsome," she mumbled.

A lot of women told me I was good looking or hot. But hearing Lauren call me handsome, even though she was drunk and exhausted, made me feel almost giddy.

"So where is home?" I asked her.

"Miles into the ocean," she giggled.

Yup. Definitely drunk.

"You can stay here, if that's okay?"

Her eyes fluttered closed.

I slipped my arm under hers, lifted her off the couch, and took her to one of the guest rooms.

She woke up when I sat her on the bed. I deliberately hadn't put her on her back just to keep things platonic.

"Do you want to take a nap, and then I'll take you home?" I asked, holding her by her shoulders so she didn't lose her balance.

She smiled at me. Our faces were inches apart again.

Her gaze drifted to my lips. I looked down at hers. They were slightly parted.

I didn't take advantage of drunken women. I didn't have to. But it was hard not to kiss her.

"Are you okay?" I asked.

She leaned close. I thought she was going to whisper something to me. But then her lips touched mine.

Her soft lips parted for me, and her arms tightened around my neck. I didn't stop myself from kissing her back.

The sound of her moaning and her hungry kisses got me hard immediately.

I'd only slept with one woman since my broken engagement, and I'd went through the motions.

But this kiss... wow!

Her legs wrapped around my waist. She pulled me closer with her legs as we continued to kiss.

My cock bulged in my pants. She ground against me. I could feel her heat and arousal through her thin yoga pants. Fuck.

Her shirt rose, and I felt her skin on the side of my hand. I slid my hands to the small of her back—my palms on her bare skin.

So soft! So smooth. I wanted to run my hands all over every inch of her.

Instinctively, I guided her to lie back on the bed. She giggled as our kiss broke. Her sleepy eyes blinked closed.

She was definitely way too drunk. I worried that I'd taken advantage of her forwardness already.

"I'll let you..." I started as I caught my breath and forced my brain to think straight. "Rest. Is that okay?"

Her deep breathing and relaxed face showed she'd

fallen asleep again. I vowed to check on her throughout the night to make sure she was okay.

I adjusted the pillow under her head and gently took off her shoes, being mindful of her sprained ankle.

The sight of her resting on the bed, her tousled hair spread across the pillow, made me want to hold her, protect her, and fuck her.

I walked to the doorway and dimmed the lights enough so she could relax, but not enough to make her afraid if she woke up in the dark.

I forced myself to leave the room, my cock still hard from that kiss.

My mind drifted into thoughts of what it might be like to fuck Lauren. Maybe we could go out on an actual date or maybe she'd be game when she woke up.

Then reality descended on me.

I'd just gotten a female subordinate drunk at lunch, taken her back to my place, and made out with her. The part where she had made a pass at me first might be my only saving grace if she remembered it that way. She might be too drunk to remember anything.

Fuck, fuck, fuck! My first day back, and I'd already screwed up my so-called "fresh start" big time.

What was wrong with me?

16

LAUREN

I woke up in a giant bed. It took me several excruciating minutes to remember that I'd gone to Aiden's house. Flashes of watching the sunset and putting my head on my boss's brother's shoulder played back in my head.

What the hell had I been thinking?

Deep in my gut, I knew that wasn't the worst of it. I must've fallen asleep or more likely passed out. Just how drunk had I gotten, and how much had I embarrassed myself?

I was glad that I remained fully clothed and felt so stupid that I'd put myself in a position to be taken advantage of.

At the time it seemed reasonable to go with Aiden after lunch, but in retrospect it was hugely stupid. I'd just met him, and I went with him to his empty giant house with two locked gates. And I'd let him make me a drink at a bar where I couldn't see him, and then passed out his couch!

He could've murdered me or sold me into slavery. Sure, we'd been in public together, and I'd never had to deal with any harassment or general creepiness at work, but still.

Not smart, Lauren! One pretty face and a few cocktails, and you get stupid.

My shoes were set neatly next to the bed. Had I taken them off? I struggled to remember anything after the couch.

I sat up and wished I had access to a toothbrush. My head ached, and so did my wrist and ankle. My crutch was propped up next to the bed. How had that gotten there? I shook my head.

Despite not remembering much, I had the innate sense that he hadn't taken advantage of the situation. No sore lady parts. No vague feelings of danger or unease when I thought about him.

From what I could remember, he'd been a hospitable host, and I'd been the awful guest that overstayed her welcome. It wasn't like me to not be able to handle my liquor.

I stood up, grabbed my crutch, and headed for the nearest door hoping to find a bathroom. I opened the door only to find another room. It took me a moment to realize that it was one of those dressing closets, complete with a triple-view mirror, sofa, and coffee table. The room was bigger than the bedroom in my apartment.

Okay, so not the bathroom. Let's see what's behind door number two.

I exited the closet and opened the next door, hoping it led to an en suite bathroom. Instead, it led to the living room.

"Good morning," Aiden said.

He was sitting in a comfy chair, facing the hallway. I bet he'd sat there waiting for me to wake up and get the hell out of his house.

"I must've fallen asleep," I said, wanting to take the narrative from passed out to falling asleep.

"Pain can take a lot out of a person."

I nodded yes and was glad that he took a generous view of my inappropriate behavior. I limped further into the living room. "What time is it?"

"About 5:30 in the morning."

I looked out toward the ocean, but all I saw was darkness. "That explains why the sun isn't up." I calculated I must've slept for at least ten hours. Sheesh.

"That's how it works," he said, setting the book that he was reading down onto the side table. Men who read are always so sexy.

I thought I'd go with a light joke to relieve the awkward tension. "I was looking for a bathroom, but I got lost in your closet apartment."

"Well, you were almost there," he said.

"So there's another door in there?" I asked, looking back into the bedroom.

"This is only the second time I've been in this house," he said, getting up from his chair, "but if I remember correctly, in your room the bathroom is on the other side of the dressing room."

"Thanks," I said, scooting on my crutch back into the bedroom, eager to get away.

Aiden walked around me and beat me to the closet door. "Let's make sure I've got this right, before you do all the work to get there."

He opened the closet door and walked to the back.

I waited in the closet doorway and noticed a box for the Super Storage Max on one of the shelves. I pointed to it. "What do you need that for with an almost-empty closet this large?"

Aiden turned around and looked at what I was pointing at. "Oh, that's from Dad. He loves to order things off TV. If there's a gadget, he's going to buy it."

"A man after my own heart," I said.

Aiden opened the door at the far end of the closet. "Looks like we've found it."

I must've been too overwhelmed by the apartment-sized "dressing room" to notice.

He must think I'm an idiot, I thought.

I hurried to the bathroom, eager to get a handle on my funky breath and bed head. "Good to know it isn't a portal to another universe." I'd wanted to be funny, but worried I sounded weird.

He just looked at me. I couldn't tell what he was thinking, but under the circumstances, it probably wasn't good. His tousled hair and effortless good looks made me self-conscious. That, and the way he seemed to study me. It made me worried I had a booger in my nose or dried drool on my face.

"I wouldn't suppose you had a toothbrush and toothpaste in there, would you?" I asked just to change the subject and to get him to stop looking at me.

He entered the bathroom and checked the drawers. "Weston usually keeps everything well stocked." He reached into the bottom drawer and held up a new, still-in-its-package toothbrush. "Here we go."

"Weston?" I asked, joining Aiden in the spacious bathroom. Had he given me the master bedroom, or was every room in this place like this?

"The house manager."

It took me a moment to register that he was answering my question. "I'm surprised you have full time staff and haven't outsourced," I said, trying to sound casual.

"Dad is old school, and it's a shared staff throughout the family," he explained.

What the hell was I doing asking stupid questions?

He opened up a cabinet, grabbed something, and then walked toward me. My eyes locked onto his as he approached me. My heart pounded as he neared. A spark of a memory from last night lit at the back of my brain.

We'd kissed! Holy shit! We'd kissed last night!

Aiden handed me the toothbrush. His fingers brushed my palm, and my brain went into overload. My brain played back the pass I'd drunkenly made, and how he'd kissed me back. The feeling of his hands on my back, and the memory of his tongue, actually made my knees weak.

"Do you need a hand?" he asked.

I realized I'd just been standing there staring at the toothbrush and toothpaste in my hand for god knew how long. Pull it together, Lauren.

"I'm gonna need the privacy thing again," I said, trying to make a joking reference to us at the restaurant bathroom. Not the smartest thing to say. If he remembered, he remembered way too much of my drunken behavior, and if he didn't, he'd just think I was weird.

I guess I was hoping for weird.

I glanced up at him. He was staring down. I couldn't tell if he was amused, bewildered, or being polite. But god, those dark eyes and long lashes! Even his jet black eyebrows were sexy.

More memories of last night flooded my brain. I'd wrapped my legs around his waist and practically dry humped him. I'd dry humped my boss's brother!

"There is a robe over there between the shower and the tub," he said, breaking the silence. "Use either for as long as you like. I found a few things of mine that might fit you. It's a little early to send someone to pick up clothes."

"Yes. I mean, no need to have anyone go anywhere. I can wear these clothes," I volunteered. I definitely didn't want anyone knowing I'd spent the night. Holy shit! The rumor mill at work would go crazy! My guess was I smelled pretty bad if he was suggesting the shower.

"I'll see what clothes I scrounged up and leave them on the bed. You're welcome to do whatever you like. Absolutely no pressure. Totally your choice," he said, his tone polite.

I nodded, and after another awkward silence, he turned and left. The sound of the closet door shutting let me know he'd left.

I shuffled over to the shower and tub. The all glass shower was probably my best bet. The tub looked like it would be hard for me to get in and out of. The shower was fully stocked with some really nice looking shampoo and conditioner.

I didn't want to ask Aiden for a plastic bag or help to take off the cast, so I decided I'd try to hold my hand out of the way of the water.

I undressed. My stretchy yoga pants proved tricky. It

was hard with one hand, and getting them off my ankle was excruciating. Maybe I could've used Aiden's help.

My brain conjured up visions of him helping me in the shower. No, no, no.

He seemed content with ignoring my inappropriate advances. Although, if my drunken brain remembered correctly, he'd been rock hard when he kissed me back.

God! How he kissed me back.

Stop it, Lauren. He'd been drinking as well. Get in the shower and get home before you ruin your entire life.

I showered as quickly as I could with my one hand and then carefully exited the shower. It was helpful that the shower was nearly flush with the floor, so I didn't have to hop over anything.

I caught sight of myself in the mirror. I wasn't sure whether it was that I'd been drinking and was partially dehydrated, or there was something about the expensive lighting, but my lower stomach that I always called my "pooch" looked flatter.

The one good thing about working all the time and not going out much meant it was easy for me to lose the weight I'd gained during college. I felt like my old, regular-bodied self. Not model thin or Kim Kardashian curvy, but a flattering weight for me.

Mental note: When I buy a house I actually live in, have great lighting in the bathroom. Looking into this mirror under these lights was like having my body airbrushed, and my self-esteem needed the boost.

I hopped over to the robe, pulled it on, grabbed my crutch and soiled clothes, and headed to the bedroom to sit on the bed and get dressed.

It was a shame that I didn't remember to ask my

coworker to grab my luggage when she grabbed my purse. Then I would've had something to wear.

I got into the bedroom to find a pair of jogging pants with the drawstring and elastic around the ankles, along with a few t-shirts.

One t-shirt was from UCLA, my alma mater. I wondered if Aiden had gone to college at UCLA first before moving on to a school in New York.

I looked at my sweaty clothes from yesterday. Then, I took a whiff of my shirt. Nope. The UCLA t-shirt would definitely be better. I debated not putting on my bra and underwear, but my thirty-four Cs and overall self-consciousness eliminated that option.

I sat on the bed and reached for my yoga pants. It would be a bear to get those over my sprained ankle. Aiden had put on a pair of sweatpants with the elastic around the ankles and a drawstring. Sure, he was a good six inches taller than me, but maybe with a little folding and the elastic, it would work.

Putting on his pants was easier. They were loose-fitting, so it made it easier for my ankle to slip through. I stood up on one leg and looked down and laughed at myself. They were very baggy, but they'd do.

Okay, now the puzzle of putting on my bra one handed came into play. And my left hand wasn't my dominant hand.

Ten minutes of abject frustration followed, and I wasn't any closer to getting my bra on, but I was right on the edge of either screaming or bursting into tears. I looked down at the bed.

There was a small tote bag laying out on the bed.

Aiden must've put it there so I could put my other clothes inside of it. His thoughtfulness made me smile.

More bits of yesterday filtered into my brain. I imagined, for a moment, what it would be like to have a boyfriend like Aiden. Someone who was thoughtful and did stuff like this for me.

I had boyfriends in college, but they were mostly the oblivious type. The ones that could plan nothing. My life was more complicated for having them in it. After everything with my parents in my first few years of college, I couldn't handle that anymore. As lonely as I got sometimes, I wasn't in the mood for someone else to take care of.

That was why Ivan, my last boyfriend, seemed like a better choice. Boy, had that gone wrong. His commanding personality had been great for making plans, but he'd been the first person who'd actively undermined all of my decisions.

At first, it didn't faze me. But over time, I doubted myself. Sometimes I still did.

I shook that thought out of my mind. There was way too much for me to be worrying about. I needed to get home.

A faint knock on the bedroom door distracted me from my post breakdown reverie.

"I don't mean to intrude, but I just need to be sure that you're okay," Aiden said. "I heard the water stop a while ago."

Dammit. How long had I been trying to get dressed?

"I'm fine," I said, but my voice didn't sound as light and unstressed as I'd hoped it would be.

"Do you need a hand? I can close my eyes," he volunteered. "It can't be easy to get dressed with only one hand."

I looked down at my bra in my lap. What would be more embarrassing? Me hopping on my crutches without a bra and my boobs shaking all over the place, or letting Aiden help me?

"I can hear you thinking from out here," Aiden joked. "One of the first steps to finding a solution is admitting that you have a problem."

I laughed.

"I learned that at my Assholes Anonymous meeting," he added.

He remembered that, but he'd forgiven me.

"Just give me two seconds," I said, slipping my bra straps over my shoulders and sliding on the t-shirt over it. I crammed my dirty clothes into the tote bag. "Okay, come in."

Aiden stepped in with his hands over his eyes.

I laughed again. "You can open your eyes."

He opened his eyes and looked at me. "It looks like you got it all handled. Do you need me to help you up?"

I took a deep breath. I needed the help. "Actually, I need you to fasten my bra in the back."

"So you have it on now?"

"If by 'on' you mean just sort of draped over my shoulders and not at all supporting any of my relevant," I thought of a word, "front lady parts, then yes."

He looked amazing in his casual wear—a pair of jogging pants, a chest-hugging, thin t-shirt. "Okay, let's do this." He crossed the room and sat down next to me on the bed. "You look good in my clothes," he said, as he reached under the t-shirt and fastened the bra lickety split.

My heart jumped at his compliment, but then I looked down at myself. "I look like a hobo."

"An adorable, wounded hobo."

I shook my head no. Was he flirting with me? No, that couldn't be it. Did he want to sleep with me?

No, Lauren. Knock it off. He was just being nice, trying to keep me from feeling bad about how I'd acted.

Think about something else. Change the subject.

My mind kicked up a bit of conversation from yesterday. Something about Aiden saying he was going to tow my car to my address.

They wouldn't be able to get behind the gate of my apartment complex, and I didn't live in the best neighborhood. "Oh no!"

"What's wrong?"

"I just remembered that my luggage and my car are still at the retreat. You mentioned something about making arrangements," I started.

"Yes, I know I said that, but yesterday when we were" He paused. He was obviously trying to explain yesterday. "Well, when I got—"

"No, that's okay," I interrupted, not wanting him to think or describe any of yesterday's events out loud. "It's just that they won't be able to get into the gated parking lot of my apartment complex. I don't want to risk somebody stealing my tires or my battery."

"Stealing your battery?" Aiden asked.

"A few months ago, my clicker to the garage didn't work, so I parked my car outside. That night someone cut the clasp to my hood and took the battery right out of my car."

"Isn't a car battery less than $100 new?" Aiden asked.

"Exactly!" I said, impressed he knew the price of a car battery. "But they caused $400 worth of damage to my Honda."

"That's terrible!"

"So you can see why I was glad that you hadn't had time to have my car towed."

"Chalk one up for procrastination," Aiden said.

Aiden's stomach let out a huge growl, and almost like whales calling across the vast sea, my stomached growled back a reply.

We stared at each other for a moment and then laughed. I gathered he had eaten nothing since Geoffrey's either.

"How about we get a ride to the retreat center, grab your car and stuff, get some breakfast, and then I'll drop you off at home," he said.

"I live far from here."

"I believe it's somewhere near the beautiful town of Van Nuys," he replied.

"You've obviously never been to Van Nuys."

"You can show me around. But seriously, as long as I'm taking care of you, I don't have to go to that retreat. And there's no food here. They weren't expecting me until Monday."

Guilt seeped into my mind. I'd kept the man from eating. "And you're going to drive my car?" I asked.

"Yes, I can drive cars. You saw me driving my brother's yesterday."

"You better be careful, because you're not on my insurance," I said. I smiled, thinking of the rich billionaire driving my old Honda.

Aiden laughed. "I'll try to keep under ninety on the freeway."

"I warn you," I said continuing with the joke to fight back any awkwardness, "it will cost literally dozens of dollars for you to replace."

"I'll sell my plasma if I must."

I told myself things were fine between us as long as we were joking around. Now, I just needed to not fuck up things up for the next couple of hours until I got home.

17

AIDEN

*L*auren had asked for a hair dryer and was blow drying her hair. I texted Gerard to let him know to be ready to take us to the retreat center.

In the meantime, I figured I should let Damien know I was taking care of Lauren and wouldn't be at the retreat until at least noon. We needed to pick up her car and her things from the center, and I needed to convince Damien it would be best no one saw us.

I had already forced the family to squelch baseless tabloid rumors on my behalf. I didn't want Dad to call in favors again.

I hoped my brother was sleeping, and I didn't want to wake him up. So, I sent him a text.

I'll try to get to the retreat by noon. I'm still taking care of Lauren.

He texted back. *What do you mean by taking care of Lauren?*

I didn't feel comfortable leaving her alone with her injuries and the pain medicine, so she spent the night at my house here in Malibu.

There was a long pause before he texted me back. I watched the dots on my phone tap dance for what seemed like ages as he texted his reply. The dots stopped, and my phone rang.

"Hello, brother. How are you this fine morning?" I said, as if nothing had happened. Here comes hell, I thought.

"What are you doing with Lauren?"

"We went to lunch, she took her pain meds, and..." I figured out what to say next. "She fell asleep."

"She doesn't think you took advantage of her when she was passed out, does she?" my brother interrupted.

"For crying out loud, Damien, of course not."

"You can't possibly be indignant! Remember how many favors Dad had to call in to keep you out of the tabloids," my brother argued. "You know one story like this in the papers will trigger an onslaught of frivolous lawsuits and other bullshit that'll tank our stock."

I exhaled and tried to control my temper. Would I ever fucking live that down? I hurried across the living room, and stepped out of the sliding glass doors and onto the deck so Lauren didn't overhear.

"She was falling asleep in the car, and I asked her if she would be alright alone or if she wanted to rest here," I lied.

"Okay, the consent part is good. The going to your place part is bad. Very bad," he said, emphasizing the last two words.

"What did you want me to do? Put her in a hotel alone? What if she went into shock, and we're liable then? Keep in mind, she's your assistant, and a very loyal one at that.

Or do we care more about covering our asses than the health and welfare of our employees, Damien?"

"We can't do both?"

"I am doing fucking both," I said, trying to calm down. "We weren't far from here, so I put her in the guest room, and now we're going to go over to that retreat center, to grab her car and her stuff, and I'll drive her home."

"Maybe we'll have a female employee drive her home," Damien said.

I didn't want that to happen, so my mind made up a good reason for it not to. "She needed fresh clothes. I gave her mine. Do you want one of our female employees to see her like that and ask her where she's been?"

Damien paused, and I relaxed, knowing that I'd won this argument.

"I'll go to her room, grab her things, and meet you by her car in the parking lot. It's still early so we can do it so no one else sees her, and I'll expect to see you at this retreat in a few hours," Damien said.

"I'm taking her to breakfast, and she lives in Van Nuys," I explained.

"Van Nuys?" Damien asked.

"Van Nuys," I confirmed.

"And you think breakfast is a good idea?"

"Don't you think us being seen in public having a friendly breakfast is a good idea?" I said.

"Get here as soon as you can."

"Don't worry. Everything's fine."

"I'm serious, Aiden. She's my assistant for crying out loud."

I hung up the phone without saying another word. My

brother was being a pain in the ass, but he had a point. I would nip this Lauren situation in the bud. My entire family thought I was a fuckup, and if I made the same mistake twice, I knew I'd be irredeemable.

18

LAUREN

*I*t surprised me how easily Aiden had adapted to driving my humble vehicle. Naturally, the seat had to be moved all the way back to fit his long legs. I stole a glance at him. The way the t-shirt hugged him made my heart speed up a bit.

Get control of yourself, Lauren, I thought. He's your boss's brother. But another evil part of me thought: it's not like he's my actual boss.

"You're awfully quiet over there," Aiden said.

"I haven't had my coffee yet," I replied, hoping he hadn't noticed me checking him out.

"Sorry about that," he said. "The staff wasn't expecting me until after this damn retreat."

"You're not looking forward to the team-building fun?" I asked.

"I'm not the type of person who needs the motivation of some artificial bonding exercise to do my work," he said.

"I've always felt like you should either do your job,

because it's your job, or get another job. The part where everyone has to be motivated by something other than themselves just made no sense to me."

Aiden smiled. "I guess that's why people end up in those weird multi-level marketing schemes and religious cults. They need something outside of themselves to feel like they have a purpose."

"Exactly! I feel bad for people who are taken advantage of, but I just never understood what motivated them. I've always known what I wanted to do."

"I can't say that I've always known what I wanted to do," Aiden confessed. "But if I have to do something, I'll do it. Although, I always questioned if I really have to."

"This is where we're different," I said.

"So my brother has told me," he said.

"What did Mr. Damien say about me?"

"Mr. Damien!" Aiden laughed as he merged onto the 101 freeway.

"I'm assuming that Van Nuys is south," he said.

"Yes, very south," I said.

"Before or after the 405?" he asked.

"A few exits after."

"Oh, so it's near Sherman Oaks," he said. "And you had me thinking that you lived in a bad neighborhood."

"It's not bad, it's just a little breaking and entering-y."

"That sounds worse."

I laughed. Something told me he never had to worry about having his car parked inside the gates.

Although he had two gates. So maybe he understood what that was like.

"Going back to what you were saying before, what is it

you've always known that you want to do in life?" he asked me.

"Um," I stalled. I didn't want to admit that I'd always wanted to be rich. It seemed like it might be something that could offend him. Or maybe he'd think I was some type of gold-digging friend.

"I know it's not working for Bronson, Inc.," he said.

"What makes you say that? I love my job," I lied. It wasn't a good idea to tell my boss's brother and the owner's son that I was just waiting until I had enough money from my real estate deals to quit.

"I believe you referred to it as your 'shitty job.'"

"I don't know what you're talking about," I said, pretending that I didn't remember what I'd said when he was trying to steal my Uber.

"Dad says you've turned down every promotion we have offered you."

"I didn't think he'd remember that," I said. I volunteered no additional information about my plans.

Aiden nodded and let it go.

He'd been great about letting a lot go—particularly the embarrassing way I'd acted last night.

I liked Aiden. Even if I had a chance with him, there'd be no way the two of us could date while I worked at Bronson, Inc. And I'd vowed to myself that this would be the last job that I ever had working for someone else. No one ever got rich working for someone else. Well, except for those initial employees at Facebook. But still.

I stifled a sigh. The idea of not knowing Aiden saddened me. Sure, there'd be a nod in the elevator or a conversation at a Christmas party, but it wouldn't be like this.

Yesterday's lunch had been fun, even if I took any hint of romance out of the equation. The idea of a friendship with Aiden came back into my mind. After all, they say hanging out with successful people makes you more successful. Who better for me to be friends with than a billionaire?

Except I didn't want to know Aiden for his money. At least I hoped I didn't.

I knew what to do. If you wanted a friend, you needed to be a friend.

"I've got the perfect place for us to go to breakfast," I said.

"I'm all ears."

"I'm taking you to The Hungry Fox," I said. "You're gonna love it."

"You don't have to take me to breakfast."

"I insist."

I glanced over at Aiden. The corners of his mouth turned up in a half smile. "I can't think of a time when someone outside my family took me out for a meal," he said, almost to himself.

I wondered what it was like for everyone to expect you'd pick up the check.

That kind of thing would make it hard to know if anyone ever wanted to know you for yourself or your money, and I found it hard to get to know people as it was.

It would be something that I'd have to get used to when I was rich, but it worried me.

We drove without talking for a while. The lack of awkwardness between us surprised me, especially considering last night's kiss. I instructed him to exit Woodman.

He instinctively wanted to head toward the mountain, and I told him to turn the other way.

"So this is Van Nuys," he said as we cruised down Woodman Avenue.

I laughed. "We're on the border of Van Nuys and North Hollywood. There's some little places like Valley Glenn that we'll drive through too, so you're getting a nice tour of the Valley."

"There's a strip mall for everything here," he said, looking at the window as if this place was interesting.

"All the check cashing outlets, liquor stores, and laundromats a person could ever need."

"This reminds me of my first car," he said, tapping my steering wheel.

"Wasn't your first car a limousine?" I asked.

"I'll have you know my first car was a Toyota Corolla."

"Your first car was a Toyota Corolla," I repeated in disbelief.

"A used one at that."

"Your father is one of the richest people in the world, and he bought you a used Toyota as your first car?"

"Oh no," Aiden corrected. "I bought it myself, and it was a used 2003 Toyota. I got the money from working at McDonald's and buying and selling baseball cards on eBay."

"You worked at McDonald's!"

"It was the hardest I've worked in my entire life," he said.

I nodded in agreement. "If you've got time to lean, you've got time to clean," I said, reciting the words of my McDonald's manager.

His eyes widened with recognition. "Do they all say

that?"

"I don't know. Maybe they got it in some sort of McDonald's manager manual or something, but that job was terrible. It was my second job."

"What was your first?"

"I got a job when I was fourteen working at a place called Mr. Donut in Margate, Florida," I answered.

"Isn't it illegal to work at fourteen?"

I shrugged. "Kind of."

We chatted easily as I directed him to turn onto Sherman Way and into the parking lot of The Hungry Fox. His down-to-earth-ness surprised me. He wasn't the cocky billionaire that I thought he'd be.

"What?" he asked as he parked the car.

"You're not what I thought you'd be."

"I'd ask what you thought I'd be, but I think I know," he said.

I motioned to his tight gray t-shirt and jogging pants. "I like you like this."

"Casual?" he asked, raising an eyebrow.

"Relaxed and comfortable."

He chuckled. "Maybe I'm only this way with you," he said, reaching for his door handle. "Stay right there."

He rushed around the car and opened my door for me.

He reached for my crutch in the backseat. "Hold on while I get this for you."

He helped me out of the car, and although I probably could've made it on my own, I appreciated it. I'd always had trouble asking for help.

As he helped me out of the car, I caught myself blushing. The feeling of his arm under mine and his hands on my back made me blush.

I wasn't exactly the blushing type, but there was something about being close to him. He smelled so good: a mix of fresh, soapy skin and his clean citrus and linen aftershave. Damn. My mind thought thoughts it shouldn't have been thinking.

I balanced on one leg and motioned to him for my crutch.

"Would it be easier if I carried you?" he asked.

"The entrance isn't far," I said, although a part of me loved the way he carried me.

Aiden handed me my crutch and the two of us headed to the front door. He stayed right by my side with his hand on the small of my back, ready to help me if I stumbled. The warmth of his hand and his protective nature felt couple-like. I fought the urge to smile.

When we got to the door, he held it open for me.

"I imagine it's a little different from the places you usually go to," I said, "but you'll love the homemade jam."

"I'll have you know, I specifically went to college on the East Coast so that I could go to places just like this."

"You didn't go to UCLA?" I asked.

"My brothers did, but I went to a small school in upstate New York."

"A place where you could be a whole new person," I said.

His eyes snapped straight to meet mine. "That's exactly why I did it."

"Did it work?"

"For a little while."

I nodded. I knew what he meant. It's why I moved to California. I sighed. "No matter how far you go, when you get there, you're still you."

"Yeah."

"Sit anywhere you like," the server called out to us.

Returning his hand on the small of my back, Aiden guided me to the last booth at the far end of the small diner.

I slid into the booth. "This is where I always sit."

"I always prefer a booth in the back," he said. "But thinking about it more considerately, I should have picked someplace closer to the door because of your crutch."

"It's worth the extra fifteen steps."

"You're one tough cookie, you know that?" he said with admiration.

"Tough cookie, nothing," I joked. "I'm a badass."

"Yes, you are," he said, looking me straight in the eye.

Our eyes locked again. A zing of excitement shot through my whole body.

The server came with our menus, and we ordered drinks.

"What do you recommend?" Aiden asked.

"Everything here is great, but," I said as I motioned toward the metal stand holding four different containers of jam, "they're known for their homemade jams. Order something that comes with toast or get toast on the side."

When our food arrived, he grabbed his toast and went straight for the jam. After sampling all four, he said, "These are fantastic."

"It's the simple things in life," I agreed, spreading homemade marmalade onto one slice of toast.

"Do they sell these?"

"Yup, at the register. They've got a 4-pack with all the flavors."

"I might just have toast for dinner," he said.

"I bought a pack to give away as a Christmas gift," I said.

"Did they like it?" he asked.

"I imagine they might've liked it, if I'd put it in the mail."

He laughed. "You should have bought two."

I looked down at the table in mock shame.

"You bought two?" he asked.

I nodded. "I couldn't control myself, and for the record, toast with this jam makes for a great dinner."

"Maybe I should get three packs."

"Three is such an odd number, though," I goaded.

"A half dozen it is."

Breakfast flew by. We had a great time chatting. It surprised me how the conversation flowed even easier than it had when we were drinking.

After we ate, we both went up to the register. He offered to pay, but I insisted and was happy that he let me. Afterward, he bought four variety packs of jam.

"This was fun," Aiden said as we exited the restaurant. He held the door open for me again, and then returned his hand to the small of my back to help me to the car.

"Yeah," I said, feeling awkward and sad. Our time was over, and it bummed me out to think that we might not hang out like this again.

"We should do this again sometime," he suggested.

"Yeah," I agreed, not being able to hide my broad smile. Then I felt awkward again as I realized that I just given the same one-syllable answer twice.

Aiden helped me into the car. He insisted we go to the pharmacy to pick up my medication. We went through the drive-thru, and then I gave him directions back to my apartment.

"So you have to go to the retreat now," I said with a sigh.

"I should break my wrist so I don't have to go either."

"Everybody can't be as lucky as me," I said.

When we reached the front gate of my apartment, I pointed to the clicker on the driver's side sun visor.

"You're not the only one who lives in a gated community," I joked.

"We have that in common," he replied, going along with my joke as he drove through the gate. I guided him to my parking spot.

"And you've got a covered spot," he said, making an impressed face.

"Only the best."

I open the door of the car, grateful that this spot next to mine was empty. It would've been a pain in the ass to get out of it with my neighbor parked there. Aiden rushed around to help me. It'd become a routine of ours. Once again, he lifted me, and once again, the smell of his aftershave and being close to him excited me. I pushed those thoughts out of my mind.

"Where to?" he asked, handing me my crutch.

"Just unlock the gate over there, and we'll take the staircase on the right."

"No elevator?" he asked.

"Don't worry. It's only a two-story building."

He found the right key for my apartment complex, and we made our way to the stairs. When we reached the bottom of the staircase, he reached for my crutch and slid his arm around me like he was going to pick me up again.

I pushed him away, my hand touching his hard chest through his thin t-shirt. Touching his solid chest, even for that second, made my heart speed up.

"There's no way you're making it up the stairs," he said.

"Do you have some weird obsession with carrying me?"

He waggled his eyebrows. "I just love sweeping you off your feet."

Damn, he was cute. But I needed to reign in all those thoughts. "As true as that may be, you carrying me up the stairs is more dangerous than me crawling up on my own."

"Don't worry, I've got it handled," he countered.

I shook my head now. "You wouldn't be able to see the steps. I'd rather crawl on my hands and knees."

"As sexy as it would be to see you on your hands and knees, it would be even worse for your wrist and ankle," he argued.

"Don't worry," I said as I handed him my crutch and hopped over to the left side of the stairs, "I've got this." I put my left hand on the railing and tried to figure out if I'd be better off hopping up each stair or putting a little weight on my ankle for a second.

He made the buzzer sound. "Nope, times up." Then he hoisted me over his shoulder in a fireman's carry.

I shrieked as we started up the stairs.

"Aiden! Put me down!" I demanded, breaking into a nervous giggle.

"Can't stop won't stop."

With each step up the stairs, I giggled more and my crush on Aiden grew. Damn. Nothing about that would be good. Heartache loomed on the horizon.

19

AIDEN

*T*he sound of her breathless shrieks made my cock twitch. Thank god she was over my shoulder and couldn't see me getting hard.

"Aiden!" she panted, out of breath from giggling and nervousness.

"Watch your ankle and your wrist," I instructed.

"Put me down," she demanded again.

"It would be more dangerous for me to put you down at this point."

I wobbled a little so that I could hear her gasp again.

"Aiden!" she cried out again.

Damn. I could get used to that.

"I got you," I reassured. We got to the landing at the halfway point, and I wished there were more flights.

"Now, calm down," I said, "and watch your head when we get to the top."

"It would be easier if you weren't so damn tall."

"Some women love a man who's six foot three," I bragged.

"Well, it's not coming in handy right now," she said, her voice still high and breathless from being on my shoulder. With every stair I climbed, I could hear her exhale and her voice hitch.

"Sometimes it comes in handy," I answered, my mind conjuring images of lifting her up and fucking her on a countertop, or maybe bending her over—

"Like getting stuff off the top shelves at the grocery store," she said, interrupting my thoughts.

"Sure."

I turned when I reached the top of the stairs. Her hand brushed my butt.

"Are you grabbing my butt, you cheeky girl?" I teased.

"No, but you can put me down. We're at the top."

I walked down the open hallway and ignored her pleas. "I only provide door-to-door service." Then, I tried to change the subject. "I like that your building is open air, like a motel. It makes things quieter."

"Don't you ignore me, Aiden. Put me down!" she demanded, slapping me on the ass.

That took me by surprise.

"So you're going to play that game." I gently slapped her ass back.

"You'll be sorry you did that." She poked at my ribs a little, which made me laugh.

But her comment triggered thoughts of HR and what my father would say if he saw me like this. I scanned the hallway for security cameras. Nothing that I could tell.

I jingled her keys and stopped in front of apartment twenty-five. "Which one of these opens this door?"

"None. I'm apartment twenty-seven."

I handed her the key ring as I walked two doors down. "Be useful instead of just hanging around up there."

She found her key and handed it back to me.

"You do impressive work for somebody who's upside down," I said.

"You don't know the half of it," she replied, her voice dark and sexy.

I laughed, but it came out a lot more gravelly and husky that I'd intended. Damn. I'd have loved to know more than the half of it.

"Are you going to open the door, or are you hoping to break your shoulder so you don't have to go back to the retreat?"

"Patience, patience." I put the key into the door, opened it. "Watch your head."

I ducked down in the doorway, made sure we got in without knocking into anything, and looked at her small apartment. I couldn't explain why it made me happy, but I enjoyed seeing where Lauren lived.

It felt like I knew something about her that few people knew.

I liked her place. The clean lines and modern furniture made the space look bigger.

She had a white loveseat that was a lot like my sofa, but smaller.

"We have the same couch," I said, walking over to it and swinging her off my shoulder.

She let out a slight gasp as I set her down. My cock twitched again. I concentrated on reining in my excitement.

"It's the same in the same way that cubic zirconia is like a diamond," she said.

It took me a moment to remember that she was talking about our sofas. "I prefer the cubic zirconia," I said, taking a seat on the small loveseat next to her.

The size of the loveseat forced us to sit close to each other. Her thigh touched mine, and my brain replayed how she'd called out my name. Damn. I needed to reel in my dirty thoughts.

"Genuine diamonds are a scam," she said.

"I can't believe you're a woman and you said that," I agreed. "Because you know they're not really rare."

"It's a real racket."

"I prefer rubies," I said. "My mom had a ruby engagement ring."

"If I ever got engaged, it's the stone I'd like. It's my birthstone."

"I thought you would never get married," I said.

"I used the word 'if'," she said.

"Oh!" I said, remembering her luggage from the retreat was in her trunk. She might need some of that stuff. I got up. "I'll be right back."

For a moment, I thought I caught a disappointed look on her face. Did she want me to stay?

"Of course, you need to return to the retreat," she said.

Remembering that I had to leave soon depressed me.

"Yes, but first I'll dash downstairs and get your luggage out of your car," I said.

"Thanks. It'll save me a trip downstairs."

I rushed down the stairs, went to the car, and wondered what it would be like to live in Lauren's world. In college, I tried to live an ordinary life, but pretending to not be rich wasn't the same as being not rich. It was a foolish endeavor, but a part of me longed for a more authentic life. Being with Lauren today had given me a lot of what I craved my whole life.

Reality descended on me as I got the stuff out of the car and headed back up to Lauren's apartment.

Lauren and I couldn't be friends. My feelings for her were too strong, and I'd only known her for a day.

We were just slapping each other's asses, for crying out loud. If anyone saw us, especially someone from work, all of this would blow up in my face.

I told myself being able to flirt with Lauren meant I was healing from my past relationship, and that it was time to be an adult and move on and make better choices.

Lauren and I couldn't be friends. I needed to get to the retreat and start my life fresh and not make the same mistakes I'd made before. My mood plummeted as I gathered Lauren's things. I looked down at the jars of jam I'd bought. Wistfulness welled inside my chest.

What the hell was wrong with me? I'd only known this girl for a day. This had to be residual grief over my last breakup. I couldn't be this heartbroken over someone I'd just met.

For fuck's sake! My brothers were right about me. I was too damn emotional about everything, and that had no place in our family business.

I forced myself to be professional and headed back to say goodbye to Lauren, and I knew that meant we'd never be able to be friends.

20

LAUREN

I sat on the couch and stared into space for a half-hour after he left. When Aiden had returned from getting my things in the car, it was as if a spell had broken. We'd gone from flirty friends to polite co-workers.

There was no future for us. Nothing could come from us dating. We lived different lives. Our flirting couldn't mean as much to him as it did to me.

Man, I felt like a loser.

My ankle and wrist ached. Time for me to take the medicine we picked up from the pharmacy.

Aiden had put everything into my luggage and duffel bag. I leaned over and unzipped my suitcase and found the four packs of jam in there.

I smiled.

What the hell was wrong with me? How could I be so maudlin over a drunken flirtation with a guy I'd known for less than twenty-four hours? I wasn't the type of woman who dreamed of falling in love and being rescued by some rich guy. Okay, I did a bit, but I always thought that I would make it on my own.

Sure, I dated and hoped to fall in love, but it always felt like it was so much more work to be in a relationship than it was to be on my own. Except I cynically believed that men benefited more from relationships than women did.

There've been countless studies talking about how women's mental health improved after a divorce and men's declined.

According to an article I'd read, men were statistically more likely to die within one year of losing their spouse, but the death of their male partners did not affect women's mortality rates.

I was better off on my own. Judging from the pain I was feeling now after just twenty-four hours of flirting, that very much was right.

I dug through my things, found the ice packs that I got from the clinic, grabbed my crutch, and headed to the kitchen.

It was time to take care of myself. I took my medication, put the ice packs in the freezer for later, and went to my bedroom to lie down.

As I undressed, I caught sight of myself in my mirrored closet doors. I looked terrible with messy hair, unflattering clothes, and no makeup.

I didn't know why I tortured myself, but I grabbed my phone and googled Aiden's name along with the term fiancée. Several pictures of him and his ex at various society events in New York popped up.

She was gorgeous—large dark eyes, perfect skin, wavy black hair, and an hourglass bombshell figure. She was a dead ringer for Megan Fox.

I looked up at my reflection again and shook my head.

In an act of self-preservation, I forced myself to put my phone away and change into my own clothes to go to sleep.

It was easier to slip off Aiden's baggy sweatpants than it had been to take off my yoga pants. I hopped over to my dresser drawer, pulled out a fresh pair of underwear and a pair of shorts, and reached for one of my t-shirts.

But instead of grabbing one of my t-shirts, I decided to just take off my bra and throw it into the hamper.

Yeah, I didn't want to take off Aiden's shirt. It smelled like him.

I hopped back to the bed and put on my fresh clothes.

My phone rang. The caller ID read "Aiden Bronson." My heart soared.

"Hey!" I said into the phone, my voice a little breathless with excitement.

"Hey!"

"Thanks for the jam."

"I thought it might soothe your pain."

I laughed. "It was very thoughtful of you, but you're going to wish you kept a few more packs for yourself."

"You're probably right. You'll never guess where I'm at right now."

"Well, you can't be at the retreat yet. There's no cell phone service." I knew I wasn't saying anything amazing, but I just wanted to keep the conversation going.

"I'm dreading that!" he said. "It's why I pulled over and called you from the parking lot of the Starbucks at the bottom of the hill where—"

I'd almost sensed that he was going to say where we met, but he'd stopped himself.

I couldn't stand the silence, so I rushed to fill it. "Stalling about getting back to the retreat, huh?"

He chuckled, but it didn't sound the same as the laughs we'd shared at breakfast or dinner. Reality had dawned on both of us.

"I just wanted to make sure you were okay, and I wanted to reassure you that the paperwork for your care will be done."

His tone was professional and heartbreaking.

I took a second to make sure my tone didn't come out as heartbroken as I felt. "I appreciate that. And I appreciate all of your help this weekend with my injuries. I know you're going to be very busy when things get underway with your new position here on the West Coast."

"Yes, I imagine that will be the case."

"Well, then I'm glad I had time to get to know you a bit before all that started." My tone came out colder than I intended.

"Yes, the same to you," Aiden said.

There was another silence, followed by a deep exhale on the other line.

"I enjoyed Geoffrey's. It was a treat for me," I said.

"And I loved The Hungry Fox."

I wanted to say that we should do it again soon, but I couldn't risk hearing him agreeing in that fake way that people do. That phony talk hadn't permeated most of our conversations, and I didn't want to spoil my memory of our time together.

It'd never be the same way between us again. Sure, we might see each other at a company function or in the elevator. But it would be like being friends with someone at summer camp and then running into them with their real friends at school. Occasionally, you shared a knowing nod, but it was never like camp again.

"Well, I just took some of my medicine, so I better hang up so I can get some sleep," I said.

"Take care of yourself, Lauren."

"You too," I said, leaving out his name. I didn't know if I should call him Aiden or Mr. Aiden now.

I hung up the phone, laid down on my bed, and cried until I fell into a nap.

21

LAUREN

*W*hen I woke up, my wrist and ankle ached, but my heart ached more.

Everything would heal. It always did. Life hurts some-times. You just feel the pain until it stops. Anyone who tries to avoid that fact ends up hurting more over a longer time. I'd learned that lesson the hard way.

So that was my plan. Feel the hurt and heal. Not the grandest plan, but the only way to go from here.

I grabbed my crutch and went to the kitchen. The fridge and cupboards were bare. I wanted to have a slice of toast with jam, but the bread that I had smelled funky. My retreat attendance had postponed my weekly shopping.

I sighed and crutched my way to the couch to fetch my laptop out of the duffel bag. Time to splurge on a delivery service since driving and the stairs were out of the ques-tion for now.

First, I researched what supplements would help my

wrist and ankle heal, and then I ordered those and two weeks' worth of groceries.

A wave of loneliness swept over me. I'd been so excited to have my own apartment after years of sharing with roommates. It was a big splurge for me. It doubled my cost-of-living, but I told myself I deserved it. I'd always enjoyed the peace and order of living alone.

Now, after having so much fun with Aiden and being injured, I wished my old roommates were here. At the very least, they'd get the groceries if I bought them snacks, and I'd have someone to talk to.

My roommates had been potheads who spent most of their time playing video games and getting high on the sofa. They were both dudes, but there was never any sexual tension between us.

But one of them had a friend from work, and that was how I met Ivan, my ex. If I was totally honest, the thing I liked about Ivan was that he liked me.

When he first came over, I figured he was just going to smoke weed in the living room and play video games, like the rest of my roommates' friends.

He made it a point to talk to me, and over time, Ivan won me over. But once we were officially a couple, he started acting more like a jerk.

He claimed I was trying to trap him into getting married, and that I was too uptight. He insisted I needed to learn to go with the flow and have fun. Sometimes, I thought he might've been right. Except, his version of go with the flow meant he could never make plans, and the few times he did, it always ended in disaster.

My mood plummeted, further thinking about my failed relationship. I needed to hear from a friendly face.

I called Carolyn, but there was no answer, so I dialed my other best friend, Mackenzie. We'd met in college while working at the same drugstore near campus. She was a freshman when I was a junior. I thought she was so cool. She was a music major and wrote songs and played gigs around town. Going to her shows made me feel cool.

Mackenzie answered the phone on the fifth ring. "Hey, I thought you were at that retreat with no cell reception."

"I was, but I got out of it because I broke my wrist and sprained my ankle."

"That's awful! How did it happen? Was it one of those trust exercises? Like during rock climbing, except they didn't hold the rope tight enough? Or the one where you're supposed to fall back and they'll catch you? Did someone not catch you?"

Mackenzie was always a flurry of energy and ideas.

"I never trusted those things, but it wasn't that."

"I need to see!" A video chat request from Mackenzie popped up on my phone.

I hit the accept button. Mackenzie appeared. She'd restyled her hair and changed her makeup. It wasn't her usual edgy look, but she looked great.

"You changed your look. It's very professional."

She smiled, but it didn't reach her eyes. "I needed a change."

Her voice didn't sound like its perky self. "What's wrong?"

Mackenzie wasn't one to share her feelings. It was probably why we became best friends. But over time we both had to admit that it was better to get these things out.

"It's too much to get into right now, but I promise I'll

tell you all about it later. It's not as bad as breaking my wrist and my ankle."

I could tell from her expression that she was trying to look more upbeat than she was. Her brown eyes look tired. I wondered if she'd been crying as well.

"Are you sure you don't want to talk about it? It would probably be good for me to think about someone else," I said.

"Stop stalling and show me."

I knew that meant that she wasn't ready to talk just yet. I held up my wrist. "Broken wrist," I said, and then panned down with my phone to show the ankle. "Sprained ankle."

"Does it hurt?"

"Not as much as the rest of me," I replied.

"What happened?"

I launched into the entire story, intending to not talk too much about Aiden, so, of course, I talked way too much about Aiden.

"Wait, you fought with your boss's brother over an Uber, and then by the end of the day he took you back to his place. After drinks?"

"That's not exactly how it happened, and I think you're missing the point about me almost losing my job for acting like an idiot."

"It's exactly how it happened, and you're not an idiot. I didn't know you were so smooth. Way to go!"

"I am the exact opposite of smooth. I'm very bumpy or sharp or whatever the opposite of smooth is."

"Stubbly?"

"Yes, I'm the stubbly, seven-day after growth of smooth," I joked.

"You shouldn't put yourself down."

"Don't be fooled by the patriarchy. Having unshaven or stubbly legs are just as valid a choice as smooth, shaved legs."

"Is this your way of telling me you stopped shaving your legs?" Mackenzie asked.

"The time that I save not grooming is my key to getting ahead in a man's world."

"I support your choices, but I'm not sure I want to hear any details."

"I'll just add that bush is back!"

Mackenzie screamed with laughter. "TMI!"

I enjoyed making her squirm. "I'm just telling you proudly that I have epic hair down there."

She shook her head no. "Congratulations."

"I should be on a double album with a Beatle."

"That's fantastic. Maybe your new billionaire is really into retro, seventies-style grooming."

"I'll make him enjoy it," I joked.

"How can I get out of this conversation?"

I laughed. "You can encourage me to get rid of any notion about having a relationship with my boss's brother, also known as the son of the big boss of the entire company."

"Fine. I'll be this cynical, stubbly curmudgeon that you want me to be. How long is it going to be before you get back to work?"

"We'll have to see how fast I heal, but I think I can do it pretty quick."

"You can't force yourself to heal fast."

"I can try," I said.

Mackenzie shook her head no. "Sometimes trying to force things to be fast only makes them take longer."

"Are you referring to the Thanksgiving mishap?"

"I promised never to bring it up, so I won't."

I appreciated my friend's discretion. For the record, jacking up the heat on a turkey doesn't make it quick cook twice as fast, and may end up setting off the smoke alarms and causing half a floor of people to evacuate.

We talked a little about old times, and then I thought I'd give it one more try to ask what was happening with her. "Mackenzie, what's going on? We don't have to do too many details."

She looked down. "They made budget cuts to the music program."

"At the middle school or the high school?" I asked. Mackenzie taught band, orchestra, and chorus at both the middle school and high school.

"Both."

"They can't! What about your promotion?"

"They're going to share a music teacher from another school. She has seniority."

"I'm so sorry. I know you put your heart and soul into that program. You even taught in the elementary schools for free to get kids interested."

Mackenzie nodded. "You know, Charles always wanted me to manage a store." She shrugged. "Maybe I'll take him up on it. In the long run, I'll probably make more money."

I nodded, but said nothing to give her space to talk out her thoughts.

"It's going to be hard to say goodbye to all the kids. But you know what bothers me the most?"

"What?"

"I wonder what would've happened if I'd never quit being a musician. I thought it was time to grow up, but maybe sometimes you just have to take a chance and go for something outlandish. Go for a dream."

A sense of guilt settled in the pit of my stomach. Mackenzie had come to me for advice about what to do when she broke up with Jett, and her band, Seldon Crisis, was on the rocks.

They played a few gigs in Los Angeles, but the bass player had gotten too deep into drugs, and things looked rocky. When all the drama with her ex left her broken hearted, and she talked about finishing her degree, I'd encouraged her to go back to school.

But Carolyn had always wanted Mackenzie to stick with it.

"I'm sorry if I steered you wrong," I said.

"It wasn't you. It was me. I talked a big game, but I never felt special enough. It was like I was a fraud every time we played a gig. And when Jett took credit for that song we wrote together, it confirmed every fear I'd ever had about myself. Like maybe I never really wrote anything good."

"I can't believe you felt that way!" Mackenzie had always seemed so confident. She looked amazing onstage. She wrote great songs.

"Promise me something. The next time I want to play it safe, remind me of this conversation. Security is an illusion."

"I promise."

The two of us talked about old times until my doorbell rang. "That's my grocery delivery."

"Okay, I'll say goodbye, but Lauren?" she said, just as I got up to head for the door.

"Yes?"

"Don't be afraid to take some risks. Regret is the worst."

I nodded, but I couldn't say anything. I wasn't sure I could take risks. Routine was my thing, but somewhere I knew she was right. She waved goodbye. I waved back. The screen closed. The doorbell rang again.

"Be right there!" I called out as I hopped to the door.

I opened the door with my left hand and hopped back to open it.

"There weren't many good oranges, so I substituted with tangerines. Is that going to be okay?" he asked. Then, he noticed my foot and wrist.

I smiled to let him know it was okay. "Even better."

"Do you want me to bring these all the way in?" the delivery guy asked, motioning to my wrapped-up ankle and wrist.

"That would be great."

Ordinarily, I would've thought the delivery guy was hot, but after being in the company of Aiden, the guy just didn't compare.

I hopped out of the way and pointed to the counter separating my kitchenette from the living room. "You can set them on the counter, and I'll take care of it from there."

"Shouldn't you have a crutch?" the delivery guy asked.

I motioned to the crutch next to the sofa. "It's my first day, so I'm just getting used to it."

I hopped over to the sofa and grabbed the crutch.

He waved at me to sit. "Relax. There are only a few

more things outside. I can handle it on my own. I'm a trained professional." He winked at his joke.

It felt awkward to sit down and let the guy just drag everything into the kitchen for me, but I told myself I'd give him a big tip on the app. When he returned, he was carrying nine grocery bags all at once. The plastic handles looked as if they were digging into his fingers.

"It looks like your fingers are going to fall off. You can just leave them on the floor by the door."

The delivery guy laughed. "I think I can make it. They're practically numb already."

Would hitting on the delivery guy keep me from missing Aiden? I considered it and decided against it. It wouldn't be fair to the delivery guy. Well, that, and I remembered I wasn't wearing any makeup and had bed head. God only knew what my breath smelled like. Remaining on the couch was probably the best idea.

"Everything's on the counter. Are you sure you don't want me to put the milk and other stuff away for you?"

"You've done more than enough."

"If you give me a five-star rating, that would really help me out."

"Of course."

He waved and headed for the door. I thought he was flirting with me, but he probably just wanted a top rating.

I put away the groceries, hopping from the refrigerator to the bags and to the cabinet. When I finished, I was sweaty and exhausted.

Knowing that I would be home for ages, and not wanting to dwell too much on thinking about Aiden, I turned on the TV and went to my favorite channel: The Home Shopping Network.

They were promoting kitchen gadgets. Yes!

I watched for a while, but the salespeople were mediocre. My glum mood needed the best.

I dialed up YouTube on my remote, then looked for videos featuring my hero, Ron Popeil.

When I'm depressed, I love watching infomercials. The cheesiness of it all combined with the simple solutions to simple problems relaxes and reassures me.

I rarely buy what's advertised, but I love to watch them. There's something about the idea that there's "gotta be a better way." And the phrase, "but wait, there's more" makes me smile.

Of all the infomercial hosts in the world, Ron Popeil is the best of the best. He invented the infomercial. He honed his pitch over years at fairgrounds across the country before bringing his skills to TV.

I'd even read his book. If I could be anybody, I'd be somebody who made gadgets and sold them on TV. Or I guess on the Internet these days.

I rested back on the couch and watched him pitch his Showtime Rotisserie. I smiled. The one good thing about being out for the next couple of weeks, or maybe even months, was that I didn't have to feel guilty about watching television. I could watch as many infomercials as I wanted.

The thing about an excellent product is that it solves a problem. People spend tons of money on rotisserie chickens or time on chopping things in the kitchen. I'd come up with a few invention ideas, but nothing that solved a problem.

My mind wandered. What kind of problem did most people have these days? I thought about the delivery guy and how his fingers had gone numb carrying all my bags. Then I remembered all the times that my own fingers had turned purple, lugging grocery bags up the stairs.

My mind imagined an announcer saying, "There's got to be a better way."

I grabbed my sketchbook out of my duffel bag. All that would really take would be a molded piece of plastic or something that you could hook the bags on to keep your fingers from getting all purple. The name Bag Buddy popped into my mind.

I laughed. Sure, it was ridiculous, but a project would be a great way to distract me from thinking too much about Aiden. Plus, with all this time off, I could easily send out for prototypes and fill out the provisional paperwork for a patent.

What I needed was a schedule! For me, having a routine created order. So I drew up a schedule for my new project, going to therapy appointments, making calls, doing chores, watching television, and getting sleep.

Time to get my life back and forget about Aiden.

22

LAUREN

*T*oday was going to be my first day back at work. I was told I'd be on light duty, but at least my ankle had healed enough so that I could walk.

My budget had tightened while I was out of work. In California, if you're on temporary disability, you only get a portion of your salary. Even before I purchased that property in Florida, my emergency fund had been half gone. Now, my financial situation teetered on the edge of disaster.

I knew it was dangerous to buy Tess's house, but I'd gotten such a good deal. The catch was, it'd be at least another two weeks before the spring semester started. Please, let it rent out soon, I thought.

After dealing with my parents' illnesses, I knew how dangerous living from paycheck to paycheck could be. I needed to get back to work, and if possible, pick up some overtime.

My behavior with Aiden embarrassed me. At least we

didn't work on the same floor, and my behavior hadn't gotten me fired.

I stared down at the empty marmalade on the table as I ate my toast. It reminded me of Aiden. My schedule had helped me finish my design and patent work for my invention, but it hadn't erased my feelings for Aiden.

It bothered me how much I missed him. I'd known him for less than twenty-four hours. We hadn't spoken since his call from Starbucks. It was for the best.

I cleared the table and put my dishes into the dish-washer. I couldn't carry anything with my right hand, but I could move my fingers.

My physical therapist had given me shoulder, elbow, and finger flexion and extension exercises. I did them exactly as instructed. My hard work had paid off. I could write and type a bit with my right hand.

Thank goodness they were letting me come back, even though I was told that my duties would be "modified." I hoped my modified duties included full time hours. There was no way I could pick up an extra job to get back on track financially.

Since the doctor had insisted that driving was still out of the question, I had to use Uber to get to work. Initially, I'd worried about the cost because I lived so far away from our offices in Woodland Hills.

But HR had told me to put it on the company credit card. Had Aiden arranged that?

I'd developed a dangerous habit of thinking about Aiden all the time. How he carried me in his arms. The smell of his aftershave. Looking into his eyes at The Hungry Fox. When we kissed.

I checked my ride share app. The driver had already exited the freeway. I had around ten minutes.

Time to grab my stuff and get downstairs. My ankle had healed, but I needed to give myself plenty of time. It hurt when I tried to walk too fast.

I got downstairs and waited a few minutes for my driver. He pulled over. I hopped into the backseat and relaxed. I smiled. It was nice not to have to fight LA traffic.

After a few minutes, I dug into my purse for my compact and checked my hair and makeup. I told myself that it was because I had the time to do it. But I knew deep down the real reason was that I was hoping I might see Aiden in the elevator.

My mind couldn't stop picturing his strong shoulders, gorgeous dark eyes, and hard chest. I could almost hear his laugh. We laughed a lot, and even just remembering it made me smile.

Despite the Los Angeles traffic, it felt like the car ride was over way too soon. My heart fluttered as I stepped out of the car.

It almost felt like it was my first day at work. I told myself to calm down. I had it bad for Aiden Bronson, and I needed to get over it.

I straightened my shoulders and headed up the cement stairs of the twenty-four story office building that Bronson, Inc. shared. My office was on the seventeenth floor. Aiden worked on the twenty-second floor.

Yes, I'd looked it up. Not a good sign. I grabbed my key card out of the outer flap of my purse, stood up straight, and headed to the front door.

Ronnie, the security guard, nodded to me. I walked

past him to the second set of double doors and scanned my key card. The light flashed red.

I headed back to Ronnie to get it reprogrammed. "I guess it expired while I was on leave."

Ronnie took my key card. "Lauren! Welcome back."

"How are your kids?"

"They're doing great in school, but I gotta say, the two boys can only be in a room together for fifteen minutes before they try killing each other."

Ronnie's forehead furrowed.

"Is there something wrong?" I asked.

He picked up the telephone. "I'm sure it's nothing."

"You can't reprogram my key card?"

He put his hand over the mouthpiece of the phone. "There's a note telling me to just call HR. I'm sure it's nothing."

Nothing! A note to call HR instead of renewing my key card. This couldn't be good.

My mind went back to that day with Aiden and me. I fell asleep on his shoulder. Hell, I slapped his ass. Maybe the person who needed to be worried about office appropriateness was me.

Ronnie saying "hello" into the phone interrupted my panic. "There's a note on Ms. McCall's keycard renewal to call in," he told HR. He nodded and smiled as he listened. "I'll tell her right away."

He hung up and then turned to me. "Mr. Bronson wants to see you. I'll take you to his private elevator."

It took me a moment to register what that meant. "You mean, Mr. Bronson, himself."

Ronnie smiled. "Looks like you've attracted the attention of the big boss, Lauren."

My gut dropped. Being called to Mr. Bronson's office when it wasn't time for your review could not be a good thing.

Shit. I couldn't afford to lose this job. Mackenzie was right. Security was an illusion.

23

AIDEN

I thought that by avoiding the Lauren situation, I'd controlled the damage. Well, the professional damage. Missing her had hit me much harder than I'd expected.

But Dad had summoned me to his office for an early morning meeting on the exact day she was coming back, and Damien had returned from Florida two months early. Both of these things couldn't be a coincidence.

Had Lauren lodged a complaint with HR?

I strode into my father's office, pretending I did not know there could be a problem. Damien and Dad were both there already. Dad sat behind his antique mahogany desk. Damien stood near the wall. This wasn't good.

I walked over to the chair in front of Dad's desk. "Damien, I didn't expect to see you here." I sat down, leaned back, and stretched out my legs. Damien remained standing.

Dad swiveled in his chair from facing Damien to facing me. I pretended the silence didn't rattle me. Dad sat

141

forward in his chair. "Something has come up, and Damien won't be able to remain in Florida to oversee the Rexford Drug project."

I could tell from the way Dad said "something" that he didn't approve of whatever that something was.

I shot Damien a questioning look, but Damien avoided eye contact. He wouldn't do that if I was the one in trouble. Was it wrong that I was glad Damien might be in hot water with Dad instead of me?

I looked back at my father and forced myself to remain calm. "Are you asking me to take over in Florida?" The prospect terrified me. Let's just say, despite my gripes with my little brother, I wasn't half the businessman he was.

Dad leaned back in his chair. "You're the only one not knee deep in an extensive project."

"Okay, I'll start getting prepared—"

Dad raised a hand. I stopped speaking, and he continued. "I have someone in mind who can get you up to speed while you're onsite. She worked with Damien on the initial research."

Damien approached Dad's desk. "No, Dad. You should send Aiden to Florida with a man. We can't risk any rumors."

How dare he! I sat forward in my chair and pointed my finger at Damien's smug face. "You know I'm perfectly capable of working with women. For crying out loud! It wasn't like I had an office fling. We were engaged."

"Boys, calm down. I've already settled this," Dad said. He didn't raise his voice. He never needed to. Dad turned to me. "This is a big acquisition to implement. Do you understand?"

Shit. He meant if I fucked this up, I may actually be out on my ass from Bronson, Inc. for good.

I gave my father a solemn nod. "Yes." I wasn't sure I could do this, but I'd probably better off leaving LA, considering the Lauren situation.

"Good," Dad replied. "And luckily, Lauren is returning today from being out on injury."

I fought to keep shock off my face. Dad wanted to send me to Florida with Lauren!

The buzz of Dad's old-school telephone interrupted our meeting.

Dad pushed the button on the base to talk to his Barbara, his assistant. "Go ahead."

"Lauren McCall is here to see you, Mr. Bronson," she responded.

"Send her in." Dad took his hand off the button and smiled. "She's three minutes early."

Damien looked like he was going to object, but Lauren's entrance stopped him.

Lauren looked even more adorable than I remembered. I stifled a smile. Nobody knew how well Lauren and I had gotten along that day.

My desire had muddied my thoughts of friendship over the last few months. But maybe if we worked together, we'd become friendly colleagues.

Except it would be torture—exquisite, cock-teasing torture.

24

LAUREN

*T*his couldn't be good—not one Bronson, but three in one room. Two more, and I'd have collected the full set. I told myself that if they wanted to fire me, there wouldn't be a need for this many Bronson men.

I expected that Aiden and I were being reprimanded for our behavior. Somehow it had gotten back to Mr. Bronson himself.

Had Aiden told Mr. Damien?

My mind whirred like the wings of a hummingbird, flipping from one worst-case scenario to the other in rapid succession. Whatever brought me here couldn't be good.

I hoped they didn't bring up the kissing or the ass slapping. What the hell had come over me? Maybe I could blame it on the pain meds. It'd been Aiden's idea to order drinks and go to lunch.

I remained calm and said nothing. There was no way I was going to make the situation even worse for myself.

Maybe it'd only be a warning. A proverbial slap on the wrist for an actual slap on the ass.

Mr. Bronson stood and motioned to the empty chair in front of his desk, next to Aiden. "Lauren, thank you for coming."

I responded with a polite nod. My goal was to say as little as possible and keep my job.

"I trust you're feeling much better now," he said as he sat down.

I nodded again.

"Glad to hear it," Mr. Bronson said.

As I walked to the hot seat, I checked Mr. Damien and Aiden's expressions.

Damien didn't look happy, and Aiden was wearing a forced smile. Not good.

I sat down. In my periphery, I could see that Mr. Damien remained standing. I didn't even glance in Aiden's direction.

An awkward silence descended on the room. But I didn't let that discomfort detract me from my singular goal in this negotiation, which was to keep my job.

Besides, Mr. Bronson had called the meeting so he would have to be the one to do the talking.

"So how are you feeling, Lauren?" Mr. Bronson asked. It was easy to see where Aiden and Damien got their good looks. Despite being in his late fifties, Mr. Bronson was in great shape and had a full head of salt and pepper hair.

"Almost as good as new," I exaggerated. It wasn't a total lie. I'd said 'almost.'

"Glad to hear it." Mr. Bronson picked up a stack of papers from his desk and took his time reading them.

The way he didn't feel any need to rush exuded power.

I made a mental note to not scurry around like I was prone to doing.

Mr. Bronson set down the papers and looked up. "Your doctor prescribes modified duty for you."

I nodded and tried to keep the puzzled and relieved expression off of my face. So far it looked like I could keep my job. Now, I needed to make sure that I could work full time.

"I've done well in physical therapy, and I can still type, write, and file," I said, building my case. "Answering the phones, of course, will not be a problem for me, so I anticipate my duties won't change much."

Mr. Bronson leaned back in his chair and steepled his fingers. "I'm sure you'll do everything in your power to maintain your excellent standard of work. However, things around the office move quickly."

I knew he was right. My typing speed was nowhere near where it used to be. A lie or exaggeration would only backfire on me later, so I figured I'd come out and ask for what I wanted. Mr. Bronson liked a straight shooter.

"It's my hope that I can resume full time work," I said.

"I'm glad to hear it," he responded.

I allowed myself to smile, but I couldn't relax. There was still the matter of the Aiden situation. I remained silent. Talking too much could only work against me.

Mr. Bronson smiled. But I didn't know what to make of it. "We've met a few times before, and each time you've turned down the promotions I've offered." Mr. Bronson leaned forward in his chair and made direct eye contact with me before he continued.

"Now, before you turn me down again, an opportunity has presented itself, and I recommend you take it. As you know, before your injury you were doing research on the acquisition of Rexford Drugs.

"In your absence, Damien has gone there and done our due diligence, and Bronson, Inc., has acquired the chain. Unfortunately, because of unforeseen circumstances, Damien cannot return to Florida to streamline the operation.

"You, at one time, worked for Rexford Drugs, is that correct?" Mr. Bronson asked.

"I worked at one location while I was an undergrad. A friend of mine still works there part time. It's why I knew they were slow-rolling their inventory."

Mr. Bronson raised his eyebrows and looked to Mr. Damien.

"It was Lauren who brought the idea of the acquisition to my attention," Mr. Damien said.

Mr. Bronson smiled again. "Even better."

I beamed. Mr. Bronson knew it was my idea!

Mr. Bronson reached for the stack of papers and read some more. "I understand you also had managerial duties at Rexford." His eyes returned to mine.

Mr. Bronson's stare intimidated me, but I didn't want it to show. I answered precisely, without exaggeration. "I was a senior sales clerk at one location. It meant that I could open and close the store, balance the registers, and help with the inventory, but my position was only part time."

Mr. Bronson folded his hands on his desk and leaned forward again. "What I suggest is that you allow me to promote you to analyst for this project. You've been doing analyst work for Damien as it is. This would put you on track to become an associate, which would use all your talents."

My heart sped up. I'd avoided taking a promotion at Bronson, Inc., because I knew if I built more of a career here that I'd feel more invested, and I'd be tempted to stay. But I needed to build up my emergency fund, and I really could use some extra money. Especially now.

Millions of thoughts flew across my mind and out of it. There were way too many unknown variables for me to consider. But I'd be lying if my primary hesitation was because I was afraid. Change stressed me out. Without a family, I relied on my routines to ease my anxiety and make me feel secure.

"If I don't take this promotion, will I be able to return to my job working full time in the office with Mr. Damien today?"

Mr. Bronson's face took on a more serious expression. He didn't frown, but he wasn't smiling anymore.

"Your position with Damien is fast-paced, and you're only cleared to work for up to thirty hours. As you know, your position as Damien's assistant works forty or more hours a week. You'd have to wait until you could work full time at your usual pace before you could return to your old job. If the position is still open when you've recovered, you could return. Otherwise, we'd find you the same position with another executive."

He let me absorb the new information.

Mr. Bronson wasn't exactly playing hardball. I couldn't handle his hardball. But he was playing tough, and the hope that we could just put me at my old wage and blow off the recommended thirty-hour week would not happen.

THE NEW BILLIONAIRE BOSS

I couldn't afford to lose that extra ten hours and over-time with my dwindled finances.

"As an associate, you would be on salary, a much larger salary, so the hours wouldn't matter," Mr. Bronson added.

Man, he read me like a book.

"Would I work weekends?" I asked.

Mr. Bronson smiled. "There may be the occasional weekend meeting, but I'm sure you'll be able to work out the details."

"What if, at the end of this project, I realize I don't like the promotion? Could I go back to working as Mr. Damien's assistant then?"

Mr. Bronson got up, walked around his desk, sat on its edge, and looked down at me. "This project would last about three months. I think you'll find you'll enjoy the position. However, we would do our best to have you return to your former responsibilities if you are not happy with your duties."

I took a moment. I needed to think, but Mr. Bronson knew he had me on the ropes. The other times he'd offered me a promotion, I'd been resolute in my declination. Now my mixed feelings and indecision broadcast my weakness straight onto Mr. Bronson's radar.

"Lauren, you've practically been an analyst for the last two years. I'd like you to accept this promotion to acquisitions associate and go to South Florida with Aiden. He'll need your knowledge and assistance to get up to speed. Will you do it?"

His voice was kind, but his eyes were intense. Mr. Bronson had made an ask. The entire room was silent. I knew no one would speak until I answered. There would be no way I could win a battle of silences with Mr. Bronson.

Then my brain registered that I'd be going to Florida with Aiden. My mind spun.

I shot a glance over at Aiden. He let out a tight smile. Mr. Bronson did not know about what'd happened between me and Aiden, and now we'd be on a trip away from everyone together!

My heart pounded into my throat. Working with Aiden would be a huge mistake, but there was no way I was going to tell Mr. Bronson why I was hesitant to work with his other son.

"When would you need an answer?" I asked.

"Now."

"I see." I'd been ready to take the job until he said the Aiden part. Now there were two things to be afraid of— change and embarrassing myself with Aiden.

Mr. Bronson turned to Aiden. I looked over as well. "I'm sure you're amenable to working on this deal with Lauren's assistance."

"Of course," Aiden said.

Aiden smiled at me. But I couldn't read what it meant. Did he want me to take this job, or did he know what I knew? The two of us working together was a bad idea.

Mr. Bronson stood. "I'm sure you have some things to wrap up, but I want you to head to HR straight away and sign your new contract and nondisclosure forms."

He was assuming the sale even though I hadn't officially accepted the offer, and I didn't know how to stop this.

Mr. Damien walked toward me and offered me his hand in congratulations. We shook hands. He was careful not to hurt my injured wrist. "If you need anything out of your desk, pack it up. My new assistant will move in while you're gone."

Wait! Was this really a done deal?

"Let's meet in my office to discuss details in about an hour?" Aiden asked.

"Which floor are you on?" I stalled, already knowing the answer.

"Twenty-two," he said.

Mr. Bronson headed for the door to his office. Aiden and Mr. Damien followed. "I'm very excited about your new position with us, Lauren. And I look forward to being briefed regarding yours and Aiden's progress."

I got up and headed for the door in a daze.

Aiden reached for the door and held it open for me.

I looked up at him as I walked through the doorway—his dark eyes made my knees weak. The smell of his citrus and linen aftershave reminded me of his lips on mine when I attacked him in my bedroom.

"See you at eleven," he said.

"Yes," was all I could say, and even that one word came out breathier than I'd wanted it to.

"Oh," Mr. Bronson said just as Aiden was about to follow me out. We both stopped and turned to Mr. Bronson. "We have made the arrangements for your trip to Florida. Your flight leaves at two. The details will be in your email in a few minutes."

Wait! What? Two today! I couldn't leave today!

DAMIEN

*L*auren and Aiden were already out the door. I needed to talk to Aiden about the acquisition. I started after him.

"Damien!" Dad called out to me.

I turned around to face my father.

"We're going to have to talk later."

"I know," I replied. "I just have to get some information to Aiden before he goes on his trip."

Dad gave me the nod, saying I could leave. I rushed to catch up with Aiden and Lauren, who were at the elevator.

"Aiden!" I called out as the elevator door opened. I yelled loud enough so the other people on the floor would hear me. Aiden would feel compelled to turn around. He turned to me.

"I need a word."

Aiden turned back to Lauren and motioned to her he would catch the next elevator. She nodded. The doors closed.

I caught up to him and pushed the button to call the next elevator.

"What do you need, Damien?"

"It's about the Rexford Drugs deal," I answered.

The next carriage arrived. We both walked into the elevator. We were alone. He turned to me the moment the doors closed. "Don't worry, I'll handle it."

Oh, for crying out loud! "You don't even know what I want to talk to you about."

"Don't worry about Lauren," he said.

"Is there something going on between you and her?"

"I don't need your lecture, Damien."

Until recently, I would've been very judgmental about Aiden. Hell, I was judgmental right now, but considering recent events, I didn't want to tell him anything.

"That isn't what I want to talk to you about," I said.

He folded his arms. "Then what?"

"There are a few employees at some stores that I got to know pretty well, an—"

Aiden interrupted me. "You want to make sure I will not fire some of your favorites."

"Yeah."

"You're always the one telling me I shouldn't get so attached to people and to let business be the business."

"I know, but can I send you a list? It's a short one."

"I'll look at it."

"Will you promise me not fire the person at the top of the list?"

Aiden shot me an incredulous look. He knew this was out of character for me.

I let my desperation show. "I'd owe you one."

Aiden raised an eyebrow. "You'd owe me a favor over not firing an employee?"

I nodded.

Aiden's expression softened. "No favor needed."

I took a deep breath. Deep down, I knew I could count on Aiden. What he lacked in business acumen, he made up for in magnanimity. "Thanks."

"Are you okay?" he asked. "Why aren't you going? Why are you letting me take a piece of this deal?"

"Not an enormous piece," I said.

"It's gonna be a sizeable piece."

I sighed and nodded yes.

Man, I'd really fucked up. I was losing millions of dollars on a deal I'd put thousands of man hours into. All because I didn't dare go back to South Florida and face the mess I'd made.

No, I wouldn't give Aiden any flavor of the "don't fuck up with Lauren" speech. It would make me the biggest hypocrite in the world.

26

AIDEN

*I*nstead of returning to my office, I took the elevator straight to the lobby and headed outside. I needed some advice, and I needed privacy from the office to get it.

I exited the building, bypassed the sidewalk, and cut through the lawn bound for a tree on the far side of the building.

A security guard caught up to me. "No one is allowed on the grass."

I wanted to tell him he was obviously on the grass, and from how he reeked of cigarettes, he was probably smoking on the premises, which wasn't allowed. But I couldn't be a dick, even if today's events stressed me out of my mind.

I reached into my pocket, pulled out my badge, and showed it to him.

The guard's eyes grew wide, and he took a step back. "My apologies, Mr. Aiden. We haven't met yet. I work in the parking lot—"

I cut him off. "Don't worry about it. I just need some privacy to make a call, and I like to be in the shade by the trees."

He bowed his head. "Of course, sir. I'll make sure you're not disturbed."

I smiled. He hurried away. I went over to the tree and leaned against it.

I put in my earpiece and voice commanded my phone to dial my brother Bradley. Bradley was the second oldest. We were only a year apart. But somehow, he always seemed to have the best advice, and he'd escaped working at Bronson, Inc.

He picked up on the third ring. "How's the rat race?"

Every time I called him during the day, he answered the phone that way. I gave my standard reply. "As ratty as ever."

"Oh, you're using your 'I'm trying to be lighthearted' voice."

My brother knew me too well.

"I've got a problem, and I need some advice."

"What else is new?" he asked.

"It's about a girl."

Bradley chuckled. "Like I said, what else is new?"

I'd called Brad a million times during my relationship with Christine. It was one of the few times that I hadn't taken my brother's advice.

But even after I completely made an ass out of myself, Bradley never rubbed it in my face. He just helped me through it. Sometimes I thought he was the only one in our family who didn't judge me for taking a shot at a normal life—or rather, a more normal life.

"You're quiet, and it's scaring me," he said. "You're not

thinking about getting back together with Christine again, are you?"

"Oh God no," I replied. "Even just thinking about that insanity makes my life seem calm in comparison."

Bradley laughed again. "Then, my work is halfway done."

"Do you know why Damien can't finish his deal in South Florida?"

"I couldn't say," Bradley answered.

"Ah, so you know something, but won't tell me. That's fine. Just tell me how I can make it so Damien finishes this deal instead of me?"

"I'm not saying that I know anything, and so I wouldn't know how to do that," Bradley said.

"I know you know something—"

"You know I'll never tell you if I did. And that's why you can feel safe telling me whatever you need to tell me."

I let out a sigh. "It's just, Dad wants me to go in his place, and he's having me work with Damien's assistant."

"This must be Lauren—the one that you have a crush on."

"Wait! What? Why, I mean, what would make you think that?"

"Don't get in a panic. Nobody said anything to me. You said you had girl troubles. You haven't stopped talking about her in the last few months, so I put two and two together."

"But if you—"

He interrupted me again. "If I put it together, you think other people will put it together. They might, but I am pretty good at this stuff. And I'm hoping I'm the only one you talked about her with."

"You read people like Dad does. You should close deals."

"No one reads people like Dad does."

Bradley might have thought that, but sometimes I thought he knew people even better than our father. Dad had gotten colder as he aged. He'd been lonely since Mom died.

"I don't think you should try to get out of going on the trip," Bradley suggested, breaking my reverie.

"Should I figure out a way to get someone else to assist me instead of Lauren?"

"Not if you care about Lauren getting fired."

"She wouldn't get fired."

"Dad would wonder why you didn't want to work with her, and you'd either have to lie about her or tell the truth about her. Either option puts her job in jeopardy."

"Dad practically begged her to go. She'd turned down his other promotions until now," I said.

"Then she's probably on Dad's shit list if she turns him down again. He likes to get what he wants, and he knows how to do it. Do you want to put her in that situation?"

"But I can't handle being alone with her," I said without thinking.

"What makes you say that?"

I hadn't wanted to get into the details, but there was no way that Bradley would rat me out, and I really needed his advice. "Because of that day that I mentioned where I took her to the doctor and then we went to lunch at Geoffrey's."

"That's not all of it, is there?"

"We were having Malibu Mint Martinis." My voice trailed off.

"Did you bang Damien's assistant?"

"Hey!" I yelled into the phone. "Don't talk about her like that."

"Whoa, I was just trying to be funny. But, did you?"

"No, nothing like that. I just brought her back to my place to see the sunset."

"I can't believe you get women to fall for that."

"It wasn't like that. It was just as friends. We were having so much fun, and I guess I was drinking. You've got to realize. It was my first day back here, and I was bummed about having to back come home in disgrace—"

My brother interrupted again. "Not in disgrace."

"Well, however it was, I didn't want to come home."

"You're taking forever with this. Just tell me what happened," Bradley demanded.

"She fell asleep on my arm, and then I got worried she passed out from too many drinks and pain medication, so I woke her up. But she was exhausted, and so instead of just putting her in a hotel, I put her in the guest bedroom."

"I don't understand what the problem is here, Aiden. It sounds like you guys just had a few drinks. You'll have a good time in Florida."

"I didn't get to the part where it went a little sideways."

"Okay, well then get to that part. You're starting to tell stories like cousin Madeline. In a million parts with a bunch of pointless tangents."

"For the record, most women tell stories like that."

"I hope you're not saying shit like that around the office, but get to the point already."

"Fine," I said. "When I put her on the bed, she made a pass at me."

"Well, that's on her."

"Except I really went with it, and I haven't been able to get it out of my head."

"I see," Bradley said.

"So what do I do?"

"You could tell Dad the truth and have him send somebody else, or go to Florida and hold your shit together."

"I don't like any of those options," I said.

"Why not?"

"I don't want to disappoint Dad, and I don't know if I'll be able to resist her."

"Why do you think you can't resist Lauren?"

I leaned against the tree and exhaled. What was I supposed to tell him? That I'd known her for a day, but I thought she was the one? I'd thought Christine was the one. It was obvious I knew nothing about what I truly wanted in the world.

"Are you afraid to admit that you think she could be someone special?" Bradley asked.

"Maybe."

"So that means yes. Here's the deal. How much time did you guys even spend together?"

"A day. An amazing day."

"Anybody can be amazing for a day. Maybe all you need to do to get over this Lauren girl is to just get to know her better. Go to Florida. Get the ideal version of Lauren out of your head, and learn about the real Lauren. You may just find she's not as great as your imagination thought she'd be."

"I hadn't thought of that."

"Remember how much we loved Mrs. Cummings, our nanny?" Bradley reminded me.

"We hated Mrs. Cummings."

"Not in the first week. Remember, she took us to the beach, and then Universal Studios, and then out to eat. It was the first time we'd ever gone to McDonald's."

"I felt so weird being a kid who'd never been to McDonald's. It was such a relief to have a Happy Meal like other kids," I recalled. "I'd forgotten she'd done all that."

"Exactly. She was in the honeymoon period with us. But by the end of the second week, we hated her more than any of the other nannies."

"So true." My mind drifted into thoughts about Christine. Our first date had been fun, but it turned out we weren't a match. From there, memories of friendships that later turned out to be people trying to get close to me because of my money flooded my mind.

Bradley sighed. "Go to Florida. Get to know her. It's the only way you'll get over this crush. Otherwise, your mind will create some stupid scenario about her being 'the one who got away.'"

"You're right. Thanks, man."

"Remind Damien how right I am."

"Right about what?"

"Just in general," he said.

I knew Brad was talking about something specific, but I didn't pry.

We said our goodbyes, I hung up, and pushed my way off the tree. My shirt must've hit a snag or something, because I heard and felt my shirt rip.

I looked over my shoulder to check the damage. There was a tear on the seam line between my right shoulder and the top of the sleeve.

Luckily, I had a spare dress shirt in my desk. Dad

always kept spare shirts in his desk, and we'd all done the same.

It always paid to look sharp, no matter how long of a day it was.

All of our assistants made sure that we were well-stocked.

I glanced down at my watch. I had about ten minutes to get upstairs and changed before Lauren and I were supposed to meet.

My mood had made a turn for the better after talking to my brother. It always did.

He was right. I wasn't a cynical man, but I was a realistic one. Life had proven to me that over time people could be incredibly disappointing or, at best, okay.

It was rare for me to meet anyone outside of the family that I could trust.

Even when I did, it had never been a woman. I'd only had three close friends outside of the family. One I'd met in the third grade, and the other two I met in New York. The odds of meeting somebody incredible had to be one in a million.

Even if it felt like Lauren was incredibly extraordinary, it wasn't based on knowing her all that well. And I did have a history of imagining people to be better than they actually were.

It was time for me to grow up.

I got to my office, but it took a longer than I hoped. The view from the twenty-second floor was great, but the elevator ride was annoyingly long. No wonder Dad made sure he had a private elevator that went straight to his floor.

When I got to my floor, I noticed my assistant's desk

was empty. I guessed the temp that I'd been working with had been reassigned since I was leaving for Florida. But I was sure I still had a fresh shirt.

I hurried into my office, closed the blinds, and opened the bottom right drawer of my desk. Yes! One white and one blue shirt!

I took off my shirt and tie and tossed the torn shirt in the trash. I grabbed the fresh shirt and unwrapped it, ditching the plastic wrap and cardboard back into the trash as well.

The sound of the door to my office opening startled me.

My eyes shot to the doorway.

"Oh!" Lauren exclaimed, staring at my naked chest.

Stunned, I just stood there. Before I could regain my bearings, Lauren bolted out of the room.

Shit!

27

LAUREN

*S*truggling to carry a box of stuff with one arm, I rushed out of the elevator. I knew it would be easy to find Aiden's office. It would likely be in the corner along the east wall. That's where Mr. Damien's office was on the 17th floor. That corner had the best view.

Half way down the hall, I stopped and used my thigh to push the box back up my arm. All I wanted to do was to set my stuff down, get through this meeting without mooning over Aiden, and rush home to pack.

We'd be alone together in his office! Taking this assignment was a curse and a blessing all in one.

I speed walked as fast as I could without dropping the box to the end of the hall, where I spotted an empty desk in front of the corner office. That had to be his, and if it wasn't, I'd at least have a place to put my stuff down.

I plopped the heavy box on the empty desk and then knocked on the door.

No answer, but I definitely heard a drawer opening and shutting coming from inside his office. He must've not heard me. I checked my watch, 11:00. Not wanting to be late and knowing that he expected my arrival, I decided to let myself in.

The view of Aiden's naked torso greeted me.

What the?! Why was he not wearing a shirt?

Too dumbstruck to say anything, I stood there for what could have been a year and then turned around and left.

It frazzled my brain to see half-naked Aiden totally sober.

His shoulders were more incredible than I remembered, and that light smattering of hair on his chest that trailed down to his—

"Lauren!" Aiden yelled.

I stopped and turned around to see him peeking his head out of the door.

"I can explain."

I looked down at the ground. I could still see part of his bare chest, which conjured up the image of his entire chest. None of this was appropriate. "Okay, I'll just wait out here."

"Give me a minute." He ducked back into his office and shut the door.

I glanced around to see if anybody was looking.

Nobody seemed to care.

What the fuck was I doing? The picture in my mind of half-naked Aiden burned in my brain and made my knees weak. I wanted to run my hands down his hard chest, feel that smattering of hair leading to his–

I stopped myself from thinking about the rest. My life had been chaos since the moment we'd met. Why the hell was he half undressed? What kind of impression had I given him when I went back to his place?

Duh. He might think I liked him working with his shirt off or whatever. Of course, I didn't hate it, but—

It wasn't appropriate, and I'd started it.

Shit. I couldn't go to Florida. My sanity demanded it.

AIDEN

I put my shirt on and dashed out of my office, relieved that Lauren was still there.

"I can't go," Lauren said.

Dad would be unhappy with me if I let Lauren change her mind.

"I can explain about the shirtless situation," I said. "I tore my shirt on a tree outside, and I keep a spare shirt in my desk—"

She looked down and shook her head no. "It's not that."

I tilted my head and raised my eyebrow, giving her space to explain.

Everything about her posture screamed discomfort and guilt—her shrugged shoulders, furrowed brow, the way she bit her lip. "There isn't enough time for me to get a ride home, pack, and get a ride to LAX. Traffic will be a nightmare, not to mention security. I don't even have clean laundry."

I smiled. Even though I wasn't as good at reading people as Dad, I knew enough from what he taught me that when someone was throwing up logistical reasons for not doing something, their objections were easy enough to overcome.

"That's totally understandable," I said.

Her shoulders relaxed.

"If we had more time, it would be less stressful," I said.

She nodded in agreement.

"We'll be departing from Van Nuys, which is right in your neighborhood, so you'll have plenty of time. Did you get your new corporate credit card and sign the HR papers for your new contract?"

Yes, it was manipulative to bring up the contract she'd signed, but I was desperate.

"Yes, but—"

"Let's do our meeting on the jet to save time," I said, grabbing my phone from my pocket.

I opened my ride share app and hit the hail button. "Your car will be here in seven minutes. Gerard and I will be at your place at one. We'll come up to help you with your bags."

She looked at her watch. "But we'll need time to get through security."

"There is no security line, and the plane will only take off when we get there. That's the nature of a private jet."

She looked down at the stack of boxes on my assistant's desk and reached for them.

I stopped her and grabbed the boxes. "You have a bad wrist. I'll help you downstairs."

"I haven't even been able to go to the laundromat," she said.

I grabbed her box of stuff and headed to the elevator.

She didn't follow. I stopped and turned around. "Your car will be here soon."

"Um," she stalled. She wanted to get out of this, and I suspected it was for the same reasons I worried about us going to Florida together.

"Don't worry about the laundromat. The clothes you're wearing now are perfect for our meeting tomorrow and are already clean. Hang those, wear some casual clothes on the plane, and pack your dirty laundry. We'll send for them to get cleaned when we arrive in Florida."

"What about when we get there?" she asked. Her adorable face was slightly disoriented and confused.

"Don't worry. We've handled everything. The most important thing," I said as I started walking to the elevator, hoping she'd follow me this time, "is that you wrap up things that have to happen here. I don't remember seeing a pet at your place. So no pets, right?"

She hurried to catch up with me. "No pets."

"Then it's easy. Lock all your windows and doors. Set your thermostat a little higher and unplug major appliances, so you're not wasting electricity. Throw out the stuff in your refrigerator. Make sure you pack your laptop, cellphone, and all the relevant chargers so you're ready for the meeting. If you have any medications for the pain that you'll need in the next week, pack that. Everything else—clothes, toothbrush, etc. we can get there. Only concern yourself with things that you can't get from Florida."

We reached the elevator. Lauren hit the down arrow button for us, since my hands were full.

"Thanks," I said.

"Your packing tips were very helpful. You've done this a lot."

The compliment surprised me. "The refrigerator thing I learned the hard way."

She laughed. The doors dinged open. I motioned for her to go first while I held the door open with my foot. As she passed by me, I caught a whiff of her perfume. We both liked clean, citrus-y fragrances.

I followed her into the elevator and hit the button for the lobby with my knuckle. I glanced down at her. She stared straight forward.

The silence got to me. "I understand the weather can be pretty muggy in Florida, even though it's not the dead of summer yet." For heaven's sakes. I was talking about the weather.

"I know. I grew up there."

"Right. I forgot." I felt like an idiot.

"Don't worry. Most of Florida is very well air-conditioned. I usually carry a light jacket around because of it."

Silence enveloped us again. This felt like the longest elevator ride of my life. "You used to work at Rexford. Did you like it there?"

"They had a company picnic every summer, and if you asked for time off in advance, they always tried to give it to you. There were only two times when I had to cancel my plans because I couldn't get off work, which is great compared to my friends, who worked at restaurants."

"Oh, I guess that is nice," I said.

She nodded.

It never occurred to me that being able to get days off would be a benefit for work. It wasn't that I could just not show up, but if I needed the days off, I got them.

Did what she was saying mean that they had denied her requested days off here at Bronson, Inc.? How did that work? Did employees just miss important events, or did they have to quit if it was something they couldn't miss, like a wedding or a graduation?

"You look confused," Lauren said.

"Pardon?" I stalled. I didn't want to tell her what I was thinking about.

"Why do you look so confused?"

"You might be as good at reading people as my dad," I replied, dodging the question.

"No one is as good at reading people as your father."

The elevator stopped on the seventeenth floor, and Angie stepped on.

"Lauren! You're back," she said.

"Yes, but it looks like I'm heading out again," Lauren replied.

"I wondered about that, because I was told I'd be covering Mr. Damien's desk permanently now."

"Mr. Damien is great to work with," Lauren offered diplomatically. I could tell she was not happy about being replaced.

"Lauren's been promoted," I interjected.

"Congratulations!" Angie said. "You're the only person I know who goes out on injury and comes back with a promotion."

"It was in the works before her injury," I added.

"Of course, Mr. Aiden. I was just joking," Angie said.

The elevator stopped on the seventh floor, and Angie got out.

The elevator door closed. "I wish you hadn't told her that," Lauren said without looking up at me.

"I didn't want the rumor mill to think that you were fired or demoted."

"Your father seems pretty convinced that I'm going to keep this promotion, but he assured me I could return to my former position."

"My father said he would do his best," I corrected.

"Tell me how Mr. Bronson's best isn't good enough to make something happen in his own company," she argued.

I nodded. She had a point. "Still, you never know. You might like the promotion."

Lauren looked up and glared at me. We finally reached the ground floor, and she stepped out ahead of me.

I followed her outside to the curb. We waited together in silence.

"About that day we spent together," Lauren started.

Panic struck in my heart. I didn't want to screw up this project or say something to upset Lauren. Her help was the only thing that would get me through this acquisition. I wasn't like Damien. Business never came naturally to me.

"What about it?" I asked, feigning ignorance to stall.

Her eyes locked on mine. My stomach dropped as I looked into her stern eyes. Her jaw tightened, and her mouth was a hard line. She turned away without saying a word.

My mind blanked. I needed to say something to clear the air.

Her Uber pulled up to the curb before I could think of anything.

She darted for the car without even looking back. Just as she opened the car door, I called out to her. "Lauren!"

She paused, but she didn't turn around. I rushed to the

car, but the door remained between us. She looked up at me, but it was as if she was looking through me. Her expression seemed as blank as my mind.

Not knowing what to say, I said, "We'll be by to pick you up at one."

"Yes, Mr. Aiden," she said. Then she got into the car and shut the door, and her Uber drove away.

I stood there, dumbstruck, holding the box of files, and watched her car turn the corner. Her use of Mr. Aiden stabbed at my heart. The reality of what this trip was descended on me.

Neither of us would follow through on our feelings. We both had too much at stake. Lauren and I would be work colleagues.

She knew it, and so did I.

The grief for what I'd secretly hoped for balled up in my throat and threatened to choke me.

It made no sense that I'd be so heartbroken. I'd thought getting to know Lauren better might cure my crush, but nothing about that rang true.

The prospect of working so closely with her but not being able to hold her or kiss her again made my chest ache.

LAUREN

The moment I closed the door to my apartment, tears poured down my face.

I slumped on the couch and let myself cry. I allowed myself the sweet tension release that only tears could provide.

Carolyn once told me to regard my emotions as information. According to her, my feelings presented me with valuable information about who I was, and that I needed to get to know myself when they came rushing out.

After a few minutes, I got up, got a tissue, and grabbed my luggage. I picked my largest bag and an overnight bag with a pouch for my laptop.

I discovered I had several clean work outfits. There'd been no need for me to wear my work clothes until today. I'd spent most of time off in my comfy pajamas or sweatpants. So it was mostly my pajamas and casual clothes that I needed to pack.

While I packed, I took Carolyn's advice. What were my tears telling me? Why had I been in tears?

My mind replayed the negotiation with Mr. Bronson and then that moment by the curb, when I'd gotten the courage to discuss that night at Aiden's house. His blank expression and the way he replied gutted me.

Aiden Bronson barely remembered us kissing. Or if he did, he didn't think it was something we needed to talk about. A few more tears escaped from my eyes. I didn't stop them. No more bottling up feelings for me. I'd learned my lesson about that the year I lost both my parents.

It was hard packing one-handed, but it gave me something to do while I cried.

The idea that I was going to leave my apartment, live in a whole new place, and do a higher-level job with a guy that I have a crush on that obviously didn't feel the same way about me made my insides tremble.

Was I over-reacting to this? How could I be so heartbroken?

I needed an objective opinion or two. Yeah, two would be better. Time to call both my best friends, and I could tell them I'd be in town.

My mood improved with that thought. I opened my phone to favorites, put in my earbuds, and hit the button for Mackenzie first.

It went straight to voicemail. Not like Mackenzie at all.

"Hey," I said. "It turns out I'll be in Florida for work tonight! Call me when you get a chance. I'll be on a flight in a few hours. If I don't hear from you, I'll call you tomorrow."

After I hung up, I realized things might get weird between Mackenzie and me. The nondisclosure meant that I couldn't talk about the details of the acquisition.

Last we spoke, she'd gone full time at Rexford Drugs. Although I hadn't talked to her much in the last month and a half.

I've been so consumed with Aiden that I'd been neglecting her at a tough time.

Here I was, with the raise that amounted to an extra $20,000, getting ready to go on a private jet, and I was about to tell my best friend, who'd just lost her job and had to go back to working full time in retail, about my "problem." Thank goodness I'd gotten her voicemail.

I unplugged the wall-unit air conditioner. Then I went about packing up my computer. It only took me a few minutes to empty the fridge.

Having been trapped at home for the last few months, my routine had included cleaning out the fridge regularly. The only thing it didn't include was doing laundry, because the basket was so damn heavy.

Well, at least now I could send the laundry out and charge it to the company.

I grabbed my suitcase out of the closet. It hadn't been used in over a year and a half.

I told myself I should be happy. After all, I got to spend time with Mackenzie and Carolyn. Although the Rexford Drug situation would be difficult, I knew Mackie would understand.

I sat on my bed and looked at my phone.

There was still some time before I had to leave. I guess it didn't really take that much for me to wrap up my life. That was one advantage to not having much of a life, I guess.

Between the Aiden situation and not being able to get

in touch with Mackenzie, there was only one thing to do. I hit the button and dialed Carolyn.

"Hey," she said.

"Are you in the car?" I asked. Carolyn was always in the car.

"Yup, but I'll be on the road for at least a half-hour. What's up?"

"I don't even know where to begin, but I haven't been able to get in touch with Mackie."

Carolyn exhaled. "She's been having a rough time since she lost her teaching job."

"Damn, I've been a shitty friend. I haven't talked to her much about it. Did she end up working full time at Rexford?"

"Yeah, but something went down, and she quit."

"What happened?" I asked.

"She said she didn't want to get into it, but she's doing a lot of temp work and answering phones at a used car lot on the weekends."

"I guess she can't take calls at work," I said.

"Between you and me, I think there was some sort of guy trouble at work," Carolyn said. "But that's just a guess. She didn't come out and say it."

I groaned. "Guy trouble at work. That seems to be going around."

"I take it your first day back to work didn't go well."

"I don't know if I can say that. Technically, I got a raise and a promotion."

Carolyn let out a gasp of excitement, and her voice jumped an octave. "How much of a raise?"

"About $20,000 a year."

"You are not allowed to call this a bad day. That's a huge raise. Congratulations! Give me all the details."

"I skipped a pay grade because Mr. Bronson needed me to take a special assignment, and I'm thinking there wasn't anyone else available," I said.

"Why don't you sound happy?"

"It's a lot of change all at once. I'm leaving for the airport in like, forty-five minutes. And you know when things happen quickly, it usually isn't good."

"I know you think that because of your folks, and how fast everything changed when they got sick. And it makes sense, but that's not always how it goes. Sometimes change can be good."

"Yeah, you're right. Plus, at least I'm coming to Florida."

Carolyn let out a squeal. "Where in Florida? Is it within driving distance?"

"It's definitely South Florida, but I don't know where exactly. I was told to pack and be ready to get on a private jet about an hour ago. My ride will be here in an hour."

"Okay, now I get it."

"Get what?"

"You are not good with last-minute changes or surprises, and wow, this is a lot even for someone who isn't risk averse. You should be proud of yourself. Look at you! Leaving town on a moment's notice! You rose to the challenge. Way to go!"

I couldn't help but laugh. Carolyn was great at motivating people. In every way that I felt awkward being around others, Carolyn was totally the opposite. If I hadn't met her my freshman year, I don't think I would've made any friends in college. As it was, I'd only really made two. But every party I was ever invited to, and any fun I ever had, was because of Carolyn.

"I feel ridiculous," I said.

"There are details you're leaving out. Spill it."

"I'm traveling with Aiden," I said. I figured that summed up pretty much everything.

Carolyn let out another squeal. "Oh my God! I know you have a big crush on this guy, and you two traveling together is perfect. How many other people are going?"

"I don't know, but I get the vibe that it may just be us on the jet tonight."

"My life is so boring. I needed this. What are you going to wear?"

"He said wear something comfortable, so I'm just gonna wear my yoga pants and sweatshirt," I said.

"Seriously?"

"I am not getting dressed up. And I'm not having an affair with my boss, and I don't even think he wants to have an affair back with me."

"What if you find out he does?" Carolyn asked.

My mind locked up. I wanted him to want me, but I was afraid of losing my job and everything I'd worked for. "I'm freaking out. I can't go. This is insane!"

"No, it'll be fine. We'll make a plan. You're great with plans."

"But that's the point. I don't know what to plan for!" I said.

"We'll come up with two plans. Plan one goes into effect if you decide to get busy with your hot boss. And another one if you end up keeping it professional. You can do this."

My mind whirred with ideas. "I feel like it's gonna go

the way of being professional, and that's probably for the best."

"Okay. Then enjoy the raise and be professional. And if things change—"

"I know you're the one rooting for romance, but that's not my thing."

"Love is everybody's thing, and love with a billionaire should definitely be everyone's thing."

"The last woman he was engaged to was someone from work, and no one's heard from her since."

"Let's say that you decide not to go on this trip, and you decide to not take this promotion. What happens?" Carolyn asked.

"I lose out on the extra $20,000, and I may not even get my old job back. Plus, I signed a contract."

"So you're going no matter what. Even if it blows up in your face, you're about where you'd be if you decided against going," Carolyn reasoned.

"Ever since that stupid retreat, my life has careened out of order."

"Just go. If you love it, keep the job. If you hate it, quit the job. Figure out how to maximize either of those options. Then, when you get more information, execute that plan."

"What if neither happens?"

"Freak out, cry it out, and then call me so we can make a new plan."

I was already feeling better. "You make it sound so easy."

"When have you ever been the person who didn't do the work?"

I smiled. "Never."

"Exactly. You work harder when things are hard. You can do anything."

"You should be an inspirational speaker."

"I've been thinking about writing a book," she joked.

"I'd buy it," I said. And I wasn't joking.

"But just in case," she said. "Be open to the idea that it may be time for love. And if you get a signal to go for it from the universe, from him, from everything, remember that life is short. You'll always find another job. But you may never find another Aiden."

"Really? That's what you want to leave it on? I felt so much better before you said that," I said.

Carolyn laughed. "I speak the truth. That's why you trust me. If you get a shot at love or even a chance at the possibility, take it. They say you regret the shots you don't take the most."

We wrapped the call, and I hung up.

Time to get my comfy clothes on, freak out, and ace this job.

As I changed, my brain cooked up my plans. For now, I'd keep things all business. In the off chance things turned romantic, I'd look for a way to explore that without losing my livelihood.

30

AIDEN

*W*hen Gerard and I picked her up at her apartment, she was waiting outside on the curb. I told her I'd help her with her luggage, but she didn't want my help.

At least she let Gerard put her bags into the trunk, and now the baggage handlers were taking care of them. If it was just me, I bet she would have carried everything herself in one hand.

I needed to put us back on the right foot, and if that meant that I had to have the uncomfortable conversation about our day together, I would. The problem was, I wasn't sure if the moment had passed.

"Are we flying in the big one?" she asked.

"Yes, it's the Gulfstream," I said.

"I don't know what that means."

I admired her straightforward answer. "It's the one with the G700 on the tail. We just got it, so it hasn't been painted with the corporate logo yet."

"Maybe it's still got that new plane smell."

I laughed. It was a good sign that she was joking with me. I figured this might be a time to push my luck a little. "Would you mind calling me Aiden?"

"It doesn't seem very professional," she said.

"Now that you're an associate instead of an assistant, it's better people see us as equals. I'll be leaning on your expertise a great deal. People are less likely to take an underling's recommendations."

"But we're not equals. They'll see you as a Bronson and me as the other person standing next to a Bronson."

Her reply wasn't short or angry. It was very matter of fact, and it disarmed me. "You know more about this deal than I do. Frankly, my acquisitions and mergers experience is at zero. That's why I need you to make me look good. So, even if you don't feel it, can you call me Aiden?"

She looked at me. I didn't know what to make of her expression. Screw it. I decided to say what I was thinking. Sincerity and truth worked before.

"You seemed to do it easily enough before, and I just like it," I said.

"That was different."

Damn, a part of me had hoped it wasn't different, but she was right. "Okay, but can we at least be friendly? It would mean a lot to me, and it'd be good for business."

She remained quiet. I hoped it meant she was mulling it over. "Okay, Aiden."

I smiled.

We began boarding the aircraft. I was glad Dad booked us on the new jet. The Gulfstream would take us straight to Florida in one shot. It'd be a long flight, but we could have something to eat, create a strategy, and maybe even take a quick nap.

Lauren reached the top of the stairs and peeked into the aircraft. "Wow!"

The crew was there to greet us.

"Welcome," the flight attendant said to us.

"Welcome aboard," Charles, our pilot said.

"Good to see you again, Charles," I said.

"This is Evan, he's our copilot for the day," Charles said, motioning to the man next to him.

"Nice to meet you, Evan and Charles," Lauren said, shaking hands with each. She turned to the flight attendant. "I didn't catch your name."

"Beth," she answered.

Lauren shook her hand. "Nice to meet you, Beth. I'm Lauren."

After our brief hellos, we entered the main cabin area. Lauren looked back at me. "Which one is my seat?"

"Anywhere you like."

"How many people are joining us?" she asked.

"It's just us."

"Cool!" She scanned the cabin and then called out, "Dibs on the right side of the plane." She set her carry-on bag on one desk and slung herself into a seat.

I laughed. "I guess I have no choice but to take the left."

She smiled at her victory.

I sat across the aisle from her and pivoted my seat to face her.

"I didn't know they did that." She smiled and pivoted her seat toward me. Then, she looked around and marveled at the aircraft. "This is freaking cool! This plane is huge."

I took in the aircraft's interior and admired it, too. "It's my first time riding on this big one. We usually have smaller ones that we lease, but dad wanted to get a bigger one so when we to go to Europe, the flight would be shorter."

"Good thinking."

Beth came over and asked if we wanted something to drink.

"A Diet Coke," Lauren said.

"Same for me."

Beth left to get our drinks, and I turned my gaze to Lauren. She was checking out everything on the aircraft. Her adorable face and obvious joy made me smile.

Lauren wasn't like other people. She didn't pretend like being on a private jet was something that happened every day. She wasn't trying to be cool.

I still found the experience thrilling. And dad's new plane was impressive. It was nice to see someone appreciated the fun of it.

"Do you think they have some snacks?" Lauren asked me. "I skipped lunch. I was busy getting ready."

"We have snacks and full meals," I said.

"I'm so glad I didn't have the Uber go through Taco Bell drive-through like I originally thought," she said. "I'm sure they're serving something better, right?"

"I've never had Taco Bell, although I hear it's very impressive, but I think we may have something better on board. So, Taco Bell. It seems to be a favorite of yours."

"How did you know?"

"You brought it up at the clinic before I took you to Geoffrey's."

"I must've forgotten in the haze of Malibu Mint Martinis."

"I hope you didn't forget too much about that day," I said before I thought better of it.

She fought back a smile as she blushed, and then turned her face away from me to look out the window. My heart soared.

Well, at least for a few minutes. But as I looked over at her adorable face, reality set in.

We'd only known each other for a short while, and even if we both were interested in something more, wasn't it still impossible? Was it worth risking so much?

Dad had forbidden dating anyone in the company, and I'd already made this mistake before.

Beth brought us our drinks. Then we prepared for takeoff.

As the plane taxied down the runway, I couldn't help but think that Lauren and I could be more than colleagues or friends. But she might not even want that. What I needed was a sign—something that told me she was up for it and willing to take the risk.

31

LAUREN

*I*t took a Herculean effort to not smile like an idiot. Aiden hadn't forgotten our day together!

Giddiness swept through me as I tried to hide my excitement by staring out the window as the plane took off.

Even though there wasn't much that I could do as far as pursuing Aiden, it comforted me to think that my crush wasn't completely unrequited. But it changed nothing. Except, maybe we could have a friendly work relationship.

Beth peeked her head into the main cabin, told us we could move about the aircraft freely, and then left again.

I swiveled my chair to face Aiden again. "How about I brief you on the acquisition?"

"Let's get something to eat, and then we'll work. It's a long flight."

I nodded in agreement, and within minutes I was eating a gourmet meal on a private jet with a billionaire.

How had this become my life? I made a mental note to be more open to change, even if it was stressful.

Time onboard flew by. Aiden had a lot of questions about the acquisition, and I realized that although he was smart, he knew little about the deal. It made me wonder why the hell Mr. Bronson chose him to replace Mr. Damien.

"What division did you work in on the East Coast?" I asked after I finished the briefing.

Aiden laughed. "Is that your polite way of trying to figure out why Dad sent me on this deal?"

Damn. I was so busted. I decided to avoid the question with a compliment. "You're so easygoing. I wish I was like that."

"I was in operations for the East Coast, but my focus was on corporate culture. There were some problems with morale, and I stepped in."

I nodded, but Aiden's former position surprised me. The other Bronson brothers were heads of divisions. His job seemed fluffy and less prestigious.

I'd quit a job I wasn't qualified for, especially one that was obviously tied to nepotism. I decided not to dwell on that.

My judgmental mind had ruined so many relationships. Aiden and I were getting along now, and I didn't want to ruin it. It would be like me to build rapport for most of the flight and then blow it in the last hour.

"I'm not the business mogul that the rest of my family is," he confessed. "But I'm determined to contribute and learn. I do well motivating underperforming divisions, and I enjoy working with people, but dealmaking isn't my thing. My father could always drive a hard bargain, but

I'm more like my mom. I just want everyone to be happy." Aiden sighed. "The truth is the only thing I ever envisioned for my future was having a family, you know? I've always wanted to be a dad."

"I don't think I've ever heard a man say that," I blurted out.

"Don't you want to have a family?"

"I guess. It's just that there's so much that I want to do with my career. But I'm still young. I'd like to think that it is possible to have it all."

"If you're really excited about your career, why have you turned down so many promotions?" he asked.

Shit. How the hell was I going to tell the big boss's son that I didn't see my future being at Bronson, Inc.?

"I always thought I'd learn a lot here at Bronson and then start my own business. But now that I'm doing this project, I may actually want to stay."

Aiden laughed. "Nice way to say, you never intended to stay this long."

My eyes widened.

"Don't worry. I won't rat you out to my dad."

I hoped that was true.

Aiden took another sip of his diet soda. "Dad doesn't want to hear it, anyway. He sees a lot in you. And you just might find that you like it here."

"I appreciate that, Aiden," I said, deliberately using his name. "Besides, taking this promotion may really be the next step to building a future at Bronson."

I wasn't lying. There was a chance that was true. The main reason I turned down the promotions was my dad always told me you'd never get rich working for someone else.

I worried that I'd get sucked into this new position, and my ambition would trigger a climb up the corporate ladder, and I'd never strike off on my own.

"But if you didn't work here, and you had your own business, would it be real estate?"

I shook my head no. "I'd invent gadgets like the stuff you see on TV."

Aiden laughed. "Wait, like those cheesy commercials?"

I grinned and nodded.

"Don't tell anybody, but Dad buys all that shit."

"He can afford it," I said.

"So have you invented anything?"

"I'm working on something now."

"What is it?" he asked.

I gave him a quick pitch on the Bag Buddy.

"Can I see your drawings of it? It sounds cool."

"It's top secret," I said jokingly.

"Please."

"Fine, I'll put it in the cloud folder with my recommendation proposal for the merger."

Beth approached us at the long conference table. "Can I get you anything else to drink? We'll be landing in about an hour."

Aiden looked at me. I shook my head no. I'd gotten my fill of drinks and food. It was like we were flying in a restaurant.

"No thank you, Beth," Aiden said.

Just as she walked away, the aircraft shook and then I heard a sickening crack. Beth stumbled and then turned back to us. "Fasten your seatbelts."

"Is there a problem?" Aiden asked.

"I'm sure it's just turbulence, but I'll go check with our pilot," she answered, and then hurried toward the cockpit.

I shot Aiden a worried look.

"It's fine," he said, "but we should get back to our seats."

I stood up from the table. The plane jolted up and then down, knocking me off balance. Out of habit, I reached for the side of my chair with my right hand, but couldn't grasp it enough to steady myself with my not-yet-healed wrist.

The plane shook again. To keep my fragile wrist from slamming into the chair, I leaned left and lost my balance.

Aiden grabbed me by the waist to steady me. "I got you," he said as he led me to a secure seat. Just as I sat down and snapped on my safety belt, I heard a sickening sound like we'd hit something. The plane plummeted.

An audible, high-pitched gasp leapt from my throat.

"Shit!" Aiden swore as he dove into the seat to the left of me and quickly fastened his seat belt.

"Are you two okay?" Beth called out. I realized she hadn't made it all the way back to the cockpit.

The captain came onto the loudspeaker. "Fasten your seatbelts and brace for landing."

His voice sounded calm, but I could tell from the hard shaking of the aircraft that all was not well, and the brevity of his words alarmed me. I looked out the window. All I could see was the ocean.

"Should we get our life vests from under the seat?" I yelled to Beth.

"Yes, just in case, but don't expand them," Beth called back, reaching under a nearby seat.

Before I could reach for the life vest, Aiden had already bent over and grabbed our vests.

He handed me my vest. I put it over my head.

The sound of the engine seemed to cut in half at the exact moment the plane dropped into a free fall.

"Oh god!" I yelped as my stomach rolled.

Without thinking, I grabbed Aiden's hand. His muscular hand encircled mine.

My mind went into overdrive. This could be the last moment of my life. How had all my plans for the future mattered? All the saving for a rainy day. All the times I played it smart. None of it mattered now.

The free fall stopped, but the plane shook hard.

My eyes closed and started an internal dialogue between me and God. "Please, if you let me live, I'll never waste a day again. I'll never postpone being happy until I'm successful. I'll live in the now. I'll go with flow. I'll do anything!"

I gripped Aiden's hand harder. With my eyes still closed, I felt him lift my hand. His soft lips kissed the top of my hand.

I opened my eyes and turned to him. Our eyes locked.

The plane shook again.

"Aiden!" I heard myself call out.

"It'll be okay, Lauren. We'll get through this," he said, but I could tell from his expression, he was scared, too.

It was night now. I peered out the window. Instead of the dark horizon, inky black waves filled my vision. Were we going to crash into the sea?

I turned to Aiden. The tension in his face mirrored my own. But he was still handsome. His dark hair and eyes. His long, yet muscular neck.

Images of us that day replayed in my memory. Even though it was only a day together, it was a day I felt alive.

A day that was rooted in enjoying the moment instead of sacrificing for the future.

I leaned closer to him. My heart pounded in my chest as my gaze dropped from his eyes to his lips.

As I closed the distance between us, my breathing sped up. The smell of his body and cologne made me feel dizzy.

The plane shook again, followed by the sickening sound of scraping metal. My gaze shot to the window just in time to see debris. Holy shit!

The imminence of death filled me with terror, tinged with regret. I'd played it smart, but never lived.

I turned back to Aiden.

He pulled me toward him. I wrapped my arms around his neck. His firm, satiny lips met mine. It ignited my hunger for more. I parted my lips. Aiden accepted my invitation. Our kiss deepened as our tongues entwined.

I wanted to get even closer, but my seatbelt stopped me. The shaking plane faded from my mind as I ran my non-injured hand down the front of his shirt. His heaving chest felt hard under my palm. His heartbeat pounded against my hand.

I pushed my fingers between the buttons of his shirt, craving the feel of Aiden's skin. His undershirt blocked my plans, but I stroked his chest through the thin, tight cotton.

Aiden growled as he kissed me even harder. I gasped for breath.

A hard jolt of the aircraft forced us apart.

"Brace for landing," the pilot announced.

Landing!

"Brace, brace, head down by your ankles!" the pilot instructed.

Beth yelled, "Feet flat on the floor, hug your knees!"

Aiden and I whipped our heads into our laps. I gripped my knees with my one good hand, and used my arm to hug on the right side.

"Stay down! Stay down!" Beth yelled over the noise of the shaking aircraft and sputtering engine.

The aircraft didn't remain on the ground. It bounced back into the air, then banged down again and again.

I heard a yelp, and it wasn't until I felt the strain on my vocal cords that I realized it'd been me. The wheels finally remained on the ground, but a sickening scraping sound reverberated throughout the cabin. My teeth clenched as I winced from the racket.

The jet pitched forward so hard I worried the aircraft would somersault. My right arm slipped from around my knee and slammed against the side of the plane. I yelped.

"Lauren! Are you okay?" Aiden asked.

I remained bent over with my eyes closed as I held my right forearm with my left hand. The hot pain of the impact on my wrist echoed as the plane shook. The plane ground to a stop. I opened my eyes. Sirens wailed. The smell of acrid smoke stung my nostrils and eyes.

"We gotta get out of here," Aiden yelled over the sirens as he undid his seatbelt and turned to help me with mine.

32

AIDEN

*I*t took a while for the ambulance to check us out. We needed to get out of here before the news media arrived. The local crew at the airport had arranged for a nearby limo service to pick us up. I would've preferred something less conspicuous, but beggars couldn't be choosers.

At least it was dark out, so it would be difficult for the press to confirm it's me if they caught up to us. The driver opened the door for us. I motioned for Lauren to go in first.

I slid in beside her, sitting close so I could feel her body next to mine.

"Take us to the nearest five-star hotel," I said, looking around to see if there were any reporters or news crews around.

"We don't have one of those here in Pensacola," the driver said, making eye contact with me in the rearview mirror. "But the Gulf Breeze Beach Hotel is one of the best in town. But they may not have rooms. There's a convention in town."

"Is it far from here?" I asked.

"About forty-five minutes."

"That's too far to drive only to find out there're no rooms," Lauren said, grabbing her phone.

I thought I caught sight of a news van. "Listen, get us out of the airport. I don't want to get held up by any reporters."

I looked over to Lauren, regretting not handling the hotel arrangements. She was already holding the phone to her ear. I could hear the ring.

"Ask for suites," I said.

"Yes, I was wondering if you had any vacancies, preferably suites," Lauren said, and then listened. "We'll keep looking."

I shot her a questioning look. She hung up. "They only have the one room."

I nodded and grabbed my phone to help her look. "Let's keep looking."

We both dialed a dozen other hotels without luck.

"Maybe we should get that one room before it goes," Lauren said, but I could tell she was uncomfortable with it.

"We'll relax and look for something else while we're there," I said, but I worried what it would look like to the staff.

"I'm not supposed to do this, but I'm only suggesting it because there's no other place for you to go," the driver said. "And I'll only do it if you promise not to get me in trouble with my car service."

"Please, you'd be doing us a favor," I said.

"A friend of mine has a nice beach cottage he rents out. He had a last-minute cancellation and hasn't been able to rent it. It's a tad pricey because it's on the beach."

"Can you call him?" I asked.

The driver pulled over to the side of the road "Absolutely." Within minutes he'd planned for his friend to meet us at the cottage, and we were on our way there.

He looked into his rear-view mirror and made eye contact with me. "You'll love the place. It's on the beach and private. Although we may have some thunderstorms rolling in tonight. It'll probably clear up by the afternoon."

Having privacy and being on the beach with Lauren sounded perfect.

"I'm glad I packed my swimsuit," I said. I turned to Lauren as if to ask her if she packed hers.

"I'm a native Floridian. Of course, I packed my swimsuit, but I doubt your father will want us staying here long enough to get a lot of swimming in."

"He'll just have to be disappointed then."

She gave me a questioning look.

"We deserve a day off. We could've died up there."

She nodded in agreement and then turned her attention to the window. "I've never been to this part of Florida."

"Me neither." A silence engulfed the backseat.

The reality of what I'd said aloud hit me. We could've died.

I scooted even closer to Lauren and reached for her hand. She let me take it and gave my hand a gentle squeeze in return. That slight gesture soothed my nerves and then turned me on.

Lauren put her head on my shoulder. I kissed her on the top of the head and tried to relax as we rode in silence.

Somehow we were still alive. When I thought we might not make it, all I could imagine was how I needed to live, and how I wouldn't let my past mistakes or my family dictate my future choices. I needed to be my own man.

My mind thought back to Lauren and me on the plane. Had she leaned in to kiss me first, or had I? Maybe it was at the same time.

That kiss.

Even when I thought I was going to die on that plane, my cock sprang to attention when her lips touched mine.

But it was more than passion. Well, it was for me, and judging by the way Lauren was letting me hold her right now, I hoped it was for her, too.

LAUREN

I closed the bathroom door, grabbed my comfy t-shirt and shorts from my carry-on, and changed.

"They'll deliver our luggage in the morning," Aiden called out to me from the living room. With all the shock of our emergency landing, neither of us realized we didn't have our luggage until after we'd arrived here at the cottage. I was glad that I'd instinctively grabbed my overnight bag when we left the plane.

My hands gripped the bathroom counter as I stared at my reflection in the mirror. I forced myself to relax my grip as my mind struggled to make sense of what had happened on the plane.

We'd learned that inclement weather had caused the turbulence and had diverted our landing. In Florida, hurricane season starts in the summer. Man, I thought I was going to die up there. But what bothered me was that my life hadn't flashed in front of me.

Not one moment. The only thing that came to my

mind had been regret—the regret of living for a future that never came. Was that what my parents would have wanted for me?

Maybe this was a sign I needed to change like Scrooge in *A Christmas Carol* with my near-death experience as a stand-in for the Ghost of Christmas Future. If that was true, now what?

I took a deep breath and tried to get present in my life —live in the here and now. And what was happening right now? I was here on some beach with my hot boss, thinking of that kiss on the plane and that kiss at his house, pretending like everything was normal when nothing was normal.

No more doubts. Doubt was for people who couldn't think or make a plan. So what was my plan now?

Go back to my life?

The life that didn't even flash in front of my eyes. My life far away from my friends and my life with no family.

The existential realization that my days were truly numbered took hold. My face heated with panic. I turned on the faucet and washed my face.

Out of habit, I reached into my carry-on bag, pulled out my toothbrush, and brushed my teeth. I returned my toothbrush into its holder and stared at my reflection.

Think, Lauren, think.

"There's no food in the fridge," Aiden called out from the other side of the bathroom door. "But there's a menu here for Italian delivery. Does that sound good to you?"

I knew what I wanted.

I took two quick steps to the door and threw it open. The suddenness startled Aiden and made him jump.

He grabbed at the wall to slow his fall before he crashed onto the hardwood floor with a thud.

I rushed to kneel and help him. "I'm so sorry!"

"I just didn't expect you to come out like that," he said, his voice breathless from his fall.

I frantically looked over his body for injury. "Are you hurt?"

"I'm fine," he said, laughing and grabbing my hand. "If you were trying to get me back for making you fall at the retreat, you'll need to try a lot harder."

Whatever courage I'd tried to muster by acting fast drowned in a pool of embarrassment. "I wasn't trying to get you back."

"What were you trying to do?" he asked, leaning back on his forearms, stretched out next to me on the hallway floor.

I stared into his dark eyes. My gaze dipped to his full lips. "I had a thought I wanted to share with you, but—" Embarrassment stopped me.

What had I been trying to do? What the hell had I been thinking? Here I was with the owner's son, wearing no makeup, in my old t-shirt and shorts, thinking I was going to what? Sweep him off his feet? The closest I'd come was knocking him down.

We weren't drunk. We weren't dying. And we were stone cold sober. Was he even interested?

"Don't stop there," he said, his voice husky. "I think I'd like to hear your thoughts."

He pulled me closer. One of my arms rested on his chest, and the other propped me up next to him.

Our faces were inches apart.

"It wasn't a fully formed thought or anything. More of just a feeling or a vibe. I guess."

His gaze took in my face and drifted to my lips. "I've had a lot of those myself."

"About me?"

He nodded yes.

"Good ones?"

"Some of them, but others..." He shook his head in mock horror. "They were bad. Very bad thoughts."

I leaned closer. "How bad?"

He sat up. "So fucking bad." In one fell swoop, he swept his arms around me and rolled on top of me.

My breath turned ragged.

His face turned serious. "Lauren," he started, but then stopped.

"I know. It's complicated."

"What I feel isn't."

"And what's that?"

He pushed himself between my legs. I felt his hardness against my inner thigh.

A moan escaped my mouth. Fire burned between my legs. "I see."

"But I respect you, and I don't—"

I stopped him. "No."

He froze.

I knew if we talked it over or thought it over, the moment would pass. I couldn't risk losing this moment. Returning to living for a future that may never come wasn't an option.

"Lauren?" Aiden searched my face for a clue about what he should do.

I closed my eyes, took a deep breath, and tried to find

the right words. "I don't want to think things over. Can you help me with that?"

He wrapped his arms around me, and I looked up at him.

"I'm the perfect man for the job," he said and leaned in for a kiss.

Our lips touched. My worried thoughts evaporated. Nothing existed but Aiden and me. I spread my lips, hungry for more. He responded to my invitation without hesitation.

His chest pressed against mine. The heat and hardness of Aiden's body made me ache for more.

His kisses drifted from my lips to my neck.

"Aiden!" I gasped.

He broke away from me and looked down at me, his expression incredulous. "Fuck! Lauren!"

The gap between us disoriented me. I needed his body against mine.

"Don't worry, we're not stopping. Just relocating," he said, standing up and offering his hand to help me off the hallway floor.

I gave him my good hand, and he swept me up and into his arms. He carried me bridal style to the bedroom.

He turned me sideways to ease me through the doorway, crossed the room, and tossed me on the bed.

I yelped in surprise.

He stood at the side of the bed, looking down at me. His dark gaze took me in. "I like the sound of that."

Fuck!

That look made me pant. He unbuttoned his shirt slowly. He'd already removed his tie.

"I didn't pack any condoms with me. I'm clean, but if

you're not on any birth control, we can still have a lot of fun."

My face heated with embarrassment, but it was good he was talking about this. "I'm on the pill, and I haven't—"

I stopped myself from telling him I hadn't had sex for two years and cut to the point. I couldn't look him in the eye, but I eked out, "Clean bill of health here."

The sound of his pant zipper got my attention. I turned toward him. "Somebody's getting shy, and it's not me." He looked me dead in the eye as he pulled down his pants, underwear and all.

His rock hard cock displayed zero signs of shyness. Holy shit!

"We'll only do what you're comfortable with, but I'll do my best to make you comfortable," he said.

I froze on the bed. This man was so fucking gorgeous. Abs. Smooth, tanned skin. The smattering of hair from his chest down to his you know what.

And here I was in my crappy t-shirt and shorts. Did he expect me to be totally shaved—like everywhere?

I tried to do that for my last boyfriend, and let's just say my private parts looked like a fricken' angry strawberry.

Aiden crawled closer to me on the bed. "Where'd you go, Lauren? I'm in charge of keeping you from thinking."

He put his hand to my cheek and steered me to a deep kiss.

Yes, more kisses.

Aiden's hand slid under my shirt. My breath hiccuped in my throat. His firm hands felt so good on my skin. He slid his hand up my rib cage.

My nipples hardened in anticipation.

Liquid heat pooled in between my legs. He continued to kiss me. His hard, wet mouth mesmerized me.

I felt alive! Sexy, even!

His palm cupped my breast, and he toyed with my hard nipple with his long fingers.

Electricity shot through me. My back arched under his expert hands.

"You're so fucking hot," he whispered as he pushed up my shirt and put his lips onto my nipple.

A moan escaped from my throat. I'd never heard myself moan before, but as he went from one nipple to the next, I did it again.

He groaned in return.

He pulled himself away, got up on his knees, and removed my shirt and pulled down my shorts and panties in a rush of motion.

The cool air on my naked skin excited me and made me feel exposed.

Aiden was on his knees between my legs, staring down at me.

"You're perfect," he whispered.

Relief washed over me. I reached for him, not being able to take our bodies being separated for long. Okay, and I felt a little weird about him looking at me.

Aiden let out an easy chuckle. "Getting too close to thinking again, are we?"

He kissed my neck and made his way downward.

"Thinking bad," I joked.

"I'll show you bad," he said, taking a sudden detour from kissing my neck to down between my legs.

I sat up in shock and attempted to wriggle away without thinking.

He ignored me.

"Aiden!" I gasped out as his mouth went there. I mean right there!

He paused for a second, looked up at me, and shot me a sexy smile. "Get used to calling out my name like that!"

So cocky!

His mouth went back to its task, and I leaned back and braced myself.

My ab and leg muscles tightened as I hiked up O Mountain. "Oh, my god!"

How did he know the exact right pressure? He made slow, steady strokes with his tongue as his powerful arms held me still.

His tongue worked my clit.

I held my breath as the mother of all orgasms built up. "Just like that!"

As if sensing how close I was, Aiden picked up speed with his mouth and teased my slit with his finger.

"Aiden!" I gasped, my voice loud and high pitched. Waves of elation swept through me. It was almost too much, but he knew exactly how to keep it going. I felt like I was floating above the bed, and when the peak ebbed, he got up on his knees, put himself between my legs, and propped himself onto me.

"Ready?" he said, his hot breath in my ear.

I barely had any breath left, so I whispered back, "Yes."

He slid into me. Holy crap!

He gasped in my ear. "Fuck, you feel so good!"

My hips bucked up to meet his strokes into me. He groaned more. I couldn't believe how good he felt inside of me.

I wanted more. My legs wrapped around his waist and pulled him deeper and closer.

His face bent close to mine. "I've dreamed about this since the first day I met you," he whispered. My heart soared.

Our lips met again, and our kisses deepened.

My insides tightened. I broke our kiss to catch my breath. "Aiden!"

"Yes! Right there!" he grunted back, making his strokes more deliberate.

My brow furrowed as he hit that exact spot that I needed. Our breathing picked up as we both focused on reaching that peak.

"So close," I whispered to Aiden.

"Fuck! Me, too!"

My orgasm threatened again. "Aiden! I'm almost there!"

"Come for me, Lauren!"

The sound of his commanding, sexy voice pushed me over the top.

I screamed his name as I tumbled over the edge.

"Lauren!" he grunted out as he fucked me hard and came inside of me.

We both rode the wave and milked every ounce of pleasure until we were exhausted.

Aiden kissed me one more time and then rolled onto his side. "Wow!"

I couldn't agree more. Had that just happened? A stupid grin threatened to take over my entire face as a shy laugh bubbled out of me.

He wrapped his arm around me and pulled me closer to rest on his broad chest. "What are you giggling about?"

I shrugged, not wanting to sound like an idiot. I was out of my element. At work, in the world, just about anywhere I felt confident and in charge, but this situation was unique. I'd never had mind-blowing, double-orgasming sex with a Mr. Malibu type before.

My insecurity threatened to rear its head. My mind pumped out questions. What did this mean to him? Was this a onetime thing? Was I falling in love with him? How did he feel about me?

Aiden planted a sweet kiss on the top of my head. "I can feel you thinking, and I'm in charge of making that not happen."

I looked up at him, but I didn't want to ruin the moment with my thoughts.

He gave me a sweet kiss on the lips and then stared into my eyes. "You're so beautiful."

"You're pretty good looking yourself," I replied without thinking.

He laughed. I wasn't sure what to make of it, but it made me happy.

"How about we order some dinner before the next round?" he asked.

I smiled at the idea of a next round and dinner. "Didn't you say something about an Italian menu?"

Aiden waggled his eyebrows. "Don't move!"

He got up and padded out of the bedroom without bothering to put his clothes on. I stifled another giggle as I caught the view of his tight ass walking away from me. Damn.

Italian food and sex with a hot man in a cottage on the beach. So not where I thought I'd be when I woke this morning!

Worries about the future of my job and the lack of a future with Aiden threatened my contentedness.

I exhaled and pushed those thoughts out of my mind. No matter what tomorrow brought, I'd always have the memories of tonight. For once I'd live for now, instead of a future that might never come.

Aiden returned to the bed with his cell phone and the menu. He shot me a wolfish grin. "I know what I want."

"Lasagna?"

He shook his head and handed me the menu. "What do you think about splitting a bottle of red as well?"

"Sounds good. And could you grab a few sodas?" I forced myself to focus on the menu. "Do you want to split a pizza?"

"We can get one."

I turned over the menu and looked at the dinners. "The fettuccini Alfredo sounds great."

Aiden picked up his phone and dialed. He ordered practically one of everything, including the desserts and two bottles of wine. He hung up the phone and wrapped his arms around me. "That'll take them a little while to put together. What ever will we do to pass the time?"

I smiled and shrugged. "Maybe they have some board games in the closet?"

He pulled me closer. "I'm not sure I can compete with Parcheesi or Checkers, but I'll try." He laid a mind-numbing, toe-curling kiss on me. "What's the verdict?"

I pretended to think about it. "I think I need another sample."

Aiden pulled me closer for another kiss, but his cell phone rang.

"Maybe it's the Italian restaurant saying we need to leave food for the rest of Florida," I said.

Aiden smiled and reached for his phone. "Ugh. It's my brother." Aiden rolled his eyes and declined the call.

"Maybe it's something important."

He tossed the phone on the bed and leaned in to kiss me again. "Nothing is more important than this."

We kissed for a couple more seconds before his cell phone interrupted us again.

"Maybe he heard about the plane," I suggested.

Aiden declined the call and looked like he was about to shut his phone off until Dolly Parton's "Nine to Five" blasted from my cell phone somewhere on the bedroom floor.

"I take it that's the ringtone for my brother?" Aiden asked.

I nodded. "Yep."

I knew I had to get out of bed to search for the phone, but I suddenly felt shy about Aiden seeing me naked. I didn't want to come out from under the covers.

Aiden let out a loud exhale, rolled over, and picked up his phone. "Don't pick it up," Aiden said, pulling me back into the bed. His face looked angry as he read the message from his phone. "I'll handle my damn brother."

Aiden pushed on his boxer briefs and stormed out of the bedroom, shutting the door behind him hard.

"Damien!" Aiden growled into the phone before I heard the sliding glass doors outside open and shut. I couldn't make out what Aiden was saying anymore.

Something was up, and it wasn't good.

AIDEN

*D*espite my rage, I took it easy on the sliding glass door. I'd inadvertently slammed the bedroom door, which probably worried Lauren. All I wanted to do was get my brother off my fucking back and get back to Lauren before she got cold feet or cold anything.

"We're not flying there tomorrow!" I said through gritted teeth.

"What do you mean you're not flying out tomorrow?" he had the nerve to demand.

"We almost died, for fuck's sake! A situation we wouldn't be in if you were doing your damn job." Yes, it was a brutal thing to say, but I was sick of his holier than thou attitude.

"You and I both know the longer you're there with her, the deeper in trouble you're going to get."

"And what do you mean by trouble?"

"I saw how close you two were sitting in the car after the diverted landing."

How had my brother spied on me all the way from California? "I don't know what you're talking about."

"You made the news. And Dad's not happy about it."

Shit! Somehow someone must've caught us in the car.

"I can tell by your silence and how defensive you are that something has already happened."

"It's none of your business."

"You know damn well that it is. It's all of our business. How bad is it? How far have you gone?"

It was none of his damn business. Time to turn the tables. "Why exactly can't you go to Florida to close this deal? I mean everyone knows I'm the son who's the fuck up who diddles all the women at the company. But since when does the golden boy, Damien, have someone else close his deals for him?"

"Dad isn't happy with either of us." His voice wasn't as snide as it usually was. Now, I really wondered what was going on with Damien.

"Maybe I'm tired of worrying about what makes Dad happy and I'm going to concern myself with what makes me happy." Immediately after saying it, I felt like an idiot.

"Shortsighted and selfish. That's all you've ever been," Damien said. "Why did you even bother coming to the West Coast if you were going to do the exact fucking thing you did before? Have you slept with her? Have you slept with my assistant?"

"Go to hell!"

"Jesus Christ, Aiden! You fucked Lauren! How dare you! Lauren is a genuinely good person and a really responsible employee. She deserves better than this. Does she know that you're on the rebound? Does she know that you've done this before?"

His low blows cut me like a knife. "I'm not on the fucking rebound, and this is nothing like before."

"It's exactly like before, but worse, because now it's a pattern! Does she even know about your engagement to another former employee?"

"Don't you tell Lauren anything about it."

"Doesn't she deserve to know?" Damien asked.

"I'll tell her when I'm ready, but you stay out of this. And we will not close that God damn deal this week. If it can't wait until next week, then you get your shit together and you take care of it your damn self." I hung up my phone and turned it off.

It took all of my willpower not to chuck the thing into the ocean.

"What are you going to tell me about in your own good time?" Lauren asked.

I turned to see her dressed in her t-shirt and shorts standing with the sliding glass doors open.

35

LAUREN

I knew I shouldn't have eavesdropped. When I'd opened the sliding glass door, I had deliberately made noise hoping that Aiden would see me. I would've announced myself, but there wasn't a moment I felt comfortable butting in.

I gripped the sliding glass door with my right hand and kept my other hand on the wall to steady myself. If I let go, I thought I'd fall to the ground in tears or shake to death.

"It's nothing, Lauren."

"Then, it's no big deal to tell me." My voice quivered when I spoke, and I hated myself for it.

"Baby—" Aiden said as he took a step toward me.

I stepped back, and he stopped walking towards me.

I hadn't intended to back away, but my self-protective instinct took over. It hurt to look at him. I stared at my feet on the tile of the cottage. "We don't know each other all that well."

"I wouldn't say that."

"We only spent one day together—"

"Two, and today," he corrected. "But we'll have more time to get to know each other this week. We've got the week off."

"I don't think Mr. Bronson or Mr. Damien would be happy with that."

The wind picked up, and I wrapped my arms around myself to keep warm. I looked out at the water. It was dark out, and I couldn't see the waves, but I could tell by the sound that they were choppy. I could tell that there was a storm brewing.

"Let's go inside," Aiden suggested. "It's too cold out here. Plus, we want to hear when the food delivery arrives."

The two of us walked in silence into the living room of the cottage. There was an L-shaped couch, and two easy chairs across from it. I opted to sit in one of the easy chairs so that Aiden couldn't sit next to me. I wanted to look him in the eye, and I didn't want to be distracted by him holding me.

Aiden exhaled and sat down on the couch across from me.

"Do you think there's something here?" he asked.

"I'm going to need you to be more specific," I said, even though I knew what he meant.

"You're thinking too much about this," Aiden said.

I shook my head and then looked down at the arm on the couch, staring at the individual light blue threads. I ran my finger along with fabric. It was rougher than I thought it would be. "Why don't you just tell me what I need to know? I'll find out anyway."

I glanced up at Aiden.

His shoulders slumped. He looked down at the floor as he ran his hands through his hair. "I'm not always good at this, especially when it's important."

When he looked up, his eyes looked directly into mine. His eyebrows furrowed. His expression seemed worried, almost pleading. "There's something here," he said, motioning between us. "I know we haven't known each other a long time, but I feel like whatever we have is something that could be something great."

My heartbeat sped up, but I remained cautious. His statement was so vague. Did he mean we should date? Did he think we could fall in love?

I exhaled and looked away from Aiden's pleading stare. No, no more of that, only worrying about what the guy wanted from our relationship in some vague future. What did I want from Aiden right now?

If I was honest with myself, I wanted him to pledge his undying love for me, but could I be sure I felt the same?

No. My answer disappointed me. Even though I thought I might be in love with Aiden, my practical nature couldn't turn off the fact that we hadn't known each other that long. The uncertainty of my job, Aiden's job, what people would think, our differences in social classes—it all worried me.

"What are you thinking?" he asked.

"That everything feels so tenuous."

"Tenuous," he said, nodding. "Are you feeling anything else? Anything for me?"

I opened my mouth, but no words came out. Could I say I loved him right now? I shook my head 'no' without thinking.

"Nothing? What about what just happened in there?"

he said, his voice getting louder as he motioned to the bedroom. "What about all of those kisses? Those were nothing?"

"I didn't say that!" I yelled back.

"You just shook your head no!" He threw his arms up and then leaned forward and sat on the edge of the couch. "Did what happened in the bedroom mean anything at all to you?"

"Of course it did, but what about you? What did it mean to you?"

"It absolutely meant something to me! There's something here. Something that could be special."

I rolled my eyes. "'Could be special?' What does that even mean? Does that mean I'm your special friend with benefits? Special employee that everyone spreads rumors about?"

"Of course that's what you think of me! I'm Mr. Malibu to you. Some playboy rich guy that doesn't give a shit about anybody!"

Anger swept over me. My muscles tensed and my stomach turned. I didn't like his tone. I felt stupid for sleeping with him. "What am I supposed to think? We spend a day together. You bring me back to your place, but you barely even call me even though I'm injured. We sleep together, and when I come out onto the balcony, you're screaming at my boss that there's something you're not telling me, which you still haven't told me about! And now you're accusing me of calling you names when you're the one withholding from me?"

Aiden held up his hands in the surrender position. "This isn't how I wanted this to go."

"What is this?"

"This discussion about us!" he said, his arms in the air again, but this time he was motioning between us.

A small smile crept onto my lips. "Well, at least you think there's an 'us'."

"Of course I do." Aiden got up from the couch and kneeled in front of me. "I think we're both too afraid of saying what this is, and what it could be, because it's so early."

I exhaled and looked back down at the threads on the armchair. He was right about being afraid to define what I was feeling. Could I fault him for not doing the same?

"What if we spend the week getting to know each other?" Aiden suggested. "Let's see if we even still like each other by the end of our stay, or if we yell at each other every day."

I looked up from the armchair again. Aiden looked up at me with his dark eyes. He looked so hopeful.

But how could his idea work? What would happen after a week?

Aiden took my hand. "You're trying to figure out a puzzle that doesn't have enough information yet. Listen, I get we can't know for sure we're meant to be together forever after only a week. But we'll know for sure if we shouldn't be together. You could walk away and never worry about regretting it if it turns out we only like the idea of each other instead of the reality."

"But what if we don't find out that we shouldn't be together, and we find out that we might have a future?"

Aiden took my hands in his. "You don't want to try this because it might work out? Listen to what you're saying!"

I realized why I was hesitating. Fear. I was afraid that I'd be heartbroken. "What is it you're not telling me?"

"I got engaged two years ago to someone I worked with, but it didn't work out. Dad and my brothers were mad because we have a no dating policy at work, and I broke it."

"So what happens if we end up dating? I'm out of a job?"

"Shouldn't we at least find out if it's worth the risk? I haven't been to an Assholes Anonymous meeting in months. You could hate me by tomorrow."

The last part caught me by surprise. I couldn't help but smile.

"Please, Lauren."

"Won't your brother and your dad be angry about us staying here for an entire week?" I asked.

"I'll take care of it. That'll all be on me."

"Maybe they'd be okay if we took just a couple days," I suggested.

Aiden smiled. "Don't worry about a thing. I've got it covered." He hugged me and gave me a kiss on the cheek. I could tell he was hesitant to be super physical.

I hugged him hard, hoping his strong arms would ease my worried thoughts. But I worried. If I fell in love with Aiden, I'd be the one taking all the risks, and I was the one who didn't have as much means to recover if it didn't work out. Could a relationship, starting with so much inequality, work out?

36

AIDEN

*T*hunder clapped in the distance. The weather that diverted our flight must've come this way. The sound of rain hitting the roof went from a gentle tapping to a full downpour.

Lauren was in the shower while I waited for dinner. It'd taken everything I could think of to convince Lauren to stay with me this week. She'd handled my confession that I'd already dated a coworker pretty well, considering the circumstances. I couldn't help but be hurt that she needed so much convincing.

By the end of this week, I vowed to know everything about Lauren, and she would know me. Okay, and deep down, I wanted her to fall for me. And that would start with tonight.

If things worked out between us, she'd have to leave her job at Bronson. But I could more than afford to take care of us. She wouldn't even have to work. We could start a family. That's if she wanted to start a family. Did she?

I realized I'd been so invested in convincing Lauren to

give us a chance that I hadn't truly entertained the idea that we might not be a match.

Could my brother have been right? Was I on the rebound?

That couldn't be true. I'd never felt like this about anyone in my life. But I needed to be sure, and so did Lauren.

I wish Damien hadn't called. If only we had more time together before we confronted all this awkwardness. I flopped onto the sofa, grabbed my phone, and turned it back on. My damn brother better not call again. I would've kept the phone off, but I worried the restaurant might need to call us about the food.

Bored, I Googled news of our diverted flight and turbulence. But after a few minutes of futile searches, I gave up. I was too aggravated.

Was I being ridiculous about Lauren? The last time I thought I was in love, I'd been wrong. Then, I realized this was the first time that I'd said "love" in my mind about Lauren. I'd been avoiding it.

But there was something here between us, wasn't there? I'd never felt so comfortable and excited and happy with anyone in my life. Well, not since I was a kid–before Mom died–when our whole family was still together.

The doorbell rang, and I rushed to the front door.

"You're the last delivery of the night," the young man at the door said. He was wearing a raincoat and didn't seem to be bothered by the weather at all.

He handed me a large box and told me to wait while he got the next one. I hadn't realized exactly how much I'd ordered. He was back in seconds.

"My boss at the restaurant was psyched that you

called," the young kid said, as he followed me into the kitchen. "I didn't know you were a famous rich guy until the owner told me. The kitchen staff and I thought the big order was for people from the convention."

It was a lot of food. I stifled a laugh as I reached into my pocket and pulled out my wallet. There were only hundreds.

"Here you go," I said to the kid. He looked like he was about seventeen years old.

"You already paid with a credit card, sir," he answered, staring at the bill.

"That's your tip."

He waved off the tip. "I couldn't—"

"Of course you could. I'm a famous rich guy, remember?" I said, putting the bill into his wet hand.

He smiled. "Thank you, sir. If you need anything, call me. I deliver all kinds of stuff. Plus, with a tropical storm coming through, you may want groceries for tomorrow," the young man volunteered.

"Tropical storm?"

"Oh yeah. It was supposed to hit south of here, but it just turned in our direction. It's hurricane season, you know. I doubt it's going to be that big of a deal. We get them all the time. But you probably want to put those storm shutters down, and get some supplies together."

"I appreciate you letting me know. Do you have a card?" I asked.

"No, sir, but I'll call you so you'll have my number," he said. He picked up his phone, looked at the telephone number written on my receipt, and dialed me.

My phone rang.

He hung up. "That's me. You can call me anytime.

There's no school tomorrow because we're on summer break," he said.

"What's your name?"

"Jared."

"Thanks, Jared. I'll call you tomorrow."

The young man beamed. "I'll be ready and waiting, sir." Then he left.

At least I'd made one person happy.

I stared at the food on the table. This needed to be more romantic dinner for two and less buffet for a hungry fraternity.

Looking over at the hutch in the dining room, I decided setting the table would make things more romantic. Since I'd ordered so much food, I grabbed some larger bowls with covers and transferred some of the food into nicer containers, grabbed the good plates, and went to the kitchen for silverware.

I finished setting the table and sighed. I never appreciated how much work it was preparing to have someone over for dinner until now. Whenever I'd wanted to impress someone, I had one of our staff set things up and clean up after. Boy, I hoped this place had a dishwasher.

I sighed again. It all looked so boring. The paper napkins hadn't helped.

I peered back into the dining room hutch and spotted two candleholders. That meant there ought to be candles somewhere in the place. I rummaged through the kitchen drawers, found matches and candles, and lit them. Then I dimmed the lights. Candlelight hid a lot.

I stood back to see how it might look when Lauren entered the dining room. It looked better. The candlelight added to the ambience. I needed all the help I could get to restore Lauren's amorous mood.

Man, the way she'd kissed me on the plane and in the hallway. I did not know how sexy she was. My mind wandered off to thoughts of Lauren naked in the shower right now. Man, what I wouldn't give to join her. Hopefully, there'd be time for that later.

I took a deep breath. Sleeping with Lauren couldn't be my top priority. We were obviously compatible in the bedroom—highly fucking compatible—but I needed to show her we were well matched as a couple.

The bowl of meatballs on the table presented a pleasant distraction from my libido. Not wanting to dirty one utensil and ruin my table setting, I reached over and snagged one.

"Looks nice," Lauren said, startling me.

A short, embarrassingly high-pitched yelp erupted from somewhere in my vocal cords as the meatball flew from my fingers and hit the table, rolling. I lunged for it to keep it from rolling onto the floor. In my panic, I smooshed the meatball under my palm, which wasn't appetizing, but I didn't have time to dwell on that.

In capturing the runaway meatball, I shook the table and caused not one, but both of the candles, to fall out of their holders and onto the table. A nearby napkin caught fire.

"Oh, my god!" Lauren yelled as she ran into the kitchen.

I rushed to smother the flames, grabbing the nearest thing available to me and pushing it over the burning napkin. The smell of burnt styrofoam and plastic permeated the air as the flame pushed through the bag and burned my index finger.

I yelped again as I pulled my hand away, pieces of hot plastic sticking to my hand.

Lauren ran over with a wet towel, pushed me out of the way, and threw it over the melting, toxic mess. The fire was extinguished, but the smoke triggered the fire alarm.

LAUREN

I changed back into my shorts and t-shirt. My robe had gotten wet and smoky from fighting the fire. I sat on the bed to give Aiden some privacy and think about our potential relationship. It'd been hard for me to focus between the emergency landing, the sex, hearing the news that Aiden was on the rebound, and the fire.

The alarm system automatically put calls into the fire station and owner. Aiden had already told the fire station it was a false alarm. Now, he was on the phone with the owner.

When I came out of the shower and saw Aiden fussing over the table, my heart warmed despite all my reservations. But was that because of his thoughtfulness, his good looks, or both? If I was going to give up my job and security for this relationship, I needed to not let the physical part of our relationship distract me.

I did not know I'd scared him, and he'd somehow set the table on fire. Let alone the part where he'd try to put out a fire with a plastic bag holding a half-empty styro-foam container of cypress salad.

I dreaded having to clean all these dishes. How much food did he think we'd eat, and why did he have to use almost every dish in the house to set it out? That was some information about Aiden right there. Did he think through what he was doing?

"The owner says he'll come by tomorrow to put down the storm shutters," Aiden called out from the hallway. I guess that was my cue to return to the living room.

When I got to the living room, I found Aiden sitting on the couch, slumped over, with his head in his hands.

"Is there a hurricane coming?" I kept my voice soft, so I didn't startle him again.

Aiden looked up at me. "Not a hurricane. Just a trop-ical storm, but the owner says we should put them down just in case."

"We should charge our devices just in case the power goes out," I said. "I've already got my computer and my phone charging now."

Aiden nodded. "I'll do that before I go to sleep."

A bright flash of lightning followed by a boom of thunder signaled that at least a part of the storm was right on top of us. I worried that the power might go out sooner. "I can plug it in for you."

He motioned for me to join him. "It can wait."

I opted to sit in the armchair next to the sofa instead of joining Aiden on the couch. If we were going to take the time to get to know each other, then we needed to spend more time talking and less time making out.

"Are you hungry?" he asked.

We'd opened the garage, which aired out some of the

toxic smoke. The smell had dampened my appetite, but now might be a good time to eat. It was almost eleven. It'd been a long day. I stood up to head to the dining room. "It seems a shame to let all that food go to waste."

Aiden followed me to the dining room. It surprised me he hadn't cleaned up anything while I was in the room. I'd cleaned up some of the immediate mess by taking the smoking bag outside in the rain and wiping everything clean.

"Maybe we should eat in the living room," he said, looking at the mess.

I nodded in agreement, but I wondered how long he intended to leave everything out on the table.

Aiden gave me a faint smile. It was like the fire had sucked away his energy.

"I appreciate how much trouble you went through to make things nice." I motioned to the remnants of the set table.

"I wanted things to be romantic."

He looked so pitiful. I felt the need to cheer him up, so I gave him a kiss on the cheek.

"I know that's a pity kiss, but I'll take it."

I gave him a peck on the lips. He smiled.

"That's the Aiden I know," I said.

I picked up a plate, grabbed a slice of pizza and some meatballs, and sliced off a piece of lasagna. "It looks delicious, and you ordered everything."

"I didn't know what you wanted or what we'd be in the mood for later," he said.

"I hope this place has a dishwasher," I said as I stared at all the bowls he'd taken from the hutch.

"I asked the owner about that while we were on the phone." His voice trailed off.

I knew what that meant. Normally, I'd volunteer to help, but I wanted to see what he'd do. This was a getting to know you in a week, after all.

I set my plate on the coffee table and sat down cross-legged on the floor to eat.

"Don't worry, I'll take care of it," he said as we walked into the living room to eat.

I smiled and nodded. In previous relationships I'd established a pattern of being the one to "take care" of things, and I'd ended up feeling more like a mother and a maid than a partner.

"So it's like that," he teased, sitting down on the ground on the other side of the coffee table.

I wasn't sure if he'd caught on that I'd deliberately refrained from helping him, but I thought he might.

"Since we're getting to know each other, I think it's really important that you know it's exactly like that."

He held his hands up in surrender. "I can clean up my own messes."

"Glad to hear it," I answered, but in the back of my mind I wondered if he really could. I wondered how somebody who'd been raised with lots of money and people to do things for him could be good at cleaning up their own messes.

Honestly, I felt like a total bitch not saying I'd help. But I forced myself not to give in on this. If Aiden and I had a future, I needed to establish the type of relationship that I wanted to be in: an equal partnership. Sure, this was small and it might not matter, but that's what I'd told myself before. If I wanted something different in my life, I needed to be different.

An uncomfortable silence engulfed us as we ate.

The lights flickered. My mind went to his phone not being fully charged. With a storm coming, the power could be out for hours.

"Maybe I should plug in your phone for you," I said.

"Lauren, I said it's fine. It can wait."

I could hear the irritation in his voice, so I stopped talking.

We continued to eat. My brain kicked up reasons it wasn't fine that he didn't charge his phone and that he couldn't possibly be sure it could wait. The storm was right on top of us.

I took a deep breath and let go of worrying.

"The food is great. I hadn't realized how hungry I was until I started eating," I said, trying to lighten the mood.

"Yeah, I really like it. The delivery boy is gonna come over tomorrow and help us with some shopping since we don't have a car here," he said.

My mood brightened. Aiden had taken care of something while I was in the shower. A point for him.

"Good thinking," I said.

Aiden smiled. "At least I got one thing right."

He reached across the coffee table and put his hand gently over mine. The pain from hitting my wrist on the plane had faded. His touch soothed and excited me.

My entire body seemed to tingle. Hell, even my nipples got hard.

I turned my hand palm up so his palm was resting in mine. He gave my hand a gentle squeeze. We continued to hold hands, and I didn't dare let go. Even if it meant that I had to eat my meatballs, pizza, and lasagna one handed.

The rain and thunder stormed outside. We enjoyed a comfortable silence as we sipped wine and ate. Aiden squeezed my hand again. I looked up at him. His smile warmed my heart.

"Call me crazy," he said. "But I kind of feel like this might be a tad romantic."

A surge of giddiness flowed from my chest through my whole body. My face warmed, and my heart sped up.

It was something about the ridiculousness of the meatball causing the fire and how he'd tried so hard, and how he was looking at me. Those dark eyes. His handsome face. His strong hand touching mine.

I couldn't help but laugh.

Here we were eating on the floor in the middle of nowhere during a tropical storm with the smell of burnt plastic and styrofoam in the air.

I still didn't know how much of what I was feeling was physical attraction versus a deeper connection, but I knew one thing for sure.

Somehow, this had turned into the most romantic night of my life.

I'd have to work hard to get to know the reality of what Aiden was like and not get swept up in the moment.

AIDEN

*A*lthough I'd utterly fucked up everything, we had salvaged the evening. What the hell was wrong with me? I'd never been such a bumbling idiot in my entire life.

On the other hand, I'd never wanted a woman this bad. Man, this sucked. Every ounce of my charm had evaded me the moment I needed it most. Time to switch things up to where I couldn't go wrong.

I abandoned my original plan of asking Lauren tons of questions and steered the evening toward the bedroom.

I needed to lean into my strengths, and frankly, those were in the bedroom. Plus, even dressed down in a t-shirt and shorts, Lauren was sexy as all hell. We were sitting cross-legged on the floor, which hid my erection but was a little painful.

"Ready for dessert?" I asked, looking straight into those beautiful green eyes of hers.

Her lips parted ever so slightly, and her breathing picked up.

"I think the cannolis survived the fire. I'll take one of those," she said.

She moved to get up, but I waved her to stay. "I'll get it."

As I stood, I grabbed the plates. My hard-on wasn't a secret, and I didn't care. I watched her eyes to see if she checked out my package.

Yup. She did. I deliberately didn't turn away. She looked up at me and blushed.

Busted, Lauren.

I gave her a sexy stare before I went to the kitchen to put the dishes in the sink and grab the cannolis.

For a second, I thought I'd grab proper plates to put them on, but then I looked at the mess I'd made with all the bowls and serving dishes. What had I been thinking?

I grabbed two paper plates from a takeout bag plus the little box of cannolis and headed back to the living room to seduce Lauren.

Lightning flickered, followed by a bark of thunder just as I neared the coffee table. Lauren yelped at the sound of the thunder.

The thunder hadn't startled me, but Lauren's yelp did.

My hand jerked hard and shook the box of cannolis. The pastries rolled in the box, slammed into the side of the box, and then the lid popped open.

Crumbs and mini chocolate chips spilled on the coffee table. I rushed forward to keep her dessert from falling. I saved the cannolis, but I stubbed my toe hard on the coffee table.

"Shit!" I groaned without thinking as I grabbed my toe. I dropped the box onto the coffee table as I half crashed, half sat down on the floor, still holding my toe.

Lauren stifled a laugh. "Are you hurt really bad?"

I let go of my toe and scooted next to Lauren. The sharp pain had faded to a light throb. "The toe isn't bad, but my pride may have taken a mortal hit between the meatball and cannoli incidents."

"Food seems to get away from you," she said.

I nudged her shoulder with mine. "It doesn't help that you keep scaring the hell out of me."

"Oh! Is that how it is?" She nudged me back a little harder.

I got up on my knees and turned to her. "Oh yeah! That's totally how it is." I grabbed a decorative pillow off the nearby sofa and tapped her with it.

She squealed and crawled over to grab another pillow off the sofa. "You're going to regret that, Aiden."

I steadied myself for her attack. She lunged to my right, but it was a fake out.

Less than a split second later, I took a hard thwack to the left side of my head.

I hit her on the shoulder with my pillow, careful to not hurt her wrist. She responded with a pillow shot to my ribs, which knocked the wind out of me.

Seizing that opening, Lauren socked me on the butt with the pillow.

"That's it! Now you've done it!" I said, aiming to hit her hard in the butt.

She rushed out of the way so my blow hit her on the back of her knees. Her knees buckled, causing her to thud to the floor.

I crawled over to her, worried she might have hurt her wrist. "Are you okay?"

I got a weak pillow hit to the face in response.

I climbed on top of her, straddling her waist. "You should surrender."

She wriggled underneath me and pelted my side with the pillow. "Never! I'll never surrender!"

Her wriggling was both adorable and fucking hot. Straddling her lap, every wiggle rubbed against my hard cock.

I wrestled the pillow out of her hand, tossed it on the couch, and grabbed both her hands, making sure to be gentle with her bad wrist.

I leaned over her adorable face as I pinned her hands down. She giggled and writhed underneath me, attempting to free herself but not trying too hard.

"Surrender!" I said again.

"Make me!" she said with the fucking sexiest smile I'd ever seen in my life.

Challenge accepted.

39

LAUREN

*W*hoa! Aiden's dark eyes smoldered. I never knew that could actually happen in real life. Before I could think of anything more, Aiden swooped in for a kiss.

Holy hell! It surprised me how me his aggressive kiss paired with the way he'd pinned my arms turned me on. I struggled to get free, but not too hard. I wasn't trying to get away, I just like the feeling of his strength, and how it made his hungry kisses even more ravenous.

I moaned and writhed on the floor.

My resolve to ignore my physical attraction to Aiden slipped away. I tried to remember why I'd thought it was important, but the heat of Aiden's kisses burned all notions of restraint out of my mind.

I stopped struggling and focused on kissing him back. Our kisses deepened. Still on top of me, Aiden's hands released mine. He put one hand in my hair and the other slipped under my shirt and grabbed my breast.

My hips bucked against the bulge in his pants. His touch became rougher and more aggressive.

New plan: Enjoy this.

I reached down to unbutton my pants. Aiden grabbed both of my wrists, put them above my head, and pinned them with one hand.

He stared into my eyes. I gasped as I stared back. Holy shit! This was so fucking hot.

My heart pounded, wondering what he was going to do next. He kissed me hard as he positioned his body in between my legs.

Without breaking eye contact, Aiden used his knees to push my legs open.

"If it gets to be too much for you, say the word 'red', and I'll stop," he said.

I eked out 'okay' as his hand slipped down my stomach, under my undies and shorts, and right to my clit.

My eyes closed. I gasped. "Aiden!"

"Look at me, Lauren. Open your eyes!"

The low, commanding sound of his voice amped up my excitement. I opened my eyes. Aiden's intense stare mesmerized me.

He slipped one finger inside me and used his thumb to toy with my clit.

My body tried to scoot away from the intensity of the stimulation, but Aiden's body held me in place.

"I got you," he growled. "Tell me if it's too much."

His finger curled inside of me and hit what I could only assume had to be my g-spot.

"Aiden!" I whispered, my breathing so heavy I could barely talk. He was going to make me cum in just a few minutes.

"Good girl," he moaned. "Look right at me when you cum. I want to see you!"

Holy fucking shit!

"Aiden!" I screamed. I was on the edge of the big O.

"Cum for me," he said, his voice commanding and his eyes locked on mine.

"Oh god! Yes!" Waves of pleasure shook my body. He eased the pressure on his fingers and expertly prolonged my orgasm for what felt like infinity.

When I couldn't cum any more, he tore off my shirt and shorts and unbuttoned his pants.

"You look so fucking hot!" he said, staring at my naked body as he got undressed.

My entire body felt so relaxed and limp from the release of every tension. It felt like I was a noodle floating in the air.

"Ready, baby?" he asked with a devilish smile as the velvety head of his hard cock rubbed against the opening of my dripping wet slit.

Even though I didn't know if I was ready, I nodded yes.

His cock rammed deep inside of me. I screamed with a combination of delight and surprise.

"You like that?" he said as he thrusted in and out inside me.

"Oh god yes!" I'd never been fucked so hard in my life, and it felt so damn good.

"Tell me!" he ordered. "Tell me how you want me to fuck you."

"Fuck me hard!" I panted.

He smiled and pulled my legs over his shoulders and fucked me even harder.

Breathy screams of pleasure joined the chorus of the

thunder and pounding rain. It took me a moment to realize that it was me.

I felt Aiden's body tense. He took my legs from his shoulders and grabbed me by the ankles, spreading them wide.

"Touch yourself!" he said.

My hand flew to my clit.

"Fuck!" he groaned as he continued to pump my pussy hard. "Baby, I'm close."

I worked my clit harder, tensing my muscles to get to my peak faster.

He released my legs and grabbed my waist. The position of his cock changed, and it rubbed my newly found sweet spot.

My hips bucked up to grind his cock into that spot. "Right there! Just like that!" I ordered, feeling my orgasm building.

Aiden groaned and continued to fuck me in a strong, constant rhythm.

"Harder! Fuck me harder," I coached.

I wrapped my legs around his waist and met his thrusts. Every time he entered me, he hit that spot until I was on the edge of exploding.

"Lauren!"

"Yes!" I came again, my pussy twitching around his cock.

"Oh god!" he called out as I continued to grip his cock inside me.

We continued to wring every ounce of ecstasy from one another until neither of us could breathe.

"Fuck!" Aiden rolled off of me and collapsed on the floor beside me. "That was incredible!"

The amazement in his voice made me smile. I'd never been so aggressive in bed before, and it surprised me how free and unself-conscious I felt with Aiden.

Aiden rolled over onto his side and propped himself up with one hand. His mouth opened as if he was going to say something, but he closed it.

I turned my head and raised my eyebrow in a question.

"You took my breath away," he said in response.

He stroked my hair and then massaged the top of my head with his hand.

I closed my eyes and took a deep breath. "That's making me want to fall asleep."

Aiden rolled onto his back, pulled my head onto his chest, and rubbed my back. At some point, I must've fallen asleep on the floor because a loud crackle of thunder followed by a boom woke me.

The entire living room was dark.

"What was that?" Aiden's voice asked in the darkness.

"I think it was the sound of a transformer blowing out," I said.

Aiden sat up. I could make out the outline of his shoulders from the bit of moonlight coming in through the sliding glass doors of the living room. "Hence the no power."

I sat up and tried to look around in the darkness, but there wasn't enough moonlight to see that far. "The power will probably be out for a while."

"Damn," he said.

40

AIDEN

I woke up early to clean the house, hoping that the electricity had come back on. Last night, when we'd woken up in the dark, I cursed myself for not listening to Lauren and charging my devices.

I'd convinced her to go to bed and told her I'd clean everything up, but I really couldn't see much of anything because I was afraid I'd burn the house down with our last two candles.

I slipped out of bed, careful not to wake Lauren, and padded barefoot and naked into the living room. My plan was to clean up fast and then slip back into bed with Lauren and see if we could do another round like last night. Damn, that'd been hot. My goal had been to show her my strengths, but the way she fucked me back blew my mind.

I snagged my boxers off the living room floor and put them on.

When was our luggage going to get here? Would the storm delay them more?

I flipped on the light switch, but no luck. I could see a little better, but I did not know what time it was. My cell phone was completely dead.

I shook my head, feeling like a dumbass.

The house was a total wreck. I wasn't sure how long food could sit out and still be good, but I imagined that time had passed. What a waste!

I rummaged through the closets, looking for garbage bags.

I finally found some and quietly tried to dump all the food into the bag.

Thank goodness the delivery driver from yesterday would be over to help us prepare for the storm. Maybe I could buy a generator or something to get things going.

I went to the table and emptied all the bowls into the trash, along with the cartons and containers.

I wanted to finish before Lauren got up, but in my haste I must've made a lot of noise.

"Good morning," Lauren said.

I turned to see her naked in the living room, bending over to get her shorts and t-shirt off the floor. Fuck. I could get used to her walking around naked for the rest of my life. I watched as she got dressed.

She looked up at me when she finished getting dressed. My gaze finally went to her face. She wasn't saying anything, but I could see her examining the mess.

Man, I'd trashed the place, and I'd promised to clean it up.

"It was too hard to see last night after the power went out, so I waited until morning," I said, feeling as if I'd gotten caught at school.

She shook her head as if she understood.

"I take it the power's still off?" she asked.

"I'm hoping to get some flashlights, and maybe a generator at a local place. I've got the delivery driver coming over today to help us."

"What time is he coming?"

I continued to chuck the leftover food into the garbage. "He said I could call him anytime."

"How much juice do you have left on your cell phone?"

"It's dead. I should've listened to you last night when you told me to charge it."

"It's no problem. Mine is charged."

That's when I remembered I didn't have the kid's number. It was on my phone. "Shit."

Lauren exhaled. "What?"

I shoveled the Italian food into the bag even faster to hurry and get everything clean. I'd really fucked up. "The kid called me so I'd have his number, but I can't get it with my phone dead."

I looked up from my panic cleaning to see her expression. She wasn't frowning, but she wasn't smiling either. I got the distinct impression she was trying to hide her disappointment.

"But he might call me to follow up," I added. After all, he'd really liked the tip I'd given him.

She stared at me, and that was when I realized he couldn't call me if my phone was dead. Duh.

"I'll call the restaurant when it opens, and see if they'll either give us his number or if they'll call him to give him my phone number," she said.

"Good thinking." I felt even more like a dumbass.

I chucked more of the spoiled food, some of which I'd never even taken out of its container, into the garbage bag. "Don't worry, I'll have this all cleaned up in no time."

"You might want to—" she started, but then stopped as I continued to work.

I stopped my work and turned to her. "What?"

She exhaled again. "I was just going to suggest you pour the soup down the garbage disposal, but I guess it'll be fine."

"Yeah, it'll be fine." I turned back to work.

"Here," she said, grabbing another trash bag. "Take that one out, and I'll start on the next one."

"Why don't you go back to bed or relax on the couch?"

"It's just that—" she started, but then stopped.

"What?"

She motioned to the garbage bag. "You might be over filling that bag a bit."

My knee-jerk reaction was to tell her it would be fine, but I looked down at the bag, and it seemed full. "I'll take this out now if it'll make you happy."

She gathered the dishes. "If you think it's fine, then don't."

I took another breath and reigned in my annoyance. "No, no, no," I said, setting the bag down to unlock the side door. "I'll take it out now to put you at ease, and when I'm done with this, I'll wash all the dishes, so you don't have to worry."

"I'm not worried, I just don't want—"

I grabbed the garbage bag to take it out.

"Wait! Wait! Wait!" Lauren said, putting the dishes down and running to me.

But the moment I lifted the bag, I felt it tear. Before I could set the bag down, the entire side ripped. The minestrone soup container plopped hard onto the floor. The top popped off and the whole container of red liquid and pasta spilled everywhere.

The tear shot down the entire side of the bag and the rest of the leftovers—spaghetti, lasagna, meatballs—splattered all over the floor and all over my bare feet.

"Fuck!" I yelled.

41

LAUREN

*M*y wrist ached a little from last night. I should've taken it easier with the pillow fight.

"Great! Just great!" Aiden muttered to himself as he threw the bag down onto the floor in anger and stared at the mess.

All I wanted to do was clean up this mess and go back to bed. I went to the hall closet to grab some towels.

"Now, she leaves," I heard Aiden mutter to himself as I left.

Seriously? It annoyed me he was acting as if this was something that wasn't easily foreseeable.

I grabbed several towels out of the hall closet and went back to the dining room area.

The marinara and soup made the place look like a crime scene. Aiden was crouched on the floor attempting to scoop up the mess with paper towels.

He'd used an entire roll.

Then, I spotted the trail of minestrone footprints,

going from the dining room to the kitchen cupboard and back to the dining room.

Sheesh.

I handed Aiden a towel and put the rest of the towels on the dining room table.

He looked so pitiful as he looked up at me. "An actual towel instead of a paper one. Yup. That's a better idea."

"Except you're probably buying these towels. Marinara stains pretty bad."

Aiden reached for the towel. "I'll break open my piggy bank."

I realized I was looking at one of the richest men in the world right now, and he was squatting over garbage in his boxers in front of me. I stifled a laugh, but Aiden caught it.

"I must look ridiculous."

"This situation isn't playing to your strengths, is it?" I went to the broom closet and pulled out a mop.

"It's humbling to admit it, but yes," he said, standing up.

I pointed to the minestrone footprints I was mopping up. "You might want to wipe your feet."

"And it just gets worse." His shoulders slumped. "You've got to believe me. I'm not usually this big of an idiot. I'm just—"

He paused.

I stopped mopping and looked up at him. "Just what?"

He exhaled. "It's like I'm nervous or something." He thought some more. "I want this to go so well that I'm fucking it up even more. I'm never like this."

My heart danced in my chest as I smiled back at Aiden. "I want it to work, too."

He motioned to the heap of spoiled takeout on the floor. "Even after I did this?"

"Yes." This time when I looked down at the mess, it didn't seem as bad.

"Let's do this," Aiden suggested. "Tell me what to do. You're in charge."

"Really?"

"I've fucked up on everything, and you knew it would happen. I should have charged my phone when you told me. I shouldn't have filled up the bag. All of it."

Had a man admitted that I was right, and he was going to listen to me? It was like a fucking Christmas miracle!

"What?" he asked, noticing my smile.

"Nothing." I finished up the mopping, putting it aside and grabbing a trash bag.

"You love to be right, don't you?" he teased.

I tried to keep my smile under wraps. "Maybe in this one instance."

Aiden laughed. "Okay, what do I do?"

"Start by wiping your feet, and we'll only fill up the garbage bags a third of the way. You can take them out one at a time."

A crackle of thunder boomed in sync with lighting. We both jumped. The rain pounded even harder.

Aiden looked at the window. I turned to look as well. The rain poured down in buckets. "How far away from the house are the garbage cans?"

"Don't worry," I said, returning to work on putting the food into a trash bag. "I dragged one can to the backdoor of the garage under the ledge last night."

Aiden said nothing in return. I looked up, wondering why he'd gone silent.

He smiled as he wiped his feet with a towel, grabbed a trash bag, and squatted next to me. "You think of everything, don't you?"

I wasn't sure what to say. In the past, people said things like that to me, but it wasn't a compliment. The tone of Aidan's voice sounded complementary, but still I hesitated.

"Does that bother you?" I asked.

"I'm thinking it's one of the things I like best about you."

A lump grew in my throat, and I had to focus on throwing away the leftovers to keep myself from tearing up. That someone might like something about me that everyone else criticized the most touched my heart.

A confusing mixture of hope, happiness, and fear flooded my brain. I might be falling for Aiden Bronson, I thought. I'd have to risk everything to see if this could be something, but I decided I didn't want to be the person who didn't go for something out of fear.

From this moment forward, I committed to seeing my relationship with Aiden through no matter the consequences.

42

AIDEN

*L*auren and I worked well together once I'd allowed myself to open up and take her suggestions. I know it must've looked like arrogance or ego when I tuned out her advice, but it was a defense mechanism born of necessity.

Most of the advice I'd gotten in my life had stemmed from people trying to get me to do something for their own benefit over mine.

But Lauren wasn't like that. Helping me and avoiding unnecessary setbacks was her only aim, and she was good at it.

With her help, it took less than an hour to clean the floor and dishes. Afterward, I used her phone to call the restaurant and got Jared's number. I jumped in the shower to clean up before he arrived.

When I returned to the living room, Lauren handed me a list.

"Are you sure you don't want to come with us?" I asked.

"I called the owner of the beach house. He's going to help with the storm shutters. Plus, one of us has to be here if they deliver our luggage."

I walked over to her and gave her a kiss on the cheek. "Good thinking."

I looked down at the list. Coming out after getting dressed to see her in the living room combined with the two of us making plans for the day felt so domestic. A surge of happiness pulsed through my body. This was us as a couple, and it worked perfectly.

The doorbell rang. I tucked the list into my pocket and headed out with Jared.

When we returned to the beach cottage after shopping, our luggage had arrived, the power had come back on, and the storm shutters were lowered. The storm shutters kept out the sunlight, so the lights were on inside.

"You're home," Lauren said, rushing from the living room to give me a quick hug and kiss.

My heart warmed. She didn't even realize that she'd used the word 'home.' I introduced her to Jared, and the three of us made quick work of putting away the groceries.

I tipped Jared, and then I was alone with Lauren. At last. I smiled.

Even with all the windows blocked by the shutters and us being trapped in a town we didn't even know existed until yesterday, I felt at home.

I put my arms around her and kissed her. It was a sweet, couple-like kiss that filled my heart with contentedness.

"When the power came on, I put your cell phone on the charger," she said, turning to me.

I pulled her cell phone out of my pocket and handed it to her. "Thanks for letting me borrow yours."

She took the phone and slipped it into her pocket. She'd changed into yoga pants similar to the ones she wore on the day we met.

"We make a great team," she said. It made my heart sing.

"We do."

"How about you change into some fresh clothes, and I'll get started on dinner," she suggested.

I gave her another peck on the lips. "Sounds great."

Yes, fresh clothes, and a relaxing home-cooked meal with Lauren!

I whistled as I headed to the bedroom to change.

It seemed as if she'd also warmed to the idea of us being together, but the reality of that and the problems that came with it weighed on me.

What would my father think?

I was certain in my heart that Lauren and I would be together, but her practicality meant that it would take her more time to feel certain.

How would we get that time? It'd be a big ask to ask her to leave her job while we merely dated. Maybe I could recommend her for an executive job at one of my cousin's companies. It seemed like a suitable solution until I remembered it would likely enrage Dad.

Lauren was an outstanding worker. It felt like he knew more about her work history than mine.

I chose a pair of shorts and a lightweight t-shirt to wear and went to change. Being out in the hot Florida sun and wearing the same clothes for so long made me feel grubby.

"I'm going to take a quick shower. Okay, babe?" I called out to Lauren. I hadn't intended to call her babe. It just came out.

"Sure thing, baby!" she yelled back.

She called me baby! I smiled as I grabbed my clothes and headed to the shower. The warm water felt good and gave me time to think.

Maybe if we kept it a secret, she'd have time to get to know me, and then losing her job wouldn't be an enormous risk.

Neither solution seemed perfect. I put off figuring everything out right now and opted to enjoy the night with Lauren instead.

I exited the bathroom in my fresh clothes and headed for the kitchen. "Nine to Five" blared from her cellphone again.

I entered the kitchen and found Lauren frowning as she looked down at the phone.

"I take it that's my brother again."

"He called while you were out, but I missed it. He didn't leave a message."

"Let it go to voicemail."

I could see the anxiety on her face.

I kissed the top of her head and took the phone from her and turned it off. "Let's just enjoy dinner together before we get into all of that."

She nodded in agreement. "Dinner will be ready in five minutes."

"So fast?"

"I found an air fryer in the cupboard."

I smiled even though I had no idea what an air fryer was. We talked as we both set the table. Just as we sat down to eat, I heard my phone ring. It had to be Damien.

"I powered it up to make sure it took the charge. It's on the nightstand," she said.

"I'll shut it off." I got to the bedroom and looked down at my screen. It wasn't my brother calling. It was Dad. "Shit!"

43

LAUREN

*A*iden returned to the dinner table holding his phone. I'd heard him swearing in the bedroom. That couldn't be good. The reality of the difficulties facing Aiden and me being together conflicted with the fantasy I'd been living in all day. We weren't an official couple yet.

"Was it Mr. Damien?" I asked, immediately realizing that I sounded ridiculous, referring to Aiden's brother as Mr. Damien. Old habits die hard.

"I have eight missed calls from Damien, but now I have a missed call from Dad."

No wonder he was swearing. Mr. Bronson himself had called. I looked into Aiden's worried eyes. "What do you think he wants?"

"I'm thinking he wants us to go to South Florida and work, but —" Aiden ran his hand through his hair and shook his head.

I didn't want to leave just yet, either.

"There is a tropical storm heading our way," I said.

"Tell him we can go down in a day or two after the storm passes."

Aiden's expression brightened. "Or maybe we can make it a week? He could've been calling to find out how we are. He could've seen what happened on the news."

It was definitely a possibility.

Aiden's phone rang again.

"I guess we're going to find out," I said.

His panicked expression reminded me of a little boy worried about getting caught for breaking a vase. "What should I say?" he asked.

"Tell him about the storm."

"I meant what should I tell him about why I wasn't answering my phone just now."

He really was flustered. This was a side of Aiden I hadn't really seen. "Tell him we were putting down the storm shutters outside."

Aiden smiled and answered the phone. "Dad! I just got back inside, the power came on an hour ago."

I eavesdropped on the conversation, wondering what Mr. Bronson was saying.

From what I could gather from Aiden's half of the conversation, Mr. Bronson had indeed heard about the weather and our diverted landing. There were a few questions that hadn't made Aiden happy, but in the end the conversation seemed to go okay.

After his goodbyes with his father, Aiden hung up the phone and turned to me with a weak smile. "Well, we've got until the storm lets up."

"What's going on with the Rexford stores in the meantime?"

"Dad didn't say, but I sense the deal is back to being Damien's domain."

I gave Aiden a questioning look. "What gave you that impression?"

"The moment the weather clears, Dad wants us to fly back to Los Angeles. He told me to forward him our recommendations, but I don't have any."

It surprised me how disappointed I was to be off the project.

Aiden scooted his chair closer to mine and put his hand on my shoulder. "I'm sure it'll work out."

"Of course it will. Tell Damien that the big money is in the store-brand ice cream," I said. "And to leverage Bronson's grocery delivery service to the pharmacy."

"We deliver in South Florida?"

"It's a pilot program, but it should expand for grocery and especially into the pharmacies. There are a lot of retirees in South Florida. The money isn't in the stores. Half don't have the square footage to compete and all of them need a remodel," I explained.

"Why did we acquire them?"

"We got a great price and being able to order groceries and medications will only feed each other. I'm sure he's probably going to do this, but just in case, tell Damien to sell off the small stores and incorporate them into the Bronson's Natural Grocers we've slated for remodeling."

"You've given this a lot of thought," Aiden said.

"It was my idea. I want it to succeed."

"Do you want me to call Dad and ask him to keep us on it?"

I looked up at him and tilted my head. "Would you

want to do that? I know you weren't happy about doing it in the first place."

"Honestly, I'm not happy working in the company business in general. I thought you wanted to go out on your own."

I nodded. He was right, but I realized it disappointed me I wouldn't get to see this deal through. It would take me forever to get to work on a deal this big. "I thought I did, too."

If things worked out between Aiden and me, my future with the company would end. It saddened me, and it wasn't just that it'd put my livelihood in danger with only a month's worth of emergency savings and an unrented rental property. But I was getting ahead of myself.

"You're not allowed to date anyone working at the company, so this discussion is in a lot of ways moot," I said.

Aiden looked down at the ground. "There may be a way around it, so you could still work on the acquisition."

"It's best for the project if it falls back into Damien's hands. It wouldn't be fair of me to ask to be a part of it knowing I won't see the acquisition all the way through."

"How about I forward your recommendations to Dad tonight? It's in the file you shared with me, right?"

I nodded. "That would be great. And tell him they can call me with questions."

Aiden grabbed his phone, and I watched him forward the email I sent him. Wow! Mr. Bronson himself would know my exact recommendations for the merger. I beamed. Then, I remembered my current predicament.

"What do we tell your dad when we get back to LA?" I asked.

"Maybe we could hide that we're dating. Give ourselves more time."

"Don't they already suspect something's going on?" I asked, but a part of me warmed to the idea. I wasn't ready to leave Bronson, Inc.

"It might be worth a try," Aiden suggested.

"And if we get caught?"

Aiden paused.

"Would you get fired or would they would ask me to leave?" I asked.

"My father would be disappointed, but—"

"Your name is on the company. It's what happened last time. It would be me leaving," I answered.

"I could recommend you for another job."

"I could get one on my own, I'm sure," I said, my lack of enthusiasm showing in my voice. Change was hard for me, but would I really give up a future with Aiden over a job?

"The job is only if you even wanted to work. You wouldn't have to," Aiden said.

I got my first job when I was fourteen years old, but I always told myself that the reason I wanted to make a lot of money was so I wouldn't have to work. But faced with the reality of not working, I realized I enjoyed it.

Plus, if I put all of my eggs in the Aiden basket, it could leave me with nothing if things didn't work out. Taking a couple of years off in the early stages of my career would definitely set back my earning potential. "I enjoy work-ing," I said.

"You sound like my dad," Aiden said.

"You've got a great job. You're at the top. How can you not like it?"

"I don't hate it," he said. "I enjoy the people, but I always wanted a family. Don't you want a family?"

"Sure, but not right away."

I could tell my answer disappointed Aiden.

"In a few years?" he asked.

"I never really thought of a timeline for it." I stopped to think about it. Quitting work to raise a family bothered me. The distraction of having a family and being a mom wasn't something that I was looking forward to. "I suppose in a few years we could afford a nanny so that might make it easier."

"Wouldn't you want to stay at home?" Aiden asked.

"I never thought of that. My mom worked when I was younger."

"Did she stop working when you were older?"

"When she got sick." I realized Aiden didn't know about my parents. Not wanting him to have to ask too much, I added, "Both my parents have passed."

"I'm sorry," Aiden said. "How long ago?"

I took me a second to add up the years. It was weird. It was almost as if time stopped when my parents died. "About seven years, give or take. It's kind of blur. Mom was sick for a while, and after she died, Dad got sick and died within the year."

"That must've been tough. My mom died when I was in the fifth grade. It's why I've always wanted to have a family and enjoy them while they're here, you know?"

I could see what he meant, and I agreed in theory. "I think you can enjoy having a family and having a career."

"Of course. I was just suggesting that you didn't have

to do both if you didn't want to." Aiden took my hand. "There's no pressure, babe. I just wanted to know how you feel."

I smiled, but a part of me felt pressured. I'd always assumed at some point I'd have kids, it was just it never occurred to me I could start a family in my twenties. The financial piece always loomed in my mind. I wanted to be as financially secure as possible before starting a family. With Aiden, that wasn't a worry.

"I can see the wheels turning in there," Aiden said. "What are you thinking about?"

"It's not that I wouldn't want to start a family right away, it's that I never thought it was an option for me so I never considered it before."

Aiden nodded and smiled. "What do you think of giving yourself time to consider it?"

The pressure I'd felt just a moment ago faded. "I think that's a good idea."

"Let me know when you want to talk about it more. You don't even have to have a decision. We can talk just so you have more information. I can tell by the way you do research that you like knowing all the possibilities."

"I do."

Aiden's eyes snapped to mine. "I like the sound of that. I like the sound of that a lot."

My heart sped up. Was he talking about marriage? Was that crazy? How would we handle life when we got back to Los Angeles?

Then Aiden pulled me close and kissed me. I decided I'd worry about everything tomorrow.

44

AIDEN

I woke up to an entirely dark room. I couldn't tell if it was day or night.

My brain registered Lauren's presence beside me. The feeling of her arm touching mine and the smell of her made me happy. I couldn't help but think that I wanted this to be the way I woke up for the rest of my life.

Sure, things hadn't always gone to plan on this trip, but I liked the way we worked through things. Wasn't that what a partner ought to be?

Lauren's level headed nature helped me think better.

I listened hard to hear if it was still storming outside, but I didn't hear any rain or thunder. My heart sank. It was odd to wish for a storm when staying on the beach, but I knew good weather meant we'd have to fly back home.

I slipped out of bed to allow Lauren to sleep a little longer. Maybe I'd make her breakfast in bed or something. I needed to know what time it was.

As I shuffled in the dark for the doorway, I stubbed my toe on what I assumed was the edge of the bed.

I stifled a yell and let out a sharp exhale in its place.

I paused in silence to see if I'd woken up Lauren, but I could hear the gentle sound of her breathing. Every once in a while, she let out a little snore. I couldn't help but think how cute it was.

Everything about Lauren made me happy. Even the way she got angry with me when I was being illogical about the mess in the kitchen.

It felt like she brought out the best in me, and I appreciated being able to trust her advice. Wasn't that what a relationship ought to be?

I finally found the door, but the hallway was even darker than the bedroom.

I wondered what time it was, and I realized that I should have just picked up the flashlight I put on the nightstand the night before.

That was why I needed Lauren. She would've thought of that.

My mind flashed back to Mom and Dad. Dad always sought Mom's advice. He said that if it wasn't for Mom, he would've never had grown Bronson, Inc. into one of the largest grocery chains in the world.

Lauren was like Mom in that way. She had a head for business. Dad always said that if Mom had grown up in a different time, or had been born a man, she would've been the billionaire.

The sound of my cell phone ringing interrupted my thoughts. Luckily, Lauren had plugged it in on the kitchen counter, and the light from it made it easier for me to maneuver over to it. I hoped the sound wouldn't wake up Lauren.

When I got to the phone, I noticed it was Damien. I debated not picking it up, but I was in enough trouble as it was.

"Hey," I said.

"Dad wants you to get back to Los Angeles today. He'll have a car to pick you up in two hours," my brother said without even saying hello.

"What time is it?" I asked.

"For crying out loud, it's already 8:30 in the morning where you are. I've been up for two hours."

"We've been battling a storm over here, and only had power for a few hours last night. We got the storm shutters down, and I can barely see a damn thing," I said.

"Do you have power now?"

"I'm not sure," I said, shuffling over to the nearest light-switch and turning it on.

The lights came on, and I realized I hadn't had to stumble in the dark all the time. "Nope. Just checked. We're entirely in the dark here."

"All the more reason you should get back to LA," Damien said.

"We'll leave tomorrow."

"You didn't hear me. Dad is sending a car for you in two hours. He's already directed the flight crew to bring you home. You know you're in a lot of trouble, right?"

"Why is that?"

"They're saying you're using the company as a dating site. And now everyone's debating about power dynamics in companies and whether women really have a choice. It's the shit show that we've been trying to avoid, Aiden."

"I don't know what you saw—"

"There are photos and even eyewitnesses! Don't even try to deny it. You should've avoided even the appearance of impropriety. Staying together in a beach cottage with a subordinate employee? Are you fucking crazy?"

"What story? What does it say?"

"Read it on *TMZ* on your plane ride back."

"There's the matter of the bad weather. It's unsafe to fly," I said, ignoring my brother's comment.

"The storm shifted south, and you're not in its path. Oh, and Dad didn't get the recommendations for the deal. You should send them pronto. It'll distract him."

"I sent him Lauren's recommendations last night!"

"That was a good move, but he didn't get them, so send it again."

"Fine. Is that all?"

"Just know that you're really fucking it up for the rest of us."

I didn't want to get into whatever the fuck he was talking about. All I knew was the cat was out of the bag, and everything was turning to shit fast. "I've got to go," I said and hung up without saying goodbye.

45

LAUREN

*T*he storm shutters had shielded us from the photographers, but running to the limousine was a whole different story. I'd seen the paparazzi pester celebrities in Los Angeles, but I never thought they would follow me—especially in such a small, out-of-the-way place.

Would it be worse in LA? All I wanted to do was to be back in my apartment, in bed, away from everyone and everything.

Aiden went to put his arm around me, but I pushed it away.

"They might see," I whispered at him, mad at him for not warning me about all of this sooner. "That's how all this got started."

Our driver had the door open for us. Aiden tried to shield me from the photographers, but we were surrounded. I slid into the limo. Aiden scooted next to me and reached for my hand.

"I don't think they can see through the tinted glass," he said.

I pointed to the cameras leaning over the front windshield, snapping away. Aiden put up the privacy window between the driver's seat and the passenger area.

"Sorry, babe. For all this," he said again, putting his head in his hands.

The backseat of the limousine was roomy, so I got up and sat on the opposite side of the car so I could think. I'd woken up to Aiden, upset from his call, to this. The emotional whiplash of it all had rattled my brain.

"Really? They can't see," he said, motioning to the tinted windows. His expression and voice were a combination of rejection and annoyance.

"I need some space." My tone came out more irritated than I'd intended. I exhaled and tried to calm myself.

I'd never been great with sudden changes. Last-minute surprises were never fun for me. Sure, I could come up with a plan on the fly, but it always stressed me out. I preferred to plan my days and to execute that plan, but ever since I'd met Aiden, it had turned my life upside down. And it felt like it never stopped.

My job had changed. This business trip had come on a few hours' notice and then we didn't even go where we wanted to go. Heck, even if I'd just woken up to suddenly having to fly back to Los Angeles, it would've rattled me. But all this!

I closed my eyes and took a deep breath to calm myself. What I needed was information so I could figure out what to do next. Step one, assess the damage. I took out my phone and figured I'd do some googling on the ride to the airport. "What site did Mr. Damien say we were on?"

"*TMZ.*"

"Have you read it?"

Aiden nodded yes, but he was quiet. Not a good sign.

There was a photo of us getting into the car from the airport with a headline that read: Bronson Billionaire Seduces Subordinate.

I speed read the article and the comments, and proceeded to go down the internet rabbit hole the entire ride to the airport. The gist of most of the stories was after a death-defying flight, the company had booked us a private beach cottage where he took advantage of the situation.

Jared, the teenager who helped us, had been quoted. Jared said that he didn't realize that Aiden was someone important until his boss at the restaurant told him. Then he said that the billionaire and his wife were down-to-earth and friendly people.

The reporter told Jared that Aiden wasn't married, and he'd replied, "I guess it was his girlfriend, then. They looked very happy."

"Have you read the entire article?" Aiden asked.

I'd been so absorbed in what I was reading that I'd almost forgotten where I was.

"I read the *TMZ* one and a few others," I said.

Aiden's expression didn't reveal his thoughts. The corners of his lips were down turned, but not in an outright frown, and his brow was furrowed with concern. Did he know he was being made out to be the villain in most of the stories?

I looked out the window. There were news vans and

cars surrounding us. I worried we might crash with how close they were. I cringed.

"It's best not to look. Our driver is good. He's not trying to outrun them. He's just keeping a steady speed," he said.

"Has this happened to you a lot?"

"When Mom was in the hospital and after my broken engagement. I dated a few actresses in my early twenties. It was worse with the actresses."

I nodded, but my brain couldn't stop trying to guess who the actresses were. They must've been beautiful to be chased down by paparazzi.

"Are the other stories as bad as the *TMZ* one?" he asked.

"Pretty much. They've got that one photo of us in the backseat of the car, but it wasn't that incriminating—"

"It was the kid calling us married that did us in, though," he said, finishing my thoughts.

"He didn't mean it."

Aiden shook his head no. "I should've told him not to give interviews. He probably thought he was helping us."

I nodded in agreement and then looked out the window. We were close to the airport. "Will they be able to follow us onto the tarmac?"

"It's a private airport," Aiden said.

I exhaled with relief. It was bad enough having my routine upended multiple times this week, but being crowded and having cameras shoved into my face almost pushed me into a dead panic.

It took all of my strength not to want to break down into tears or demand to be let out of the car. All I wanted to do was run away.

"Are you okay?" Aiden asked.

"Everything will be fine," I said. I'd tried to keep my voice steady, but it came out a little icy.

"I didn't ask if everything was going to be fine. I asked if you were okay," Aiden said, his tone bordering on harsh.

I glared at him. "What happens when we get back to Los Angeles?"

"Dad wants to see us right away."

"Any chance we can see him first thing in the morning?"

"Father isn't a man that you can just blow off. You know that."

I didn't like Aiden's tone. He didn't sound like himself. He sounded like a spoiled snob. "Fine, at least tell me what 'Father' said on the phone this morning."

"Nothing. Like I told you earlier, Damien called."

"What exactly did Damien say?"

"He said the cat was out of the bag regarding the two of us, and that Dad wanted to see us right away. He told me to be ready because a car was coming to pick us up. That's it. It's what I already told you."

I folded my arms and shook my head. "Alright. Let's get to the part you didn't tell me about. I'm assuming that one of us is going to have to lose their jobs today, and since my last name doesn't match the name of the company, it's going to be me. Do I have that right?"

Aiden's expression softened. He leaned forward in his seat, almost to the point of kneeling on the floor in front of me. "I'll take care of you."

"I resent being put in the position where I need to be taken care of. I did a great job taking care of myself for a long time until—" I stopped myself from finishing that sentence.

"Until what?"

He sat back in his seat and glared at me. I stared back at him, hard.

"Why won't you say it?"

I folded my arms on my chest. "I don't want to say anything unkind. You're not making it easy. We both know what's happened here."

"And it's all my fault?"

I exhaled and shook my head. "This isn't the time to deal with this."

"I'm tired of waiting around for you to decide whether you want to do this."

Seriously? Did he just say that?

"Is this some kind of ultimatum? Because you don't want to do that."

His eyes locked on mine. If he wanted to play hardball, I'd play hardball, and he'd lose.

We stared at each other in silence. The limousine slowed, which meant that we'd already gotten inside the airport and arrived at the plane. But I would not break eye contact.

The standoff continued, but when the door opened, Aiden's eyes went to the driver. I won.

He motioned for me to get out of the car first. "You're stubborn."

"And you're an inconsiderate, spoiled brat." I exited the car.

A thought dawned on me. Neither of us needed to lose our jobs. We could just break up. My angry brain loved the idea, but my soft heart hated it.

46

AIDEN

*H*ow dare she! Calling me a spoiled brat. I'd been tying myself up in knots just trying to get her comfortable this entire trip. Who the hell did she think she was?

I climbed out of the limo. Lauren was halfway to the plane already. I followed her, but she didn't back.

When I caught up to her at the top of the boarding stairs, I heard her exchanging pleasantries with the flight crew as if we weren't even fighting.

The flight attendant turned to me and smiled. "Welcome aboard, Mr. Bronson."

"You're new," I said and glanced at her name tag. "Call me Aiden, Emily."

Emily smiled back at me, and for a split second, I thought she was flirting with me. Would that make Lauren jealous? The idea brought a smile to my lips. Of course, I was above it, but I couldn't help but hope that Lauren might pick up on Emily's flirtation.

I entered the cabin and noticed that Lauren had

picked one recliner near the window. It tempted me to sit in the recliner next to hers, but I thought better of it. I chose the seat across from her. If she wanted to talk, she could turn her chair to face mine. This was going to be a long flight.

Lauren reached into her bag and pulled out a slim book.

"Can I get either of you anything?" Emily asked.

"I'll have a latte," Lauren said.

She reached into her bag for a pen, opened the book, and began writing and sketching in her journal as if I wasn't there.

I was sure she was writing hateful things about me now.

"I'll just have a cup of black coffee and some water."

"I'll have a bottled water as well," Lauren said.

The tension between Lauren and me deflated Emily's flirty demeanor. And she'd retreated to the crew cabin.

Lauren and I were alone.

We didn't say a word to each other for the first forty-five minutes of the flight. I pretended to read the newspaper, but the longer we sat in silence, the more a sense of impending doom took over.

"Talk to me, Lauren," I said. "I'm dying here."

She looked over at me and then swiveled her seat in my direction. I did the same, and we were facing each other. I fought the urge to rush over to her.

She needed her space. A sinking feeling overwhelmed me.

"I think I found a solution," she said.

There was something about the quietness of her voice and the sadness in her eyes that filled me with dread. I sensed what she was going to say. "Lauren, that's not a solution. We can work this out."

"Or our trip did what it was supposed to do," she said.

I wasn't sure I understood what she meant, so I waited for her to clarify.

"You said that we could use the time at the beach house to figure out whether we worked together. I think we found that out," she said.

"So we hit a bump in the road, and you just give up on us?"

"Losing my job and my independence isn't some bump in the road, Aiden. And if you could look at things from my point of view instead of your privileged life, you wouldn't classify this as some bump."

"I didn't mean it like that! We need to give things more time."

"We don't have time. Your family is making sure of that. And that's another thing that I've learned in our time together. All of this," Lauren said, motioning around to the jet. "It comes at a price. And it's a price that I don't want to pay."

"So you're holding my background against me? Does that seem fair?"

"Is it fair that I lose my job even though I'm not the one who promised not to date anyone at work?"

I didn't have an answer for her.

Lauren exhaled. "Ever since you came into my life, it's been a disaster. From minute one. You stole my ride share and almost made me late for my job. Your need to tease me cost me months of missing work. I'm financially worse off than before we ever met.

"And now I'm on the eve of losing my job. But none of

that even occurs to you, does it? You act like just because you have money that it doesn't matter that I don't. But it matters. Aiden, it really matters."

"Lauren, you've got to know that money doesn't matter to me. I don't care that you don't have any money. I have enough for both of us, I swear."

"And that's the problem."

"How can that be a problem?"

"That you don't recognize that your family and your money mean you have a security and safety net that people like me don't have. From the moment we met until this exact second, you've never thoroughly understood that.

"You act like your promise that I'm going to be okay is enough of a safety net, but it's not. Because the moment that you choose to renege on your promise is the moment that my life is no longer secure."

She leaned forward in her chair. "Aiden, I'm not asking you to put your security in my hands after only knowing you for a short period, but you're asking that of me. Your privileged life keeps you from even understanding what a big ask that is. Because you've never known what it feels like to be absolutely alone in the world, with almost no one else to count on but yourself and limited assets."

Her speech stunned me. It was a lot to take in, but my heart sank. Everything that she was saying was true. I hadn't really understood what she meant until now. How could I not have seen it? She didn't have any parents or brothers or sisters. She didn't have billions to fall back on. And here I was, asking her to trust me. I never really acknowledged what a big chance she was taking.

"I'm sorry, Lauren," was all I could think of to say.

"I know you didn't mean it. But I've got to be smart about this," she said.

My mind went back to the first day that we met. The shakiness in her voice and the tears in her eyes when she was worried that she'd make the wrong call on that medical bill. How could I have been so stupid?

"It's for the best, Aiden. I wouldn't want to get in between you and your family. Family is really important."

"But—"

"Aiden, this is hard for me, too. Please, don't make it harder."

The pleading look in her eyes broke my heart. I'd been so selfish already. How could I not honor her one simple request?

47

LAUREN

*W*hen we arrived at the Van Nuys airport, a car was waiting for us. We rode back to the Bronson, Inc. office in silence. It both relieved and disappointed me that Aiden hadn't put up more of a fight over the breakup.

The muscles in my shoulders ached from tension, and my mind whirred from worry to worry. I needed to go back to my old routine. All this change rattled me.

But I forced myself to think. One option might be for me to explain to Mr. Bronson that Aiden and I had contemplated being together, but that we both decided it was in our best interest to not pursue a relationship. Then, I'd request to be put back on Mr. Damien's desk. Then, maybe my life could go back to normal.

I worried Mr. Bronson wouldn't let me go back to my old job, but then it occurred to me. I had one advantage. I had broken no rules, and I had a stellar record on the job.

Mr. Bronson was a smart man. He'd know that I'd be able to get a lawyer and fight against a demotion or termination of employment. Not that I worried it would come to that.

"I'm going to request that I go back to my original position as your brother's assistant," I said.

"Why?"

"I just need to go back to my old routine. Do something that I'm good at. All this has been very—" I stopped to think, "—disconcerting. I need to heal, and it's not just my wrist."

Aiden nodded. "I forgot about your injuries. I guess that's another thing that I hadn't considered. Lauren, please understand—"

I held my hand up to cut him off. "I know you didn't do any of it on purpose, and it's not because you were deliberately trying to hurt me. It's just a habit."

"Ouch," Aiden said.

"I'm not trying to hurt you. I'm sure there are a million things that you have to deal with in your life, like all the paparazzi that I'd never realized came into play," I said, trying to ease the blow.

"It's hard to believe that it's over," he said, half aloud and half to himself.

I knew what he meant. I struggled to believe as well.

We rode the rest of the way back to the office with no more discussion.

Our car pulled up to the office, and the driver opened my door. I went to grab my laptop bag, but Aiden stopped me. "Let me carry this for you. You have your purse to deal with."

I wanted to argue that I could handle it, but his eyes looked so sad.

"Let me do something for you one last time. I've been so selfish," he said.

"Aiden, you haven't—"

He waved me off and grabbed the bag.

I got out of the car, and Aiden followed.

Aiden turned to the driver. "Have my bags sent to my house, and then return here to take Miss McCall home. Her luggage is in the back. Make sure she carries nothing. She has a wrist injury."

"Yes, sir," the driver said.

It was weird hearing him call me Miss McCall, but I appreciated him thinking about my luggage and how I was going to get home.

We walked to the lobby, and Ronnie, the security guard, greeted us. "Welcome back, Mr. Aiden and Miss Lauren. Glad to see the two of you safe and sound."

"Glad to be back," Aiden said, his voice professional.

"Mr. Bronson wanted me to tell you both that he's waiting for you in his office," he said. Ronnie picked up the phone, and I knew it was to let Mr. Bronson know that we'd arrived.

"Thank you, Ronnie," Aiden said, and he motioned for me to go ahead.

Aiden followed me to the private elevator. We both boarded the carriage. We didn't speak or look at each other. I didn't know what to say.

Aiden hit the emergency button. The carriage stopped between floors. The safety alarm let out a loud ring. I turned to him with a questioning look.

"What if I quit?" he asked.

It took me a moment to register what he'd meant. "You can't quit Bronson!"

"You could keep your job. We could still see each other. We'd have more time."

The sudden change in plans locked up my brain.

The alarm bell on the elevator sounded again. The emergency phone rang.

"We have to keep going," I said, reaching for the bell.

Aiden stopped my hand. "Yes, we," he said, motioning back and forth, indicating the two of us as a couple. "We have to keep going."

48

AIDEN

I picked up the emergency phone. It was building maintenance. "Everything's fine," I said.

I released the emergency stop button. The elevator resumed.

"Your father won't let you quit," Lauren said.

I hung up the phone and turned to her. "He doesn't have to let me. The thing about quitting is that I don't work for him anymore. He can't make me do anything."

"He could disown you."

"Yes, from his fortune, but I'd still have the money Mom left me."

Lauren shot me a questioning look.

"My mom was the one who had the money to help my father buy his first grocery chain. But he insisted it was only a loan. She insisted on being an investor. They didn't get married until after he made his first thirty million. By then, she'd done well with her investments. They had a prenup. When she died, she split the money between all of her children, and it went into a trust. When I became of age, I got that money."

"But it's not the same money that you get with your earnings here and from your father later," she said. I appreciated she referred to my father's future passing as later, instead of blatantly saying your inheritance or when your father died as so many other people did.

"I don't need a lot to live on, and frankly, you need even less. So, I'll be fine, you'll keep your job, and we'll have time to get to know each other."

"I can't let you lose billions of dollars just to be with me. That's too much pressure," she said.

"Well, I'm quitting. You can decide to date me or not, but when I asked you to let me take care of you, know that it wasn't because I wouldn't make the same sacrifice for you. Because I am. And I'll never regret it," I said, and exited the elevator.

"Aiden! Stop!" Lauren said, rushing to catch up with me, but I knew what I needed to do.

Barbara, my father's secretary, looked up and noticed me approaching Dad's office. I saw her reach for the buzzer to let my father know we were here. I didn't wait for her to tell us he was ready to see us. I needed to have this talk with my dad.

It was a mistake that I came to work at the West Coast headquarters. Even if things didn't work out with Lauren, this is what I needed to do. I needed to be my own man.

"I need to talk to my father alone," I said to Barbara as I sped past her.

"You'll have to wait until I buzz you in," Barbara said.

"It's an urgent family matter," I said.

Barbara let me pass, but got up from her desk to intercept Lauren as I sped into Dad's office.

"I'm sorry, Miss McCall, but you'll have to wait until Mr. Bronson—"

Lauren protested not being able to enter, but I shut the door to Dad's office behind me and couldn't make out the rest.

Dad looked up from behind his desk. His expression was inscrutable.

"Where is Lauren?" Dad asked.

I walked to his desk but did not take a seat. "This doesn't concern her."

Dad leaned back in his chair. "It's good that we talk in private, but I have to correct you. This has everything to do with Lauren."

"I quit."

Dad exhaled. "Do you think you're in love with her?"

"I know I am."

Dad motioned for me to sit down. Since he wasn't ranting and raving, I played nice and took a seat.

"Son, you've always been a romantic, and I like Lauren a great deal. But you can't know that it's love this soon."

"I can, and I do. But it wouldn't matter if I was wrong."

Dad tilted his head in a question. But he didn't speak. He waited for me to fill the void and answer, and I decided this was the time to tell him how I felt.

"I'm not a business executive, Dad. Everyone knows it, and as much as I hate to disappoint you, I think it's easier to just disappoint you all at once and get it over with than to live my entire life feeling like a disappointment."

"What do you plan to do?" Dad asked.

"Raise a family with Lauren."

Dad looked away and took a deep breath. "For a living! I mean, what do you plan to do for a living?"

"I love kids, maybe I can get a job at an elementary school or at a daycare."

"So you're going to leave this company, but you have no plan at all?"

I felt myself becoming defensive, but I fought it. I needed to be reasonable with Dad, if there was any hope for me and Lauren. "It's not like I don't have money to take the time to figure out what I want to do. I don't think it matters as much to me as it does to everyone else.

"All I know is that I want to be with Lauren. I can try a bunch of different jobs until I find something that makes me feel good about myself instead of feeling like I'm failing all the time. Spending this time with Lauren showed me how much I don't know what I'm doing.

"She's so good at this, and it showed me how much I'm not. When I listen to her, it's like I'm hearing you talk to Mom at the kitchen table when we were kids. And she noticed that I'm not good at this stuff, but she isn't—"

Dad interrupted my thought with a loud sigh. "As judgmental about it as I am."

I looked at my father. His response stunned me. Dad never admitted fault in a negotiation, and as my father always said, 'everything is a negotiation.'

Lauren burst into the office, with Barbara right behind her.

"Mr. Bronson, she just pushed past me," Barbara said.

"Don't accept his resignation, accept mine," Lauren said.

Dad turned to Lauren. "And why should I do that?"

"Because family is the most important thing, and there's always another job," Lauren said.

"I'd like to think that working for Bronson, Inc. is a very special job," Dad said.

Lauren's face fell. "I didn't mean it like that. I just meant that no job should come between family. And if it's a choice between family and a job, find a new job."

"You know you've done nothing wrong. Why should you suffer?"

"But he's your son," Lauren protested.

Dad nodded. He turned to Barbara. "I'll take care of this, everything's fine."

He turned back to Lauren and motioned for her to sit in the seat beside me.

"I'm assuming the reason you both want to quit is because of your relationship?" Dad asked.

Lauren and I spoke at the same time. I said 'no' and Lauren said 'yes.'

Lauren turned to me with her eyebrows raised.

"The solution is simple." Dad turned to Lauren. "I accept your resignation." Then Dad turned to me and said, "I don't accept yours."

"Dad!" I protested, but Dad held up his hand. I stopped talking.

"Son, you're fired. I fired you the moment the new tabloids hit, and you confirmed to your brother that you had violated company policy. You have an exit interview and your last paycheck with HR as soon as we're finished here."

What the fuck!

49

MR. BRONSON

I'd assumed my decision would upset Aiden, but Lauren's expression surprised me. When I'd told her I'd accepted her resignation, her lips went up. When I told Aiden I fired him, the corners of Lauren's mouth turned down. Then her expression went neutral, followed by a smile.

"No, Dad! Lauren shouldn't lose her job," Aiden protested.

"Aiden, don't you see?" Lauren said. "This is what's best for us."

Aiden argued with Lauren as she explained to him my reasoning.

It's a rare occasion that I'm surprised by someone's reaction in a negotiation. I couldn't help but smile. Lauren was an incredible young woman. That she was reacting like this, not knowing my next offer boded well.

Between this and some other recent experiences, I thought it was time for me to revise my earlier conclusions about billionaires and love. But that would have to wait.

"You both have to discuss this between yourselves after our meeting," I said, interrupting the two of them. They quieted and turned to me.

"Now, hear me out, originally, son. I felt bad about firing you. To be honest, I wasn't sure that you could get a job somewhere else in business. But knowing that you truly don't want to work here, and knowing that Lauren would sacrifice her position here for you, makes this next part easier.

"Now, the two of you will have the freedom to explore the relationship, and I would advise that Lauren, perhaps when she's healed or even right away, should apply for another job here at Bronson. One in research and development."

I kept my face neutral, but I could tell from their surprised looks that they didn't know what I was talking about.

"It seems that when my son here forwarded the information about the deal, with Lauren's astute tips regarding the drugstore acquisition, he also forwarded me some schematics for a fantastic little device."

"That was private," Lauren said to Aiden.

"I must've shared the wrong cloud link," Aiden said. "What do you want with the bag thing, Dad?"

"Bag Buddy," Lauren corrected.

"I want to manufacture and sell it, of course." I turned to Lauren. "You're having trouble with getting the initial prototype put together, and I feel like Bronson, Inc. can help you with that. So I suggest you work in research and development."

Lauren sat back in her chair and remained silent.

I waited to see what she said.

"Mr. Bronson, that is a very generous offer, and one I will definitely consider."

I stifled a smile. Lauren McCall was going to negotiate with me for this invention, and she knew she not only had the leverage of knowing how impressed I was about the product, but she also knew that she was family.

"Well then, I suggest we table this discussion," I said, standing up. "I imagine you two have someplace you'd like to be other than here with an old man at jobs you both no longer work at."

The two of them smiled.

"Thanks, Dad," Aiden said, standing up. He reached out to shake my hand, but I came around my desk and hugged him.

After our embrace, I looked at my son. He looked so much like his mother, and he had her heart. "I'm proud of you, son."

His eyes shined with unshed tears. My own eyes threatened to tear up in response. Why had I waited so long to tell him that? Why had I tried so hard to make him in my image?

"Thank you, Mr. Bronson," Lauren said.

"Maybe there'll be a day when you call me Dad, too," I said to Lauren.

She smiled. My son did a double take. Had I been that much of a Scrooge about love?

Someone had been trying to tell me that for years, but I hadn't listened.

"Call me when you're ready to talk about coming back to Bronson," I said to Lauren as we all walked to the door.

"I'll call you when I have a counteroffer," she said.

I laughed aloud, even though it meant I'd lose my bargaining position.

The two of them left my office, and they were in each other's arms before I shut the door.

I sat down at my desk, smiling like I hadn't smiled since I lost Mary. She would've been so happy for Aiden and Lauren.

It was definitely time for me to revise my opinion about love.

50

LAUREN

"Good morning, Sydney. Have those contracts arrived?" I asked as I stopped by my assistant's desk. So far, Sydney and I were the entire staff of my business, but we soon I'd expand.

"Not yet, but I expect them any minute now," she said, smiling.

"You're in a good mood."

She reached for her coffee mug. "Guess I'm excited about the premiere party tonight."

"It's only a commercial," I said, embarrassed about all the fuss Aiden had made about the party.

"It's way more than that," Sydney said with a smile so big it bordered on ridiculous. She took a huge swig of coffee, drinking nearly half of it.

"How many of those have you had this morning?" I joked.

"This is my second."

I headed for my office. "Don't make me cut you off."

"Do you want me to make you one?"

"Already have one in my hand," I said, holding up my cup.

"I'll let you know the moment the contracts for the shopping channel arrive."

"Thanks," I said and closed the door behind me so I could prepare my day.

Yes, I was excited about the shopping channel live appearances and commercials, but it shocked me how excited Sydney was about it. She'd been in a suspiciously smiley mood lately, and I couldn't help but wonder if maybe she had a new boyfriend or something.

I sat down at my desk with my cup of coffee, put in my ear buds, and grabbed my sketchbook. I fired up my computer and opened YouTube for some inspiration. What did I want to watch today?

In honor of my own 60-second spot, I picked out the Popeil Pocket Fisherman and hit play. My heart bubbled with joy as I sketched away.

After the Popeil spot ended, I pondered my life. I'd actually shot my very own infomercial! Aiden had been on the set, and he'd convinced me to be in it despite my initial reservations. I was one of the "before" people straining to carry the shopping bags as they dug into my fingers.

It'd turned out to be fun. Besides, it wasn't like people expected Meryl Streep quality acting in an infomercial.

Since Aiden came into my life, I had more fun. I'd never be Miss Spontaneity, but I had been more open to change and fun.

I thought about tonight's party. Maybe he was right. I needed to celebrate my "wins" more. Plus, for reasons I didn't understand, he'd set his heart on having this party. He even insisted on flying out Carolyn and Mackenzie.

It seemed silly to have a party for the "premiere" of my commercial, but Aiden promised it would only be family and a few other business associates.

Family. I liked the sound of that. It'd been so many years since I'd been in a family, and the Bronsons—especially Mr. Bronson—had felt just like that.

I smiled, thinking about Mr. Bronson. He'd been a mentor to me and even leveraged his contacts to have better prototypes made. In exchange, Bronson grocery stores and drugstores had an exclusive with the Bag Buddy for the first six months.

It was the perfect add-on item, and it thrilled me to see my product by the register when I went to the grocery store. It turned out Mr. Bronson was a big Ron Popeil fan himself. He even gave me a Showtime Rotisserie for my birthday a few months ago.

A knock on my door interrupted my thoughts.

"You can come in, Sydney."

"It's not Sydney, it's me," Aiden said as he entered, carrying a large envelope.

I got up and hugged him. "What are you doing here?"

He smiled and handed me the package. "I wanted to be here when you finalized the national ad buys."

"That's sweet of you," I said, puzzled by his excitement.

"Let's sit down," he said, guiding me to my desk. "I can't believe I'm so excited over paperwork. I'd always hated it when I worked for Bronson," he said.

"Maybe you should work for me," I joked.

"No, no, no. I like my job as cheerleader-in-chief."

He was smiling from ear to ear, but his smile seemed

strained. "You almost look nervous," I said. "These contracts are just a formality. Unless there's something—"

He tapped on the paper and kneeled next to my chair. "Stop stalling. Get to speed reading these puppies so we can celebrate."

I shook my head. It wasn't that big of a deal. I did not know why he was so eager. He'd even taken the papers out of the courier envelope for me.

I grabbed my pen and read over the contract, but when I got to the signature page, there were still some pages behind it.

Had they tried to add an addendum to our deal? How dare they!

I turned the page and at the top it read, "Prenuptial Agreement of Aiden Bronson and Lauren McCall."

Wait? What?

I turned to Aiden. And he was on one knee with a ring in his hand—a ruby engagement ring.

"I know there'll be negotiations. My future wife has assets to protect, but I'm open to anything. Pre-nup, no pre-nup."

"I told you I'd never get married without a pre-nup," I said, remembering that conversation from the first day we'd met.

"Well, my wife will handle all the negotiations. That's if you say yes. So what do you say? Will you marry me, Lauren?"

His face looked so earnest and hopeful.

Tears poured down my cheeks. "Yes! Of course, yes!"

He slid the ring on my finger.

My phone intercom beeped. "Did I hear a yes in there?" Sydney asked.

So that was why she was so damn smiley!

"You did," Aiden said, getting up off his knees.

"I guess I'm going to an engagement party tonight!" Sydney beamed.

Now it all made sense! He knew I hated surprises, so he thought of a way to prepare me for having a party while keeping it a surprise.

"Hold all my calls," I said to Sydney as I stood up. I hung up the phone and turned to Aiden.

Time to celebrate.

51

EPILOGUE - DAMIEN BRONSON

I arrived at Geoffrey's late, hoping that I'd be able to make it an early evening. There was an epic ton of work for me in the morning, and I wanted to get a jumpstart on it tonight.

Aiden had booked the entire restaurant for the "premiere." They'd decorated it with flowers and mini cloth bags on each table clasped together with a Bag Buddy. They had set a stage up with a projector screen to air the commercials at the edge of the main dining room. Flat TV screens had been placed around the entire property.

Why book a restaurant with such a gorgeous view if you wanted everyone looking at your stupid gadget ad? But then who was I to ask? I thought the entire thing seemed ridiculous, even for Aiden. Imagine creating such a fuss over a damn commercial!

I spotted Dad talking with a dark-haired Asian woman at the bar. She looked so familiar.

The older woman threw her arms out for a hug. "Damien! It's been so long!"

Within seconds, I was hugging this woman, and she seemed so familiar. I knew it sounded crazy, but there was something about her voice and her perfume that tickled my memory.

"I'm sorry for hugging you so fast," she said, breaking our embrace. "You couldn't possibly recognize me. I haven't seen you since you were..." She looked over to Dad for recollection.

"I guess he must've been about four."

Four! Who was this woman?

"It's Anita. You probably don't recognize me—"

"Aunt Anita?" I interrupted. My mind conjured up a memory of eating macaroni and cheese while sitting at a coffee table.

"Yes!" she squealed. "I've missed you! I wouldn't have recognized you if I hadn't seen your pictures. Look at you. So grown up and handsome!"

"Mom!" a feminine voice called from across the room. She was on her cell phone and waving to Anita to come out to the patio, where it was less crowded.

"That's the call from the Philippines I've been waiting for," Anita said to Dad and then excused herself.

I turned to Dad. "Wow! I didn't even remember her until just now. What's she doing here?"

"She's in town on business." He was talking to me, but his attention was on Aunt Anita and her daughter. "Why are you late? You're never late."

"The Duponts are bidding on our acquisition, and I'm looking at how to edge them out," I said.

Dad gritted his teeth. "I wouldn't be surprised if they only wanted those stores because we wanted them."

Dad hated Henry Dupont. They'd gone to school

together and had been rivals for over forty years. I figured once he knew that was what I was working on, he'd tell me to leave right away. "Well, if I'm going to beat them out, I thought I'd duck out early to get to work. Maybe stay for a half hour."

Dad shook his head no. "There's going to be an announcement and the commercial. You'll stay for both."

I did a double take. Dad couldn't be serious. "When's the commercial going to air?"

"I don't know, but it doesn't matter. You're staying. One day, son, you're going to find that there are more important things than business. And this is a very important evening for our family," Dad said, and then left to join Aunt Anita and her daughter on the patio.

Something more important than business! Had my father, the man who lived and breathed business, just told me there was something more important than business?

It was bad enough that Aiden and Lauren had gotten together. Not only had I lost an assistant, but Lauren's invention had occupied almost all of Dad's attention. And somehow Aiden just doing charity work was okay now.

It was like everything I held to be true had been wiped away.

I shook my head and went to the bar for a dirty vodka martini. The bartender at Geoffrey's knew me and even remembered to add three olives. I downed the drink fast and ordered another, hoping to get into a more festive mood.

Drink in hand, I turned from the bar and surveyed the room. All of my brothers were here: Carter, Everett, and even Bradley. What on Earth was Bradley doing here? He never went to work stuff. Well, at least I wasn't the only one being forced to attend this over-hyped non-occasion.

Everett seemed to be having a great time hitting on a young redhead that I had never met. So, of course, I figured I'd say hello to him first. Everett was such a wolf. The girl didn't know what she was in for.

"Hi Everett," I said, slapping my brother on the back. "Why don't you introduce me to your new friend?"

"I'm Sydney," she said, holding out her hand. "I work for Lauren."

I nodded.

"You better be careful around this guy, Sydney," I said. "He's got quite a reputation."

Sydney looked back at Everett. "Is that so?"

Everett glared at me. "My brother exaggerates."

I knew it was rotten to interfere with my brother's evening, but I couldn't help it. Ever since the ridiculousness of my last romantic encounter, I'd completely given up on love.

Luckily, none of my family had gotten wind of it.

I wandered the party until Lauren and Aiden arrived.

Dad took the stage and clinked his glass with a spoon as he approached the microphone. The guests quieted and gave Dad their complete attention.

"You all may think you know why you're here, but I think you're going to be even more glad that you came." Dad motioned to Lauren and Aiden. They both got onto the stage.

Aiden approached the mic first. "Thank you all for coming. It's a very special day for Lauren and me. I'm sure most of you are here to see the commercial, but there's something else we wanted to share with you." Aiden's voice cracked with emotion at the last statement, and he stopped talking.

Aiden stepped aside. He was too emotional to speak. Lauren got behind the microphone, but shot Aiden a quick look to make sure he hadn't wanted to continue.

What the fuck was going on?

Lauren held up her left hand. "I guess what my fiancé is trying to say is we're engaged. It'll be a June wedding, and we hope you all will come!"

Holy shit! Married!

I'd never thought I wanted to get married, but that was until I pretended like I was. Now, it was all I thought about.

I crossed the restaurant to join the line of well-wishers to congratulate the happy couple.

Something about the woman hugging Lauren caught my attention. From the back, she looked just like—

My heart rate shot up to over a hundred when I saw her face. There was no mistaking those beautiful brown eyes. Her hair had grown longer, but it was Mackenzie. I hadn't seen her in almost a year, but she looked even better than she did every time I imagined her.

"Everyone!" Sydney said, turning up the sound of the television. "It's on!"

The party turned its attention to the commercial. But I couldn't pay attention to anything but Mackenzie. Everyone clapped after the ad ran, but I was frozen.

How the hell had my former fake fiancée ended up at my brother's engagement?

What's Next in the *Bronson Billionaire Series*

You won't believe how one of Lauren's best friends, Mackenzie, wound up fake engaged to Aiden's brother, Damien!

It's crazy hot and hilarious.

Do you remember how Aiden and Lauren were going to take over the Rexford Drugs' acquisition? Did you wonder why Damien couldn't do it?

The answer is Mackenzie Harper.

Find out what happens in Damien and Mackenzie's story in ***The Billionaire's Faux Fiancée***!

A NOTE FROM THE AUTHOR

Thank you for reading the first book in my new series! I'm so excited to write about the Bronson family, and I'm in the middle of writing Damien and Mackenzie's story now.

You may have noticed I set the book in Southern California, which is where I live. I've even drank coffee at the Starbucks on PCH in the opening scene. When I complete the series, I plan to celebrate with a Malibu Mint Martini at Geoffrey's (which I've only read about.) Maybe a bunch of us should meet up!

Unlike Geoffrey's, I have frequented The Hungry Fox with my sister, and yes, we both recommend you order toast with whatever you're having. Their homemade jam is delicious. A real-life billionaire would be lucky to try it.

Let's keep in touch. You can join the Sparks Fly Romance VIP List for free by visiting this link:

https://sparksflyromance.com/bronson1/

Not only will you get updates and sneak previews

regarding the *Bronson Billionaires* series, you'll also get to find out what happened with Lauren and Aiden after *The New Billionaire Boss* ended. Here's a hint: It's their one-year anniversary, but the couple is in for two surprises.

Well, I should get back to writing. Until next time…

ABOUT THE AUTHOR

Tina Gabor lives in Southern California with her fiancé and a stray cat named Fred. She loves reading and writing funny contemporary romance.

ALSO BY TINA GABOR

Bronson Billionaires Romance Series

The New Billionaire Boss

The Billionaire's Faux Fiancée

Four Weddings and a Billionaire

Rebounding with the Billionaire

OTHER SPARKS FLY ROMANCE BOOKS

Check out the *Lusted Series*!

Lusted

Lusted 2: Totally Exposed

Lusted 3: Billionaire Bound

Lusted 4: Uncovered Secrets

Made in United States
North Haven, CT
29 July 2022

21979606R00173